AF825672

Journey to the Centre of the Earth

by

Jules Verne

A Journey to the Center of the Earth (Voyage au centre de la Terre) is a classic science fiction. The story involves a German professor who believes there are volcanic tubes going toward the center of the Earth. He, his nephew and their guide Hans descend the chimney of an extinct volcano near Reykjavik, Iceland. The unbelievable and terrifying journey to find what lies at the centre of the earth begins.

One of the most liked novels in the world. Complete & unabridged.

JOURNEY TO THE CENTRE OF THE EARTH

JULES VERNE

Translated from the original by
Frederick Amadeus Malleson

PAPILIO

email: projapotibooks@gmail.com
website: www.projapotibooks.com

PAPILIO is an imprint of PROJAPOTI

© PROJAPOTI
All rights reserved. No part of this publication may be reproduced, stored in or introduced into a retrieval system, or transmitted in any form or by any means (electronic, mechanical, photocopying, recording, or otherwise) without the prior written permission of the publisher.

Journey to the Center of the Earth
(Voyage au centre de la Terre)
was first published in 1864

This revised edition of *Journey to the Centre of the Earth by Jules Verne*
is published by
PROJAPOTI 22 Sitaram Ghosh Street, Kolkata-700009. India
Printed in India

IP 9/20

3 5 7 9 8 6 4

ISBN 10: 81-7606-133-6
ISBN 13: 978-81-7606-133-9

Jules Verne
(1828-1905)

Jules Verne was the founding father of science fiction with H. G. Wells.

Jules Verne was born and raised in the port of Nantes. His father was a prosperous lawyer. To continue the practice, Verne moved to Paris, where he studied law. His uncle introduced him into literary circles and he started to published plays under the influence of such writers as Victor Hugo and Alexandre Dumas (fils), whom Verne also knew personally. Verne's one-act comedy *The Broken Straws* was performed in Paris when he was 22. In spite of busy writing, Verne managed to pass his law degree. During this period Verne suffered from digestive problems which then recurred at intervals through his life.

Jules Verne wrote his first science fiction tale, *A voyage in Balloon* (1851), under the influence of Edgar Allan Poe. Later Verne would write a sequel to Poe's unfinished novel, *Narrative of A Gordon Pym*, entitled *The Sphinz of the Ice-Fileds* (1897). Verne turned to stockbroking, an occupation which he held until his successful tale *Five Weeks in a Balloon* (1863) in the series *Voyages Extraordinaries*. Pierre Jules Hetzel, a publisher and writer for children, started to publish Verne's 'Extraordinary Journeys'. This cooperation lasted until the end of Verne's career.

Verne's novels gained soon a huge popularity throughout the world. Verne did not keep to the facts and probabilities too slavishly. *Around the World in Eighty Days* was about Philèas Fogg's daring but realistic travel feat on a wager, based on a real journey by the US traveller George Francis Train (1829-1904). *A Journey to the Centre of the Earth* is vulnerable to criticism on geological grounds. In *Hector Servadac* (1877) a comet takes Hector and his servant on a trip around the Solar System. Verne's major works were written by 1880. In later novels the author's pessimism about the future of human civilization was reflected. In his tale *The Eternal Adam* a far-future historian discovers the 20th Century civilization was overthrown by geological catalysms. In *Robur the Conqueror* (1886) Verne predicted the birth of heavier-than-air craft, but in the sequel, *Master of the World* (1904), the great inventor Robur suffers from megalomania.

Verne travelled with his brother Paul in 1867 to the United States, visiting the Niagara falls. When he made a boat trip around the Mediterranean, he was celebrated in Gibraltar, North Africa, and in Rome Pope Leo XIII blessed his books. In 1871 he settled in Amiens and was elected councillor in 1888. Verne survived there in 1886 a murder attempt. His paranoid nephew, Gaston, shot him in the leg and the authors was disabled for the rest of his life. Gaston never recovered his sanity. Verne had married Honorine de Viane at age 28.

For over 40 years Verne published at least one book per year on a wide range subjects. Although Verne wrote about exotic places, he travelled relatively little—his only balloon flight lasted twenty-four minutes. Verne's works include sixty-five novels, some twenty short stories and essays, thirty plays, some geographical works, and also opera librettos. Verne died in Amiens on March 24, 1905. Verne's works have inspired a number of film makers from Georges Méliès (*A Trip to the Moon*, 1902) and Walt Disney (*20,000 Leagues Under the Sea*, 1954) to such Hollywood directors as Henry Levin (*Journey to the Centre of the Earth*, 1959) and Irwin Allen (*Five Weeks in a Balloon*, 1962).

-

Further reading:

Jules Verne by Kenneth Allott (1940);

Jules Verne and His Works by I. O. Evans (1966);

Jules Verne by B. Becker (1966);

Le Trés Curieux Jules Verne by M. More (1969);

The Political and Social Ideas of Jules Verne by Jean Chesneaux (1972);

Jules Verne by Jean-Jules Verne (1976),

Jules Verne by Peter Costello (1978);

Jules Verne: A Primary and Secondary Bibliography by Edward J. Gallagher, Judith Mistichelli and John A. Van Eerde (1980);

Jules Verne's Journey to the Centre of the Self by William Butcher (1990);

TRANSLATOR'S PREFACE

The "Voyages Extraordinaires" of M. Jules Verne deserve to be made widely known in English-speaking countries by means of carefully prepared translations. Witty and ingenious adaptations of the researches and discoveries of modern science to the popular taste, which demands that these should be presented to ordinary readers in the lighter form of cleverly mingled truth and fiction, these books will assuredly be read with profit and delight, especially by English youth. Certainly no writer before M. Jules Verne has been so happy in weaving together in judicious combination severe scientific truth with a charming exercise of playful imagination.

Iceland, the starting point of the marvellous underground journey imagined in this volume, is invested at the present time with. a painful interest in consequence of the disastrous eruptions last Easter Day, which covered with lava and ashes the poor and scanty vegetation upon which four thousand persons were partly dependent for the means of subsistence. For a long time to come the natives of that interesting island, who cleave to their desert home with all that amor patriae which is so much more easily understood than explained, will look, and look not in vain, for the help of those on whom fall the smiles of a kindlier sun in regions not torn by earthquakes nor blasted and ravaged by volcanic fires. Will the readers of this little book, who, are gifted with the means of indulging in the luxury of extended beneficence, remember the distress of their brethren in the far north, whom distance has not barred from the claim of being counted our "neighbours"? And whatever their humane feelings may prompt them to bestow will be gladly added to the Mansion-House Iceland Relief Fund.

In his desire to ascertain how far the picture of Iceland,

drawn in the work of Jules Verne is a correct one, the translator hopes in the course of a mail or two to receive a communication from a leading man of science in the island, which may furnish matter for additional information in a future edition.

The scientific portion of the French original is not without a few errors, which the translator, with the kind assistance of Mr. Cameron of H. M. Geological Survey, has ventured to point out and correct. It is scarcely to be expected in a work in which the element of amusement is intended to enter more largely than that of scientific instruction, that any great degree of accuracy should be arrived at. Yet the translator hopes that what trifling deviations from the text or corrections in foot notes he is responsible for, will have done a little towards the increased usefulness of the work.

F. A. M.

The Vicarage,
Broughton-in-Furness

ONE

THE PROFESSOR AND HIS FAMILY

On the 24th of May, 1863, my uncle, Professor Liedenbrock, rushed into his little house, No. 19 Königstrasse, one of the oldest streets in the oldest portion of the city of Hamburg.

Martha must have concluded that she was very much behindhand, for the dinner had only just been put into the oven.

'Well, now,' said I to myself, 'if that most impatient of men is hungry, what a disturbance he will make!'

'M. Liedenbrock so soon!' cried poor Martha in great alarm, half opening the dining-room door.

'Yes, Martha; but very likely the dinner is not half cooked, for it is not two yet. Saint Michael's clock has only just struck half-past one.'

'Then why has the master come home so soon?'

'Perhaps he will tell us that himself.'

'Here he is, Monsieur Axel; I will run and hide myself while you argue with him.'

And Martha retreated in safety into her own dominions.

I was left alone. But how was it possible for a man of my undecided turn of mind to argue successfully with so irascible a person as the Professor? With this persuasion I was hurrying away to my own little retreat upstairs, when the street door creaked upon its hinges; heavy feet made the whole flight of stairs to shake; and the master of the house, passing rapidly through the dining-room, threw himself in haste into his own sanctum.

But on his rapid way he had found time to fling his hazel

stick into a corner, his rough broadbrim upon the table, and these few emphatic words at his nephew:

'Axel, follow me!'

I had scarcely had time to move when the Professor was again shouting after me:

'What! not come yet?'

And I rushed into my redoubtable master's study.

Otto Liedenbrock had no mischief in him, I willingly allow that; but unless he very considerably changes as he grows older, at the end he will be a most original character.

He was professor at the Johannæum, and was delivering a series of lectures on mineralogy, in the course of every one of which he broke into a passion once or twice at least. Not at all that he was over-anxious about the improvement of his class, or about the degree of attention with which they listened to him, or the success which might eventually crown his labours. Such little matters of detail never troubled him much. His teaching was as the German philosophy calls it, 'subjective'; it was to benefit himself, not others. He was a learned egotist. He was a well of science, and the pulleys worked uneasily when you wanted to draw anything out of it. In a word, he was a learned miser.

Germany has not a few professors of this sort.

To his misfortune, my uncle was not gifted with a sufficiently rapid utterance; not, to be sure, when he was talking at home, but certainly in his public delivery; this is a want much to be deplored in a speaker. The fact is, that during the course of his lectures at the Johannæum, the Professor often came to a complete standstill; he fought with wilful words that refused to pass his struggling lips, such words as resist and distend the cheeks, and at last break out into the unasked-for shape of a round and most unscientific oath: then his fury would gradually abate.

Now in mineralogy there are many half-Greek and half-Latin terms, very hard to articulate, and which would be most trying to a poet's measures. I don't wish to say a word against so respectable a science, far be that from me. True, in the august presence of rhombohedral crystals, retinasphaltic resins, gehlenites, Fassaites, molybdenites, tungstates of manganese, and titanite of zirconium, why, the most facile of tongues may make a slip now and then.

It therefore happened that this venial fault of my uncle's came to be pretty well understood in time, and an unfair advantage was taken of it; the students laid wait for him in dangerous places, and when he began to stumble, loud was the laughter, which is not in good taste, not even in Germans. And if there was always a full audience to honour the Liedenbrock courses, I should be sorry to conjecture how many came to make merry at my uncle's expense.

Nevertheless my good uncle was a man of deep learning—a fact I am most anxious to assert and reassert. Sometimes he might irretrievably injure a specimen by his too great ardour in handling it; but still he united the genius of a true geologist with the keen eye of the mineralogist. Armed with his hammer, his steel pointer, his magnetic needles, his blowpipe, and his bottle of nitric acid, he was a powerful man of science. He would refer any mineral to its proper place among the six hundred[1] elementary substances now enumerated, by its fracture, its appearance, its hardness, its fusibility, its sonorousness, its smell, and its taste.

The name of Liedenbrock was honourably mentioned in colleges and learned societies. Humphry Davy,[2] Humboldt, Captain Sir John Franklin, General Sabine, never failed to call upon him on their way through Hamburg. Becquerel, Ebelman, Brewster, Dumas, Milne-Edwards, Saint-Claire-

1. Sixtythree. (Tr.)

2. As Sir Humphry Davy died in 1829, the translator must be pardoned for pointing out here an anachronism, unless we are to assume that the learned Professor's celebrity dawned in his earliest years. (Tr.)

Deville frequently consulted him upon the most difficult problems in chemistry, a science which was indebted to him for considerable discoveries, for in 1853 there had appeared at Leipzig an imposing folio by Otto Liedenbrock, entitled, 'A Treatise upon Transcendental Chemistry,' with plates; a work, however, which failed to cover its expenses.

To all these titles to honour let me add that my uncle was the curator of the museum of mineralogy formed by M. Struve, the Russian ambassador; a most valuable collection, the fame of which is European.

Such was the gentleman who addressed me in that impetuous manner. Fancy a tall, spare man, of an iron constitution, and with a fair complexion which took off a good ten years from the fifty he must own to. His restless eyes were in incessant motion behind his full-sized spectacles. His long, thin nose was like a knife blade. Boys have been heard to remark that that organ was magnetised and attracted iron filings. But this was merely a mischievous report; it had no attraction except for snuff, which it seemed to draw to itself in great quantities.

When I have added, to complete my portrait, that my uncle walked by mathematical strides of a yard and a half, and that in walking he kept his fists firmly closed, a sure sign of an irritable temperament, I think I shall have said enough to disenchant any one who should by mistake have coveted much of his company.

He lived in his own little house in Königstrasse, a structure half brick and half wood, with a gable cut into steps; it looked upon one of those winding canals which intersect each other in the middle of the ancient quarter of Hamburg, and which the great fire of 1842 had fortunately spared.

It is true that the old house stood slightly off the perpendicular, and bulged out a little towards the street; its roof sloped a little to one side, like the cap over the left ear of a Tugendbund student; its lines wanted accuracy; but after all, it stood firm, thanks to an old elm which buttressed it in front, and which often in spring sent its young sprays through the window panes.

My uncle was tolerably well off for a German professor. The house was his own, and everything in it. The living contents were his god-daughter Gräuben, a young Virlandaise of seventeen, Martha, and myself. As his nephew and an orphan, I became his laboratory assistant.

I freely confess that I was exceedingly fond of geology and all its kindred sciences; the blood of a mineralogist was in my veins, and in the midst of my specimens I was always happy.

In a word, a man might live happily enough in the little old house in the Königstrasse, in spite of the restless impatience of its master, for although he was a little too excitable—he was very fond of me. But the man had no notion how to wait; nature herself was too slow for him. In April, after a had planted in the terra-cotta pots outside his window seedling plants of mignonette and convolvulus, he would go and give them a little pull by their leaves to make them grow faster. In dealing with such a strange individual there was nothing for it but prompt obedience. I therefore rushed after him.

TWO

A MYSTERY TO BE SOLVED AT ANY PRICE

That study of his was a museum, and nothing else. Specimens of everything known in mineralogy lay there in their places in perfect order, and correctly named, divided into inflammable, metallic, and lithoid minerals.

How well I knew all these bits of science! Many a time, instead of enjoying the company of lads of my own age, I had preferred dusting these graphites, anthracites, coals, lignites, and peats! And there were bitumens, resins, organic salts, to be protected from the least grain of dust; and metals, from iron to gold, metals whose current value altogether disappeared in the presence of the republican equality of scientific specimens; and stones too, enough to rebuild entirely the house in Königstrasse, even with a handsome additional room, which would have suited me admirably.

But on entering this study now I thought of none of all these wonders; my uncle alone filled my thoughts. He had thrown himself into a velvet easy-chair, and was grasping between his hands a book over which he bent, pondering with intense admiration.

'Here's a remarkable book! What a wonderful book!' he was exclaiming.

These ejaculations brought to my mind the fact that my uncle was liable to occasional fits of bibliomania; but no old book had any value in his eyes unless it had the virtue of being nowhere else to be found, or, at any rate, of being illegible.

'Well, now; don't you see it yet? Why I have got a priceless treasure, that I found his morning, in rummaging in old Hevelius's shop, the Jew.'

'Magnificent!' I replied, with a good imitation of enthusiasm.

What was the good of all this fuss about an old quarto, bound in rough calf, a yellow, faded volume, with a ragged seal depending from it?

But for all that there was no lull yet in the admiring exclamations of the Professor.

'See,' he went on, both asking the questions and supplying the answers. 'Isn't it a beauty? Yes; splendid! Did you ever see such a binding? Doesn't the book open easily? Yes; it stops open anywhere. But does it shut equally well? Yes; for the binding and the leaves are flush, all in a straight line, and no gaps or openings anywhere. And look at its back, after seven hundred years. Why, Bozerian, Closs, or Purgold might have been proud of such a binding!'

While rapidly making these comments my uncle kept opening and shutting the old tome. I really could do no less than ask a question about its contents, although I did not feel the slightest interest.

'And what is the title of this marvellous work?' I asked with an affected eagerness which he must have been very blind not to see through.

'This work,' replied my uncle, firing up with renewed enthusiasm, 'this work is the Heims Kringla of Snorre Turlleson, the most famous Icelandic author of the twelfth century! It is the chronicle of the Norwegian princes who ruled in Iceland.'

'Indeed;' I cried, keeping up wonderfully, 'of course it is a German translation?'

'What!' sharply replied the Professor, 'a translation! What should I do with a translation? This is the Icelandic original, in the magnificent idiomatic vernacular, which is both rich and simple, and admits of an infinite variety of grammatical combinations and verbal modifications.'

'Like German.' I happily ventured.

'Yes.' replied my uncle, shrugging his shoulders; 'but, in addition to all this, the Icelandic has three numbers like the Greek, and irregular declensions of nouns proper like the Latin.'

'Ah!' said I, a little moved out of my indifference; 'and is the type good?'

'Type! What do you mean by talking of type, wretched Axel? Type! Do you take it for a printed book, you ignorant fool? It is a manuscript, a Runic manuscript.'

'Runic?'

'Yes. Do you want me to explain what that is?'

'Of course not,' I replied in the tone of an injured man. But my uncle persevered, and told me, against my will, of many things I cared nothing about.

'Runic characters were in use in Iceland in former ages.

They were invented, it is said, by Odin himself. Look there, and wonder, impious young man, and admire these letters, the invention of the Scandinavian god!'

Well, well! not knowing what to say, I was going to prostrate myself before this wonderful book, a way of answering equally pleasing to gods and kings, and which has the advantage of never giving them any embarrassment, when a little incident happened to divert conversation into another channel.

This was the appearance of a dirty slip of parchment, which slipped out of the volume and fell upon the floor.

My uncle pounced upon this shred with incredible avidity. An old document, enclosed an immemorial time within the folds of this old book, had for him an immeasurable value.

'What's this?' he cried.

And he laid out upon the table a piece of parchment, five inches by three, and along which were traced certain mysterious characters.

Here is the exact facsimile. I think it important to let these strange signs be publicly known, for they were the means of drawing on Professor Liedenbrock and his nephew to undertake the most wonderful expedition of the nineteenth century.

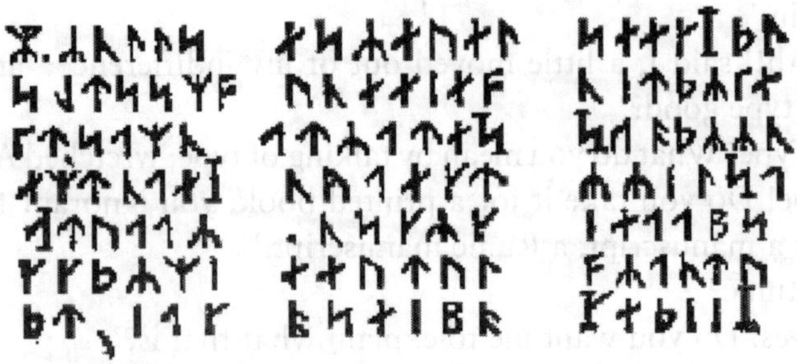

The Professor mused a few moments over this series of characters; then raising his spectacles he pronounced:

'These are Runic letters; they are exactly like those of the manuscript of Snorre Turlleson. But, what on earth is their meaning?'

Runic letters appearing to my mind to be an invention of the learned to mystify this poor world, I was not sorry to see my uncle suffering the pangs of mystification. At least, so it seemed to me, judging from his fingers, which were beginning to work with terrible energy.

'It is certainly old Icelandic,' he muttered between his teeth.

And Professor Liedenbrock must have known, for he was acknowledged to be quite a polyglot. Not that he could speak fluently in the two thousand languages and twelve thousand dialects which are spoken on the earth, but he knew at least his share of them.

So he was going, in the presence of this difficulty, to give way to all the impetuosity of his character, and I was preparing for a violent outbreak, when two o'clock struck by the little timepiece over the fireplace.

At that moment our good housekeeper Martha opened the study door, saying:

'Dinner is ready!'

I am afraid he sent that soup to where it would boil away to nothing, and Martha took to her heels for safety. I followed her, and hardly knowing how I got there I found myself seated in my usual place.

I waited a few minutes. No Professor came. Never within my remembrance had he missed the important ceremonial of dinner. And yet what a good dinner it was! There was parsley soup, an omelette of ham garnished with spiced sorrel, a fillet of veal with compote of prunes; for dessert, crystallised fruit; the whole washed down with sweet Moselle.

All this my uncle was going to sacrifice to a bit of old parchment. As an affectionate and attentive nephew I considered it my duty to eat for him as well as for myself, which I did conscientiously.

'I have never known such a thing,' said Martha. 'M. Liedenbrock is not at table!'

'Who could have believed it?' I said, with my mouth full.

'Something serious is going to happen,' said the servant, shaking her head.

My opinion was, that nothing more serious would happen than an awful scene when my uncle should have discovered that his dinner was devoured. I had come to the last of the fruit when a very loud voice tore me away from the pleasures of my dessert. With one spring I bounded out of the dining-room into the study.

THREE

THE RUNIC WRITING EXERCISES THE PROFESSOR

'Undoubtedly it is Runic,' said the Professor, bending his brows; 'but there is a secret in it, and I mean to discover the key.'

A violent gesture finished the sentence.

'Sit there,' he added, holding out his fist towards the table. 'Sit there, and write.'

I was seated in a trice.

'Now I will dictate to you every letter of our alphabet which corresponds with each of these Icelandic characters. We will see what that will give us. But, by St. Michael, if you should dare to deceive me—'

The dictation commenced. I did my best. Every letter was given me one after the other, with the following remarkable result:

mm.rnlls	esrevel	seecIde
sgtssmf	vnteief	niedrke
kt,samn	atrateS	saodrrn
emtnaeI	nvaect	rrilSa
Atsaar	.nvcrc	ieaabs
ccrmi	eevtVl	frAntv
dt,iac	oseibo	KediiI

When this work was ended my uncle tore the paper from me and examined it attentively for a long time.

'What does it all mean?' he kept repeating mechanically.

Upon my honour I could not have enlightened him. Besides he did not ask me, and he went on talking to himself.

'This is what is called a cryptogram, or cipher,' he said, 'in which letters are purposely thrown in confusion, which if properly arranged would reveal their sense. Only think that under this jargon there may lie concealed the clue to some great discovery!'

As for me, I was of opinion that there was nothing at all, in it; though, of course, I took care not to say so.

Then the Professor took the book and the parchment, and diligently compared them together.

'These two writings are not by the same hand,' he said; 'the cipher is of later date than the book, an undoubted proof of which I see in a moment. The first letter is a double m, a letter which is not to be found in Turlleson's book, and which was only added to the alphabet in the fourteenth century. Therefore there are two hundred years between the manuscript and the document.'

I admitted that this was a strictly logical conclusion.

'I am therefore led to imagine,' continued my uncle, 'that some possessor of this book wrote these mysterious letters. But who was that possessor? Is his name nowhere to be found in the manuscript?'

My uncle raised his spectacles, took up a strong lens, and carefully examined the blank pages of the book. On the front of the second, the title-page, he noticed a sort of stain which looked like an ink blot. But in looking at it very closely he thought he could distinguish some half-effaced letters. My uncle at once fastened upon this as the centre of interest, and he laboured at that blot, until by the help of his microscope he ended by making out the following Runic characters which he read without difficulty.

'Arne Saknussemm!' he cried in triumph. 'Why that is the name of another Icelander, a savant of the sixteenth century, a celebrated alchemist!'

I gazed at my uncle with satisfactory admiration.

'Those alchemists,' he resumed, 'Avicenna, Bacon, Lully, Paracelsus, were the real and only savants of their time. They made discoveries at which we are astonished. Has not this Saknussemm concealed under his cryptogram some surprising invention? It is so; it must be so!'

The Professor's imagination took fire at this hypothesis.

'No doubt,' I ventured to reply, 'but what interest would he have in thus hiding so marvellous a discovery?'

'Why? Why? How can I tell? Did not Galileo do the same by Saturn? We shall see. I will get at the secret of this document, and I will neither sleep nor eat until I have found it out.'

My comment on this was a half-suppressed 'Oh!'

'Nor you either, Axel,' he added.

'The deuce!' said I to myself; 'then it is lucky I have eaten two dinners Today!'

'First of all we must find out the key to this cipher; that cannot be difficult.'

At these words I quickly raised my head; but my uncle went on soliloquising.

'There's nothing easier. In this document there are a hundred and thirty-two letters, viz., seventy-seven consonants and fifty-five vowels. This is the proportion found in southern languages, whilst northern tongues are much richer in consonants; therefore this is in a southern language.'

These were very fair conclusions, I thought.

'But what language is it?'

Here I looked for a display of learning, but I met instead with profound analysis.

'This Saknussemm,' he went on, 'was a very well-informed man; now since he was not writing in his own mother tongue, he would naturally select that which was currently adopted by the choice spirits of the sixteenth century; I mean Latin. If I am mistaken, I can but try Spanish, French, Italian, Greek, or Hebrew. But the savants of the sixteenth century generally wrote in Latin. I am therefore entitled to pronounce this, à priori, to be Latin. It is Latin.'

I jumped up in my chair. My Latin memories rose in revolt against the notion that these barbarous words could belong to the sweet language of Virgil.

'Yes, it is Latin,' my uncle went on; 'but it is Latin confused and in disorder; 'pertubata seu inordinata,' as Euclid has it.'

'Very well,' thought I, 'if you can bring order out of that confusion, my dear uncle, you are a clever man.'

'Let us examine carefully,' said he again, taking up the leaf upon which I had written. 'Here is a series of one hundred and thirty-two letters in apparent disorder. There are words consisting of consonants only, as nrrlls; others, on the other hand, in which vowels predominate, as for instance the fifth, uneeief, or the last but one, oseibo. Now this arrangement has evidently not been premeditated; it has arisen mathematically in obedience to the unknown law which has ruled in the succession of these letters. It appears to me a certainty that the original sentence was written in a proper manner, and afterwards distorted by a law which we have yet to discover. Whoever possesses the key of this cipher will read it with fluency. What is that key? Axel, have you got it?'

I answered not a word, and for a very good reason. My eyes had fallen upon a charming picture, suspended against the wall, the portrait of Gräuben. My uncle's ward was at that time at Altona, staying with a relation, and in her absence I was very downhearted; for I may confess it to you now, the pretty Virlandaise and the professor's nephew loved each other with a patience and a calmness entirely German. We had become engaged unknown to my uncle, who was too much taken up with geology to be able to enter into such feelings as ours. Gräuben was a lovely blue-eyed blonde, rather given to gravity and seriousness; but that did not prevent her from loving me very sincerely. As for me, I adored her, if there is such a word in the German language. Thus it happened that the picture of my pretty Virlandaise threw me in a moment out of the world of realities into that of memory and fancy.

There looked down upon me the faithful companion of my labours and my recreations. Every day she helped me to arrange my uncle's precious specimens; she and I labelled them together. Mademoiselle Gräuben was an accomplished mineralogist; she could have taught a few things to a savant. She was fond of investigating abstruse scientific questions. What pleasant hours we have spent in study; and how often I envied the very stones which she handled with her charming fingers.

Then, when our leisure hours came, we used to go out together and turn into the shady avenues by the Alster, and went happily side by side up to the old windmill, which forms such an improvement to the landscape at the head of the lake. On the road we chatted hand in hand; I told her amusing tales at which she laughed heartilv. Then we reached the banks of the Elbe, and after having bid good-bye to the swan, sailing gracefully amidst the white water lilies, we returned to the quay by the steamer.

That is just where I was in my dream, when my uncle with a vehement thump on the table dragged me back to the realities of life.

'Come,' said he, 'the very first idea which would come into any one's head to confuse the letters of a sentence would be to write the words vertically instead of horizontally.'

'Indeed!' said I.

'Now we must see what would be the effect of that, Axel; put down upon this paper any sentence you like, only instead of arranging the letters in the usual way, one after the other, place them in succession in vertical columns, so as to group them together in five or six vertical lines.'

I caught his meaning, and immediately produced the following literary wonder:

I	y	l	o	a	u
l	o	l	w	r	b
o	u	,	n	G	e
v	w	m	d	r	n
e	e	y	e	a	!

'Good,' said the professor, without reading them, 'now set down those words in a horizontal line.'

I obeyed, and with this result:

Iyloau lolwrb ou,nGe vwmdrn eeyea!

'Excellent!' said my uncle, taking the paper hastily out of my hands. 'This begins to look just like an ancient document: the vowels and the consonants are grouped together in equal disorder; there are even capitals in the middle of words, and commas too, just as in Saknussemm's parchment.'

I considered these remarks very clever.

'Now,' said my uncle, looking straight at me, 'to read the sentence which you have just written, and with which I am wholly unacquainted, I shall only have to take the first letter of each word, then the second, the third, and so forth.'

And my uncle, to his great astonishment, and my much greater, read:

'I love you well, my own dear Gräuben!'

'Hallo!' cried the Professor.

Yes, indeed, without knowing what I was about, like an

awkward and unlucky lover, I had compromised myself by writing this unfortunate sentence.

'Aha! you are in love with Gräuben?' he said, with the right look for a guardian.

'Yes; no!' I stammered.

'You love Gräuben,' he went on once or twice dreamily. 'Well, let us apply the process I have suggested to the document in question.'

My uncle, falling back into his absorbing contemplations, had already forgotten my imprudent words. I merely say imprudent, for the great mind of so learned a man of course had no place for love affairs, and happily the grand business of the document gained me the victory.

Just as the moment of the supreme experiment arrived the Professor's eyes flashed right through his spectacles. There was a quivering in his fingers as he grasped the old parchment. He was deeply moved. At last he gave a preliminary cough, and with profound gravity, naming in succession the first, then the second letter of each word, he dictated me the following:

mmessvnkaSenrA.icefdoK.segnittamvrtn
ecertserrette,rotaisadva,ednecsedsadne
lacartniiilvIsiratracSarbmvtabiledmek
meretarcsilvcoIsleffenSnI.

I confess I felt considerably excited in coming to the end; these letters named, one at a time, had carried no sense to my mind; I therefore waited for the Professor with great pomp to unfold the magnificent but hidden Latin of this mysterious phrase.

But who could have foretold the result? A violent thump made the furniture rattle, and spilt some ink, and my pen dropped from between my fingers.

'That's not it,' cried my uncle, 'there's no sense in it.'

Then darting out like a shot, bowling down stairs like an avalanche, he rushed into the Königstrasse and fled.

FOUR

THE ENEMY TO BE STARVED INTO SUBMISSION

He is gone!' cried Martha, running out of her kitchen at the noise of the violent slamming of doors.

'Yes,' I replied, 'completely gone.'

'Well; and how about his dinner?' said the old servant.

'He won't have any.'

'And his supper?'

'He won't have any.'

'What?' cried Martha, with clasped hands.

'No, my dear Martha, he will eat no more. No one in the house is to eat anything at all. Uncle Liedenbrock is going to make us all fast until he has succeeded in deciphering an undecipherable scrawl.'

'Oh, my dear! must we then all die of hunger?'

I hardly dared to confess that, with so absolute a ruler as my uncle, this fate was inevitable.

The old servant, visibly moved, returned to the kitchen, moaning piteously.

When I was alone, I thought I would go and tell Gräuben all about it. But how should I be able to escape from the house? The Professor might return at any moment. And suppose he called me? And suppose he tackled me again with this logomachy, which might vainly have been set before ancient Oedipus. And if I did not obey his call, who could answer for what might happen?

The wisest course was to remain where I was. A mineralogist at Besançon had just sent us a collection of siliceous nodules, which I had to classify: so I set to work; I sorted, labelled, and arranged in their own glass case all these hollow specimens, in the cavity of each of which was a nest of little crystals.

But this work did not succeed in absorbing all my attention. That old document kept working in my brain. My head throbbed with excitement, and I felt an undefined uneasiness. I was possessed with a presentiment of coming evil.

In an hour my nodules were all arranged upon successive shelves. Then I dropped down into the old velvet arm-chair, my head thrown back and my hands joined over it. I lighted my long crooked pipe, with a painting on it of an idle-looking naiad; then I amused myself watching the process of the conversion of the tobacco into carbon, which was by slow degrees making my naiad into a negress. Now and then I listened to hear whether a well-known step was on the stairs. No. Where could my uncle be at that moment? I fancied him running under the noble trees which line the road to Altona, gesticulating, making shots with his cane, thrashing the long grass, cutting the heads off the thistles, and disturbing the contemplative storks in their peaceful solitude.

Would he return in triumph or in discouragement? Which would get the upper hand, he or the secret? I was thus asking myself questions, and mechanically taking between my fingers the sheet of paper mysteriously disfigured with the incomprehensible succession of letters I had written down; and I repeated to myself 'What does it all mean?'

I sought to group the letters so as to form words. Quite impossible! When I put them together by twos, threes, fives or sixes, nothing came of it but nonsense. To be sure the fourteenth, fifteenth and sixteenth letters made the English word 'ice'; the eighty-third and two following made 'sir'; and in the midst of the document, in the second and third lines, I observed the words, 'rots,' 'mutabile,' 'ira,' 'net,' 'atra.'

'Come now,' I thought, 'these words seem to justify my uncle's view about the language of the document. In the fourth line appeared the word 'luco', which means a sacred wood. It is true that in the third line was the word 'tabiled', which looked like Hebrew, and in the last the purely French words 'mer', 'arc', 'mere."

All this was enough to drive a poor fellow crazy. Four different languages in this ridiculous sentence! What connection could there possibly be between such words as ice, sir, anger, cruel, sacred wood, changeable, mother, bow, and sea? The first and the last might have something to do with each other; it was not at all surprising that in a document written in Iceland there should be mention of a sea of ice; but it was quite another thing to get to the end of this cryptogram with so small a clue. So I was struggling with an insurmountable difficulty; my brain got heated, my eyes watered over that sheet of paper; its hundred and thirty-two letters seemed to flutter and fly around me like those motes of mingled light and darkness which float in the air around the head when the blood is rushing upwards with undue violence. I was a prey to a kind of hallucination; I was stifling; I wanted air. Unconsciously I fanned myself with the bit of paper, the back and front of which successively came before my eyes. What was my surprise when, in one of those rapid revolutions, at the moment when the back was turned to me I thought I caught sight of the Latin words 'craterem,' 'terrestre,' and others.

A sudden light burst in upon me; these hints alone gave me the first glimpse of the truth; I had discovered the key to the cipher. To read the document, it would not even be necessary to read it through the paper. Such as it was, just such as it had been dictated to me, so it might be spelt out with ease. All those ingenious professorial combinations were coming right. He was right as to the arrangement of the letters; he was right as to the language. He had been within a hair's breadth of reading this Latin document from end to end; but that hair's breadth, chance had given it to me!

You may be sure I felt stirred up. My eyes were dim, I could scarcely see. I had laid the paper upon the table. At a glance I could tell the whole secret.

At last I became more calm. I made a wise resolve to walk twice round the room quietly and settle my nerves, and then I returned into the deep gulf of the huge armchair.

'Now I'll read it,' I cried, after having well distended my lungs with air.

I leaned over the table; I laid my finger successively upon every letter; and without a pause, without one moment's hesitation, I read off the whole sentence aloud.

Stupefaction! terror! I sat overwhelmed as if with a sudden deadly blow. What! that which I read had actually, really been done! A mortal man had had the audacity to penetrate! . . .

'Ah!' I cried, springing up. 'But no! no! My uncle shall never know it. He would insist upon doing it too. He would want to know all about it. Ropes could not hold him, such a determined geologist as he is! He would start, he would, in spite of everything and everybody, and he would take me with him, and we should never get back. No, never! never!'

My over-excitement was beyond all description.

'No! no! it shall not be,' I declared energetically; 'and as it is in my power to prevent the knowledge of it coming into the mind of my tyrant, I will do it. By dint of turning this document round and round, he too might discover the key. I will destroy it.'

There was a little fire left on the hearth. I seized not only the paper but Saknussemm's parchment; with a feverish hand I was about to fling it all upon the coals and utterly destroy and abolish this dangerous secret, when the, study door opened, and my uncle appeared.

FIVE

FAMINE, THEN VICTORY, FOLLOWED BY DISMAY

I had only just time to replace the unfortunate document upon the table.

Professor Liedenbrock seemed to be greatly abstracted.

The ruling thought gave him no rest. Evidently he had gone deeply into the matter, analytically and with profound scrutiny. He had brought all the resources of his mind to bear upon it during his walk, and he had come back to apply some new combination.

He sat in his armchair, and pen in hand he began what looked very much like algebraic formula: I followed with my eyes his trembling hands, I took count of every movement. Might not some unhoped-for result come of it? I trembled, too, very unnecessarily, since the true key was in my hands, and no other would open the secret.

For three long hours my uncle worked on without a word, without lifting his head; rubbing out, beginning again, then rubbing out again, and so on a hundred times.

I knew very well that if he succeeded in setting down these letters in every possible relative position, the sentence would come out. But I knew also that twenty letters alone could form two quintillions, four hundred and thirty-two quadrillions, nine hundred and two trillions, eight billions, a hundred and seventy-six millions, six hundred and forty thousand combinations. Now, here were a hundred and thirty-two letters in this sentence, and these hundred and thirty-two letters would give a number of different sentences, each made up of at least a hundred and thirty-three figures, a number which passed far beyond all calculation or conception.

So I felt reassured as far as regarded this heroic method of solving the difficulty.

But time was passing away; night came on; the street noises ceased; my uncle, bending over his task, noticed nothing, not even Martha half opening the door; he heard not a sound, not even that excellent woman saying:

'Will not monsieur take any supper to-night?'

And poor Martha had to go away unanswered. As for me, after long resistance, I was overcome by sleep, and fell off at the end of the sofa, while uncle Liedenbrock went on calculating and rubbing out his calculations.

When I awoke next morning that indefatigable worker was still at his post. His red eyes, his pale complexion, his hair tangled between his feverish fingers, the red spots on his cheeks, revealed his desperate struggle with impossibilities, and the weariness of spirit, the mental wrestlings he must have undergone all through that unhappy night.

To tell the plain truth, I pitied him. In spite of the reproaches which I considered I had a right to lay upon him, a certain feeling of compassion was beginning to gain upon me. The poor man was so entirely taken up with his one idea that he had even forgotten how to get angry. All the strength of his feelings was concentrated upon one point alone; and as their usual vent was closed, it was to be feared lest extreme tension should give rise to an explosion sooner or later.

I might with a word have loosened the screw of the steel vice that was crushing his brain; but that word I would not speak.

Yet I was not an ill-natured fellow. Why was I dumb at such a crisis? Why so insensible to my uncle's interests?

'No, no,' I repeated, 'I shall not speak. He would insist upon going; nothing on earth could stop him. His imagination is a volcano, and to do that which other geologists have never done he would risk his life. I will preserve silence. I will keep the secret which mere chance has revealed to me. To discover it, would be to kill Professor Liedenbrock! Let him find it out himself if he can. I will never have it laid to my door that I led him to his destruction.'

Having formed this resolution, I folded my arms and waited. But I had not reckoned upon one little incident which turned up a few hours after.

When our good Martha wanted to go to Market, she found the door locked. The big key was gone. Who could have taken it out? Assuredly, it was my uncle, when he returned the night before from his hurried walk.

Was this done on purpose? Or was it a mistake? Did he want to reduce us by famine? This seemed like going rather too far! What! should Martha and I be victims of a position of things in which we had not the smallest interest? It was a fact that a few years before this, whilst my uncle was working at his great classification of minerals, he was forty-eight hours without eating, and all his household were obliged to share in this scientific fast. As for me, what I remember is, that I got severe cramps in my stomach, which hardly suited the constitution of a hungry, growing lad.

Now it appeared to me as if breakfast was going to be wanting, just as supper had been the night before. Yet I resolved to be a hero, and not to be conquered by the pangs of hunger. Martha took it very seriously, and, poor woman, was very much distressed. As for me, the impossibility of leaving the house distressed me a good deal more, and for a very good reason. A caged lover's feelings may easily be imagined.

My uncle went on working, his imagination went off rambling into the ideal world of combinations; he was far away from earth, and really far away from earthly wants.

About noon hunger began to stimulate me severely. Martha had, without thinking any harm, cleared out the larder the night before, so that now there was nothing left in the house. Still I held out; I made it a point of honour.

Two o'clock struck. This was becoming ridiculous; worse

than that, unbearable. I began to say to myself that I was exaggerating the importance of the document; that my uncle would surely not believe in it, that he would set it down as a mere puzzle; that if it came to the worst, we should lay violent hands on him and keep him at home if he thought on venturing on the expedition that, after all, he might himself discover the key of the cipher, and that then I should be clear at the mere expense of my involuntary abstinence.

These reasons seemed excellent to me, though on the night before I should have rejected them with indignation; I even went so far as to condemn myself for my absurdity in having waited so long, and I finally resolved to let it all out.

I was therefore meditating a proper introduction to the matter, so as not to seem too abrupt, when the Professor jumped up, clapped on his hat, and prepared to go out.

Surely he was not going out, to shut us in again! no, never!

'Uncle!' I cried.

He seemed not to hear me.

'Uncle Liedenbrock!' I cried, lifting up my voice.

'Ay,' he answered like a man suddenly waking.

'Uncle, that key!'

'What key? The door key?'

'No, no!' I cried. 'The key of the document.'

The Professor stared at me over his spectacles; no doubt he saw something unusual in the expression of my countenance; for he laid hold of my arm, and speechlessly questioned me with his eyes. Yes, never was a question more forcibly put.

I nodded my head up and down.

He shook his pityingly, as if he was dealing with a lunatic. I gave a more affirmative gesture.

His eyes glistened and sparkled with live fire, his hand was shaken threateningly.

This mute conversation at such a momentous crisis would have riveted the attention of the most indifferent. And the fact really was that I dared not speak now, so intense was the excitement for fear lest my uncle should smother me in his first joyful embraces. But he became so urgent that I was at last compelled to answer.

'Yes, that key, chance—'

'What is that you are saying?' he shouted with indescribable emotion.

'There, read that!' I said, presenting a sheet of paper on which I had written.

'But there is nothing in this,' he answered, crumpling up the paper.

'No, nothing until you proceed to read from the end to the beginning.'

I had not finished my sentence when the Professor broke out into a cry, nay, a roar. A new revelation burst in upon him. He was transformed!

'Aha, clever Saknussemm!' he cried. 'You had first written out your sentence the wrong way.'

And darting upon the paper, with eyes bedimmed, and voice choked with emotion, he read the whole document from the last letter to the first.

It was conceived in the following terms:

In Sneffels Joculis craterem quem delibat
Umbra Scartaris Julii intra calendas descende,
Audax viator, et terrestre centrum attinges.
Quod feci, Arne Saknussemm.

Which bad Latin may be translated thus:

'Descend, bold traveller, into the crater of the jokul of Sneffels, which the shadow of Scartaris touches before the kalends of July, and you will attain the centre of the earth; which I have done, Arne Saknussemm.'

In reading this, my uncle gave a spring as if he had touched a Leyden jar. His audacity, his joy, and his convictions were magnificent to behold. He came and he went; he seized his head between both his hands; he pushed the chairs out of their places, he piled up his books; incredible as it may seem, he rattled his precious nodules of flints together; he sent a kick here, a thump there. At last his nerves calmed down, and like a man exhausted by too lavish an expenditure of vital power, he sank back exhausted into his armchair.

'What o'clock is it?' he asked after a few moments of silence.

'Three o'clock,' I replied.

'Is it really? The dinner-hour is past, and I did not know it. I am half dead with hunger. Come on, and after dinner—'

'Well?'

'After dinner, pack up my trunk.'

'What?' I cried.

'And yours!' replied the indefatigable Professor, entering the dining-room.

SIX

EXCITING DISCUSSIONS ABOUT AN UNPARALLELED ENTERPRISE

At these words a cold shiver ran through me. Yet I controlled myself; I even resolved to put a good face upon it. Scientific arguments alone could have any weight with Professor Liedenbrock. Now there were good ones against the practicability of such a journey. Penetrate to the centre of the earth! What nonsense! But I kept my dialectic battery in reserve for a suitable opportunity, and I interested myself in the prospect of my dinner, which was not yet forthcoming.

It is no use to tell of the rage and imprecations of my uncle before the empty table. Explanations were given, Martha was set at liberty, ran off to the market, and did her part so well that in an hour afterwards my hunger was appeased, and I was able to return to the contemplation of the gravity of the situation.

During all dinner time my uncle was almost merry; he indulged in some of those learned jokes which never do anybody any harm. Dessert over, he beckoned me into his study.

I obeyed; he sat at one end of his table, I at the other.

'Axel,' said he very mildly; 'you are a very ingenious young man, you have done me a splendid service, at a moment when, wearied out with the struggle, I was going to abandon the contest. Where should I have lost myself? None can tell. Never, my lad, shall I forget it; and you shall have your share in the glory to which your discovery will lead.'

'Oh, come!' thought I, 'he is in a good way. Now is the time for discussing that same glory.'

'Before all things,' my uncle resumed, 'I enjoin you to preserve the most inviolable secrecy: you understand? There are not a few in the scientific world who envy my success, and many would be ready to undertake this enterprise, to whom our return should be the first news of it.'

'Do you really think there are many people bold enough?' said I.

'Certainly; who would hesitate to acquire such renown? If that document were divulged, a whole army of geologists would be ready to rush into the footsteps of Arne Saknussemm.'

'I don't feel so very sure of that, uncle,' I replied; 'for we have no proof of the authenticity of this document.'

'What! not of the book, inside which we have discovered it?'

'Granted. I admit that Saknussemm may have written these lines. But does it follow that he has really accomplished such a journey? And may it not be that this old parchment is intended to mislead?'

I almost regretted having uttered this last word, which dropped from me in an unguarded moment. The Professor bent his shaggy brows, and I feared I had seriously compromised my own safety. Happily no great harm came of it. A smile flitted across the lip of my severe companion, and he answered:

'That is what we shall see.'

'Ah!' said I, rather put out. 'But do let me exhaust all the possible objections against this document.'

'Speak, my boy, don't be afraid. You are quite at liberty to express your opinions. You are no longer my nephew only, but my colleague. Pray go on.'

'Well, in the first place, I wish to ask what are this Jokul, this Sneffels, and this Scartaris, names which I have never heard before?'

'Nothing easier. I received not long ago a map from my friend, Augustus Petermann, at Liepzig. Nothing could be more apropos. Take down the third atlas in the second shelf in the large bookcase, series Z, plate 4.'

I rose, and with the help of such precise instructions could not fail to find the required atlas. My uncle opened it and said:

'Here is one of the best maps of Iceland, that of Handersen, and I believe this will solve the worst of our difficulties.'

I bent over the map.

'You see this volcanic island,' said the Professor; 'observe that all the volcanoes are called jokuls, a word which means glacier in Icelandic, and under the high latitude of Iceland nearly all the active volcanoes discharge through beds of ice. Hence this term of jokul is applied to all the eruptive mountains in Iceland.'

'Very good,' said I; 'but what of Sneffels?'

I was hoping that this question would be unanswerable; but I was mistaken. My uncle replied:

'Follow my finger along the west coast of Iceland. Do you see Rejkiavik, the capital? You do. Well; ascend the innumerable fiords that indent those sea-beaten shores, and stop at the sixty-fifth degree of latitude. What do you see there?'

'I see a peninsula looking like a thigh bone with the knee bone at the end of it.'

'A very fair comparison, my lad. Now do you see anything upon that knee bone?'

'Yes; a mountain rising out of the sea.'

'Right. That is Snæfell.'

'That Snæfell?'

'It is. It is a mountain five thousand feet high, one of the most remarkable in the world, if its crater leads down to the centre of the earth.'

'But that is impossible,' I said shrugging my shoulders, and disgusted at such a ridiculous supposition.

'Impossible?' said the Professor severely; 'and why, pray?'

'Because this crater is evidently filled with lava and burning rocks, and therefore—'

'But suppose it is an extinct volcano?'

'Extinct?'

'Yes; the number of active volcanoes on the surface of the globe is at the present time only about three hundred. But there is a very much larger number of extinct ones. Now, Snæfell is one of these. Since historic times there has been but one eruption of this mountain, that of 1219; from that time it has quieted down more and. more, and now it is no longer reckoned among active volcanoes.'

To such positive statements I could make no reply. I therefore took refuge in other dark passages of the document.

'What is the meaning of this word Scartaris, and what have the kalends of July to do with it?'

My uncle took a few minutes to consider. For one short moment I felt a ray of hope, speedily to be extinguished. For he soon answered thus:

'What is darkness to you is light to me. This proves the ingenious care with which Saknussemm guarded and defined his discovery. Sneffels, or Snæfell, has several craters. It was therefore necessary to point out which of these leads to the centre of the globe. What did the Icelandic sage do? He observed that at the approach of the kalends of July, that is to say in the last days of June, one of the peaks, called Scartaris, flung its shadow down the mouth of that particular crater, and he committed that fact to his document. Could there possibly have been a more exact guide? As soon as we have arrived at the summit of Snæfell we shall have no hesitation as to the proper road to take.'

Decidedly, my uncle had answered every one of my objections. I saw that his position on the old parchment was impregnable. I therefore ceased to press him upon that part of the subject, and as above all things he must be convinced, I passed on to scientific objections, which in my opinion were far more serious.

'Well, then,' I said, 'I am forced to admit that Saknussemm's sentence is clear, and leaves no room for doubt. I will even allow that the document bears every mark and evidence of authenticity. That learned philosopher did get to the bottom of Sneffels, he has seen the shadow of Scartaris touch the edge of the crater before the kalends of July; he may even have heard the legendary stories told in his day about that crater reaching to the centre of the world; but as for reaching it himself, as for performing the journey, and returning, if he ever went, I say no—he never, never did that.'

'Now for your reason?' said my uncle ironically.

'All the theories of science demonstrate such a feat to be impracticable.'

'The theories say that, do they?' replied the Professor in the tone of a meek disciple. 'Oh! unpleasant theories! How the theories will hinder. us, won't they?'

I saw that he was only laughing at me; but I went on all the same.

'Yes; it is perfectly well known that the internal temperature rises one degree for every 70 feet in depth; now, admitting this proportion to be constant, and the radius of the earth being fifteen hundred leagues, there must be a temperature of 360,032 degrees at the centre of the earth. Therefore, all the substances that compose the body of this earth must exist there in a state of incandescent gas; for the metals that most resist the action of heat, gold, and platinum, and the hardest rocks, can never be either solid or liquid under such a temperature. I have therefore good reason for asking if it is possible to penetrate through such a medium.'

'So, Axel, it is the heat that troubles you?'

'Of course it is. Were we to reach a depth of thirty miles we should have arrived at the limit of the terrestrial crust, for there the temperature will be more than 2372 degrees.'

'Are you afraid of being put into a state of fusion?'

'I will leave you to decide that question,' I answered rather sullenly. 'This is my decision,' replied Professor Liedenbrock, putting on one of his grandest airs. 'Neither you nor anybody else knows with any certainty what is going on in the interior of this globe, since not the twelve thousandth part of its radius is known; science is eminently perfectible; and every new theory is soon routed by a newer. Was it not always believed until Fourier that the temperature of the interplanetary spaces decreased perpetually? and is it not known at the present time that the greatest cold of the ethereal regions is never lower than 40 degrees below zero Fahr.? Why should it not be the same with the internal heat? Why should it not, at a certain depth, attain an impassable limit, instead of rising to such a point as to fuse the most infusible metals?'

As my uncle was now taking his stand upon hypotheses, of course, there was nothing to be said.

'Well, I will tell you that true savants, amongst them Poisson, have demonstrated that if a heat of 360,000 degrees[1] existed in

1. The degrees of temperature are given by Jules Verne according to the centigrade system, for which we will in each case substitute the Fahrenheit measurement. (Tr.)

the interior of the globe, the fiery gases arising from the fused matter would acquire an elastic force which the crust of the earth would be unable to resist, and that it would explode like the plates of a bursting boiler.'

'That is Poisson's opinion, my uncle, nothing more.'

'Granted. But it is likewise the creed adopted by other distinguished geologists, that the interior of the globe is neither gas nor water, nor any of the heaviest minerals known, for in none of these cases would the earth weigh what it does.'

'Oh, with figures you may prove anything!'

'But is it the same with facts! Is it not known that the number of volcanoes has diminished since the first days of creation? and if there is central heat may we not thence conclude that it is in process of diminution?'

'My good uncle, if you will enter into the legion of speculation, I can discuss the matter no longer.'

'But I have to tell you that the highest names have come to the support of my views. Do you remember a visit paid to me by the celebrated chemist, Humphry Davy, in 1825?'

'Not at all, for I was not born until nineteen years afterwards.'

'Well, Humphry Davy did call upon me on his way through Hamburg. We were long engaged in discussing, amongst other problems, the hypothesis of the liquid structure of the terrestrial nucleus. We were agreed that it could not be in a liquid state, for a reason which science has never been able to confute.'

'What is that reason?' I said, rather astonished.

'Because this liquid mass would be subject, like the ocean, to the lunar attraction, and therefore twice every day there would be internal tides, which, upheaving the terrestrial crust, would cause periodical earthquakes!'

'Yet it is evident that the surface of the globe has been subject to the action of fire,' I replied, 'and it is quite reasonable to suppose that the external crust cooled down first, whilst the heat took refuge down to the centre.'

'Quite a mistake,' my uncle answered. 'The earth has been heated by combustion on its surface, that is all. Its surface was composed of a great number of metals, such as potassium and sodium, which have the peculiar property of igniting at the mere contact with air and water; these metals kindled when the atmospheric vapours fell in rain upon the soil; and by and by, when the waters penetrated into the fissures of the crust of the earth, they broke out into fresh combustion with explosions and eruptions. Such was the cause of the numerous volcanoes at the origin of the earth.'

'Upon my word, this is a very clever hypothesis,' I exclaimed, in spite rather of myself.

'And which Humphry Davy demonstrated to me by a simple experiment. He formed a small ball of the metals which I have named, and which was a very fair representation of our globe; whenever he caused a fine dew of rain to fall upon its surface, it heaved up into little monticules, it became oxydized and formed miniature mountains; a crater broke open at one of its summits; the eruption took place, and communicated to the whole of the ball such a heat that it could not be held in the hand.'

In truth, I was beginning to be shaken by the Professor's arguments, besides which he gave additional weight to them by his usual ardour and fervent enthusiasm.

'You see, Axel,' he added, 'the condition of the terrestrial nucleus has given rise to various hypotheses among geologists; there is no proof at all for this internal heat; my opinion is that there is no such thing, it cannot be; besides we shall see for ourselves, and, like Arne Saknussemm, we shall know exactly what to hold as truth concerning this grand question.'

'Very well, we shall see,' I replied, feeling myself carried off by his contagious enthusiasm. 'Yes, we shall see; that is, if it is possible to see anything there.'

'And why not? May we not depend upon electric phenomena

to give us light? May we not even expect light from the atmosphere, the pressure of which may render it luminous as we approach the centre?'

'Yes, yes,' said I; 'that is possible, too.'

'It is certain,' exclaimed my uncle in a tone of triumph. 'But silence, do you hear me? silence upon the whole subject; and let no one get before us in this design of discovering the centre of the earth.'

SEVEN

A WOMAN'S COURAGE

Thus ended this memorable seance. That conversation threw me into a fever. I came out of my uncle's study as if I had been stunned, and as if there was not air enough in all the streets of Hamburg to put me right again. I therefore made for the banks of the Elbe, where the steamer lands her passengers, which forms the communication between the city and the Hamburg railway.

Was I convinced of the truth of what I had heard? Had I not bent under the iron rule of the Professor Liedenbrock? Was I to believe him in earnest in his intention to penetrate to the centre of this massive globe? Had I been listening to the mad speculations of a lunatic, or to the scientific conclusions of a lofty genius? Where did truth stop? Where did error begin?

I was all adrift amongst a thousand contradictory hypotheses, but I could not lay hold of one.

Yet I remembered that I had been convinced, although now my enthusiasm was beginning to cool down; but I felt a desire to start at once, and not to lose time and courage by calm reflection. I had at that moment quite courage enough to strap my knapsack to my shoulders and start.

But I must confess that in another hour this unnatural excitement abated, my nerves became unstrung, and from the depths of the abysses of this earth I ascended to its surface again.

'It is quite absurd!' I cried, 'there is no sense about it. No sensible young man should for a moment entertain such a proposal. The whole thing is non-existent. I have had a bad night, I have been dreaming of horrors.'

But I had followed the banks of the Elbe and passed the town. After passing the port too, I had reached the Altona road. I was led by a presentiment, soon to be realised; for shortly I espied my little Gräuben bravely returning with her light step to Hamburg.

'Gräuben!' I cried from afar off.

The young girl stopped, rather frightened perhaps to hear her name called after her on the high road. Ten yards more, and I had joined her.

'Axel!' she cried surprised. 'What! have you come to meet me? Is this why you are here, sir?'

But when she had looked upon me, Gräuben could not fail to see the uneasiness and distress of my mind.

'What is the matter?' she said, holding out her hand.

'What is the matter, Gräuben?' I cried.

In a couple of minutes my pretty Virlandaise was fully informed of the position of affairs. For a time she was silent. Did her heart palpitate as mine did? I don't know about that, but I know that her hand did not tremble in mine. We went on a hundred yards without speaking.

At last she said, 'Axel!'

'My dear Gräuben.'

'That will be a splendid journey!'

I gave a bound at these words.

'Yes, Axel, a journey worthy of the nephew of a savant; it is a good thing for a man to be distinguished by some great enterprise.'

'What, Gräuben, won't you dissuade me from such an undertaking?'

'No, my dear Axel, and I would willingly go with you, but that a poor girl would only be in your way.'

'Is that quite true?'

'It is true.'

Ah! women and young girls, how incomprehensible are your feminine hearts! When you are not the timidest, you are the bravest of creatures. Reason has nothing to do with your actions. What! did this child encourage me in such an expedition! Would she not be afraid to join it herself? And she was driving me to it, one whom she loved!

I was disconcerted, and, if I must tell the whole truth, I was ashamed.

'Gräuben, we will see whether you will say the same thing tomorrow.'

'Tomorrow, dear Axel, I will say what I say Today.'

Gräuben and I, hand in hand, but in silence, pursued our way. The emotions of that day were breaking my heart.

After all, I thought, the kalends of July are a long way off, and between this and then many things may take place which will cure my uncle of his desire to travel underground.

It was night when we arrived at the house in Königstrasse. I expected to find all quiet there, my uncle in bed as was his custom, and Martha giving her last touches with the feather brush.

But I had not taken into account the Professor's impatience. I found him shouting- and working himself up amidst a crowd of porters and messengers who were all depositing various loads in the passage. Our old servant was at her wits' end.

'Come, Axel, come, you miserable wretch,' my uncle cried from as far off as he could see me. 'Your boxes are not packed, and my papers are not arranged; where's the key of my carpet bag? and what have you done with my gaiters?'

I stood thunderstruck. My voice failed. Scarcely could my

lips utter the words:

'Are we really going?'

'Of course, you unhappy boy! Could I have dreamed that yon would have gone out for a walk instead of hurrying your preparations forward?'

'Are we to go?' I asked again, with sinking hopes.

'Yes; the day after Tomorrow, early.'

I could hear no more. I fled for refuge into my own little room.

All hope was now at an end. My uncle had been all the morning making purchases of a part of the tools and apparatus required for this desperate undertaking. The passage was encumbered with rope ladders, knotted cords, torches, flasks, grappling irons, alpenstocks, pickaxes, iron shod sticks, enough to load ten men.

I spent an awful night. Next morning I was called early. I had quite decided I would not open the door. But how was I to resist the sweet voice which was always music to my ears, saying, 'My dear Axel?'

I came out of my room. I thought my pale countenance and my red and sleepless eyes would work upon Gräuben's sympathies and change her mind.

'Ah! my dear Axel,' she said. 'I see you are better. A night's rest has done you good.'

'Done me good!' I exclaimed.

I rushed to the glass. Well, in fact I did look better than I had expected. I could hardly believe my own eyes.

'Axel,' she said, 'I have had a long talk with my guardian. He is a bold philosopher, a man of immense courage, and you must remember that his blood flows in your veins. He has confided to me his plans, his hopes, and why and how he hopes to attain his object. He will no doubt succeed. My dear Axel, it is a grand thing to devote yourself to science! What honour will fall upon Herr Liedenbrock, and so be reflected upon his companion! When you return, Axel, you will be a man, his equal, free to speak and to act independently, and free to—'

The dear girl only finished this sentence by blushing. Her words revived me. Yet I refused to believe we should start. I drew Gräuben into the Professor's study.

'Uncle, is it true that we are to go?'

'Why do you doubt?'

'Well, I don't doubt,' I said, not to vex him; 'but, I ask, what need is there to hurry?'

'Time, time, flying with irreparable rapidity.'

'But it is only the 16th May, and until the end of June—'

'What, you monument of ignorance! do you think you can get to Iceland in a couple of days? If you had not deserted me like a fool I should have taken you to the Copenhagen office, to Liffender & Co., and you would have learned then that there is only one trip every month from Copenhagen to Rejkiavik, on the 22nd.'

'Well?'

'Well, if we waited for the 22nd June we should be too late to see the shadow of Scartaris touch the crater of Sneffels. Therefore we must get to Copenhagen as fast as we can to secure our passage. Go and pack up.'

There was no reply to this. I went up to my room. Gräuben followed me. She undertook to pack up all things necessary for my voyage. She was no more moved than if I had been starting for a little trip to Lübeck or Heligoland. Her little hands moved without haste. She talked quietly. She supplied me with sensible reasons for our expedition. She delighted me, and yet I was angry with her. Now and then I felt I ought to break out into a passion, but she took no notice and went on her way as methodically as ever.

Finally the last strap was buckled; I came downstairs. All that day the philosophical instrument makers and the electricians kept coming and going. Martha was distracted.

'Is master mad?' she asked.

I nodded my head.

'And is he going to take you with him?'

I nodded again.

'Where to?'

I pointed with my finger downward.

'Down into the cellar?' cried the old servant.

'No,' I said. 'Lower down than that.'

Night came. But I knew nothing about the lapse of time.

'Tomorrow morning at six precisely,' my uncle decreed 'we start.'

At ten o'clock I fell upon my bed, a dead lump of inert matter. All through the night terror had hold of me. I spent it dreaming of abysses. I was a prey to delirium. I felt myself grasped by the Professor's sinewy hand, dragged along, hurled down, shattered into little bits. I dropped down unfathomable precipices with the accelerating velocity of bodies falling through space. My life had become an endless fall. I awoke at five with shattered nerves, trembling and weary. I came downstairs. My uncle was at table, devouring his breakfast. I stared at him with horror and disgust. But dear Gräuben was there; so I said nothing, and could eat nothing.

At half-past five there was a rattle of wheels outside. A large carriage was there to take us to the Altona railway station. It was soon piled up with my uncle's multifarious preparations.

'Where's your box?' he cried.

'It is ready,' I replied, with faltering voice.

'Then make haste down, or we shall lose the train.'

It was now manifestly impossible to maintain the struggle against destiny. I went up again to my room, and rolling my portmanteaus downstairs I darted after him.

At that moment my uncle was solemnly investing Gräuben with the reins of government. My pretty Virlandaise was as calm and collected as was her wont. She kissed her guardian; but could not restrain a tear in touching my cheek with her gentle lips.

'Gräuben!' I murmured.

'Go, my dear Axel, go! I am now your betrothed; and when you come back I will be your wife.'

I pressed her in my arms and took my place in the carriage. Martha and the young girl, standing at the door, waved their last farewell. Then the horses, roused by the driver's whistling, darted off at a gallop on the road to Altona.

EIGHT

SERIOUS PREPARATIONS FOR VERTICAL DESCENT

Altona, which is but a suburb of Hamburg, is the terminus of the Kiel railway, which was to carry us to the Belts. In twenty minutes we were in Holstein.

At half-past six the carriage stopped at the station; my uncle's numerous packages, his voluminous impedimenta, were unloaded, removed, labelled, weighed, put into the luggage vans, and at seven we were seated face to face in our compartment. The whistle sounded, the engine started, we were off.

Was I resigned? No, not yet. Yet the cool morning air and the scenes on the road, rapidly changed by the swiftness of the train, drew me away somewhat from my sad reflections.

As for the Professor's reflections, they went far in advance of the swiftest express. We were alone in the carriage, but we sat in silence. My uncle examined all his pockets and his travelling bag with the minutest care. I saw that he had not forgotten the smallest matter of detail.

Amongst other documents, a sheet of paper, carefully folded, bore the heading of the Danish consulate with the signature of W. Christiensen, consul at Hamburg and the Professor's friend. With this we possessed the proper introductions to the

Governor of Iceland.

I also observed the famous document most carefully laid up in a secret pocket in his portfolio. I bestowed a malediction upon it, and then proceeded to examine the country.

It was a very long succession of uninteresting loamy and fertile flats, a very easy country for the construction of railways, and propitious for the laying-down of these direct level lines so dear to railway companies.

I had no time to get tired of the monotony; for in three hours we stopped at Kiel, close to the sea.

The luggage being labelled for Copenhagen, we had no occasion to look after it. Yet the Professor watched every article with jealous vigilance, until all were safe on board. There they disappeared in the hold.

My uncle, notwithstanding his hurry, had so well calculated the relations between the train and the steamer that we had a whole day to spare. The steamer Ellenora, did not start until night. Thence sprang a feverish state of excitement in which the impatient irascible traveller devoted to perdition the railway directors and the steamboat companies and the governments which allowed such intolerable slowness. I was obliged to act chorus to him when he attacked the captain of the Ellenora upon this subject. The captain disposed of us summarily.

At Kiel, as elsewhere, we must do something to while away the time. What with walking on the verdant shores of the bay within which nestles the little town, exploring the thick woods which make it look like a nest embowered amongst thick foliage, admiring the villas, each provided with a little bathing house, and moving about and grumbling, at last ten o'clock came.

The heavy coils of smoke from the Ellenora's funnel unrolled in the sky, the bridge shook with the quivering of the struggling steam; we were on board, and owners for the time of two berths, one over the other, in the only saloon cabin on board.

At a quarter past the moorings were loosed and the throbbing steamer pursued her way over the dark waters of the Great Belt.

The night was dark; there was a sharp breeze and a rough sea, a few lights appeared on shore through the thick darkness; later on, I cannot tell when, a dazzling light from some lighthouse threw a bright stream of fire along the waves; and this is all I can remember of this first portion of our sail.

At seven in the morning we landed at Korsor, a small town on the west coast of Zealand. There we were transferred from the boat to another line of railway, which took us by just as flat a country as the plain of Holstein.

Three hours' travelling brought us to the capital of Denmark. My uncle had not shut his eyes all night. In his impatience I believe he was trying to accelerate the train with his feet.

At last he discerned a stretch of sea.

'The Sound!' he cried.

At our left was a huge building that looked like a hospital.

'That's a lunatic asylum,' said one of or travelling companions.

Very good! thought I, just the place we want to end our days in; and great as it is, that asylum is not big enough to contain all Professor Liedenbrock's madness!

At ten in the morning, at last, we set our feet in Copenhagen; the luggage was put upon a carriage and taken with ourselves to the Phoenix Hotel in Breda Gate. This took half an hour, for the station is out of the town. Then my uncle, after a hasty toilet, dragged me after him. The porter at the hotel could speak German and English; but the Professor, as a polyglot, questioned him in good Danish, and it was in the same language that that personage directed him to the Museum of Northern Antiquities.

The curator of this curious establishment, in which wonders are gathered together out of which the ancient history of the country might be reconstructed by means of its stone weapons, its cups and its jewels, was a learned savant, the friend of the Danish consul at Hamburg, Professor Thomsen.

My uncle had a cordial letter of introduction to him. As a general rule one savant greets another with coolness. But here the case was different. M. Thomsen, like a good friend, gave the Professor Liedenbrock a cordial greeting, and he even vouchsafed the same kindness to his nephew. It is hardly necessary to say the secret was sacredly kept from the excellent curator; we were simply disinterested travellers visiting Iceland out of harmless curiosity.

M. Thomsen placed his services at our disposal, and we visited the quays with the object of finding out the next vessel to sail.

I was yet in hopes that there would be no means of getting to Iceland. But there was no such luck. A small Danish schooner, the Valkyria, was to set sail for Rejkiavik on the 2nd of June. The captain, M. Bjarne, was on board. His intending passenger was so joyful that he almost squeezed his hands till they ached. That good man was rather surprised at his energy. To him it seemed a very simple thing to go to Iceland, as that was his business; but to my uncle it was sublime. The worthy captain took advantage of his enthusiasm to charge double fares; but we did not trouble ourselves about mere trifles. .

'You must be on board on Tuesday, at seven in the morning,' said Captain Bjarne, after having pocketed more dollars than were his due.

Then we thanked M. Thomsen for his kindness, and we returned to the Phoenix Hotel.

'It's all right, it's all right,' my uncle repeated. 'How fortunate we are to have found this boat ready for sailing. Now let us have some breakfast and go about the town.'

We went first to Kongens-nye-Torw, an irregular square in which are two innocent-looking guns, which need not alarm any one. Close by, at No. 5, there was a French 'restaurant,' kept by a cook of the name of Vincent, where we had an ample breakfast for four marks each (2s. 4d.).

Then I took a childish pleasure in exploring the city; my uncle let me take him with me, but he took notice of nothing, neither the insignificant king's palace, nor the pretty seventeenth century bridge, which spans the canal before the museum, nor that immense cenotaph of Thorwaldsen's, adorned with horrible mural painting, and containing within it a collection of the sculptor's works, nor in a fine park the toylike chateau of Rosenberg, nor the beautiful renaissance edifice of the Exchange, nor its spire composed of the twisted tails of four bronze dragons, nor the great windmill on the ramparts, whose huge arms dilated in the sea breeze like the sails of a ship.

What delicious walks we should have had together, my pretty Virlandaise and I, along the harbour where the two-deckers and the frigate slept peaceably by the red roofing of the warehouse, by the green banks of the strait, through the deep shades of the trees amongst which the fort is half concealed, where the guns are thrusting out their black throats between branches of alder and willow.

But, alas! Gräuben was far away; and I never hoped to see her again.

But if my uncle felt no attraction towards these romantic scenes he was very much struck with the aspect of a certain church spire situated in the island of Amak, which forms the south-west quarter of Copenhagen.

I was ordered to direct my feet that way; I embarked on a small steamer which plies on the canals, and in a few minutes she touched the quay of the dockyard.

After crossing a few narrow streets where some convicts, in trousers half yellow and half grey, were at work under the orders of the gangers, we arrived at the Vor Frelsers Kirk. There was nothing remarkable about the church; but there was a reason why its tall spire had attracted the Professor's attention. Starting from the top of the tower, an external staircase wound around the spire, the spirals circling up into the sky.

'Let us get to the top,' said my uncle.

'I shall be dizzy,' I said.

'The more reason why we should go up; we must get used to it.'

'But—'

'Come, I tell you; don't waste our time.'

I had to obey. A keeper who lived at the other end of the street handed us the key, and the ascent began.

My uncle went ahead with a light step. I followed him not without alarm, for my head was very apt to feel dizzy; I possessed neither the equilibrium of an eagle nor his fearless nature.

As long as we were protected on the inside of the winding staircase up the tower, all was well enough; but after toiling up a hundred and fifty steps the fresh air came to salute my face, and we were on the leads of the tower. There the aerial staircase began its gyrations, only guarded by a thin iron rail, and the narrowing steps seemed to ascend into infinite space!

'Never shall I be able to do it,' I said.

'Don't be a coward; come up, sir'; said my uncle with the coldest cruelty.

I had to follow, clutching at every step. The keen air made me giddy; I felt the spire rocking with every gust of wind; my knees began to fail; soon I was crawling on my knees, then creeping on my stomach; I closed my eyes; I seemed to be lost in space.

At last I reached the apex, with the assistance of my uncle dragging me up by the collar.

'Look down!' he cried. 'Look down well! You must take a lesson in abysses.'

I opened my eyes. I saw houses squashed flat as if they had all fallen down from the skies; a smoke fog seemed to drown them. Over my head ragged clouds were drifting past, and by an optical inversion they seemed stationary, while the steeple, the ball and I were all spinning along with fantastic speed.

Far away on one side was the green country, on the other the sea sparkled, bathed in sunlight. The Sound stretched away to Elsinore, dotted with a few white sails, like sea-gulls' wings; and in the misty east and away to the north-east lay outstretched the faintly-shadowed shores of Sweden. All this immensity of space whirled and wavered, fluctuating beneath my eyes.

But I was compelled to rise, to stand up, to look. My first lesson in dizziness lasted an hour. When I got permission to come down and feel the solid street pavements I was afflicted with severe lumbago.

'Tomorrow we will do it again,' said the Professor.

And it was so; for five days in succession, I was obliged to undergo this anti-vertiginous exercise; and whether I would or not, I made some improvement in the art of 'lofty contemplations.'

NINE

ICELAND! BUT WHAT NEXT?

The day for our departure arrived. The day before it our kind friend M. Thomsen brought us letters of introduction to Count Trampe, the Governor of Iceland, M. Picturssen, the bishop's suffragan, and M. Finsen, mayor of Rejkiavik. My uncle expressed his gratitude by tremendous compressions of both his hands.

On the 2nd, at six in the evening, all our precious baggage being safely on board the Valkyria, the captain took us into a very narrow cabin.

'Is the wind favourable?' my uncle asked.

'Excellent,' replied Captain Bjarne; 'a sou'-easter. We shall pass down the Sound full speed, with all sails set.'

In a few minutes the schooner, under her mizen, brigantine, topsail, and topgallant sail, loosed from her moorings and made full sail through the straits. In an hour the capital of Denmark seemed to sink below the distant waves, and the Valkyria was skirting the coast by Elsinore. In my nervous frame of mind I expected to see the ghost of Hamlet wandering on the legendary castle terrace.

'Sublime madman!' I said, 'no doubt you would approve of our expedition. Perhaps you would keep us company to the centre of the globe, to find the solution of your eternal doubts.'

But there was no ghostly shape upon the ancient walls. Indeed, the castle is much younger than the heroic prince of Denmark. It now answers the purpose of a sumptuous lodge for the doorkeeper of the straits of the Sound, before which every year there pass fifteen thousand ships of all nations.

The castle of Kronsberg soon disappeared in the mist, as well as the tower of Helsingborg, built on the Swedish coast, and the schooner passed lightly on her way urged by the breezes of the Cattegat.

The Valkyria was a splendid sailer, but on a sailing vessel you can place no dependence. She was taking to Rejkiavik coal, household goods, earthenware, woollen clothing, and a cargo of wheat. The crew consisted of five men, all Danes.

'How long will the passage take?' my uncle asked.

'Ten days,' the captain replied, 'if we don't meet a nor'-wester in passing the Faroes.'

'But are you not subject to considerable delays?'

'No, M. Liedenbrock, don't be uneasy, we shall get there in very good time.'

At evening the schooner doubled the Skaw at the northern point of Denmark, in the night passed the Skager Rack, skirted Norway by Cape Lindness, and entered the North Sea.

In two days more we sighted the coast of Scotland near Peterhead,,and the Valkyria turned her lead towards the Faroe

Islands, passing between the Orkneys and Shetlands.

Soon the schooner encountered the great Atlantic swell; she had to tack against the north wind, and reached the Faroes only with some difficulty. On the 8th the captain made out Myganness, the southernmost of these islands, and from that moment took a straight course for Cape Portland, the most southerly point of Iceland.

The passage was marked by nothing unusual. I bore the troubles of the sea pretty well; my uncle, to his own intense disgust, and his greater shame, was ill all through the voyage.

He therefore was unable to converse with the captain about Snæfell, the way to get to it, the facilities for transport, he was obliged to put off these inquiries until his arrival, and spent all his time at full length in his cabin, of which the timbers creaked and shook with every pitch she took. It must be confessed he was not undeserving of his punishment.

On the 11th we reached Cape Portland. The clear open weather gave us a good view of Myrdals jokul, which overhangs it. The cape is merely a low hill with steep sides, standing lonely by the beach.

The Valkyria kept at some distance from the coast, taking a westerly course amidst great shoals of whales and sharks. Soon we came in sight of an enormous perforated rock, through which the sea dashed furiously. The Westman islets seemed to rise out of the ocean like a group of rocks in a liquid plain. From that time the schooner took a wide berth and swept at a great distance round Cape Rejkianess, which forms the western point of Iceland.

The rough sea prevented my uncle from coming on deck to admire these shattered and surf-beaten coasts.

Forty-eight hours after, coming out of a storm which forced the schooner to scud under bare poles, we sighted east of us the beacon on Cape Skagen, where dangerous rocks extend far away seaward. An Icelandic pilot came on board, and in three hours the *Valkyria* dropped her anchor before Rejkiavik, in Faxa Bay.

The Professor at last emerged from his cabin, rather pale and wretched-looking, but still full of enthusiasm, and with ardent satisfaction shining in his eyes.

The population of the town, wonderfully interested in the arrival of a vessel from which every one expected something, formed in groups upon the quay.

My uncle left in haste his floating prison, or rather hospital. But before quitting the deck of the schooner he dragged me forward, and pointing with outstretched finger north of the bay at a distant mountain terminating in a double peak, a pair of cones covered with perpetual snow, he cried:

'Snæfell! Snæfell!'

Then recommending me, by an impressive gesture, to keep silence, he went into the boat which awaited him. I followed, and presently we were treading the soil of Iceland.

The first man we saw was a good-looking fellow enough, in a general's uniform. Yet he was not a general but a magistrate, the Governor of the island, M. le Baron Trampe himself. The Professor was soon aware of the presence he was in. He delivered him his letters from Copenhagen, and then followed a short conversation in the Danish language, the purport of which I was quite ignorant of, and for a very good reason. But the result of this first conversation was, that Baron Trampe placed himself entirely at the service of Professor Liedenbrock.

My uncle was just as courteously received by the mayor, M. Finsen, whose appearance was as military, and disposition and office as pacific, as the Governor's.

As for the bishop's suffragan, M. Picturssen, he was at that moment engaged on an episcopal visitation in the north. For the time we must be resigned to wait for the honour of being presented to him. But M. Fridrikssen, professor of natural sciences at the school of Rejkiavik, was a delightful man, and his friendship became very precious to me. This modest philosopher spoke only Danish and Latin. He came to proffer me his good offices in the language of Horace, and I felt that we were made to understand each other. In fact he was the only person in Iceland with whom I could converse at all.

This good-natured gentleman made over to us two of the three rooms which his house contained, and we were soon installed in it with all our luggage, the abundance of which rather astonished the good people of Rejkiavik.

'Well, Axel,' said my uncle, 'we are getting on, and now the worst is over.'

'The worst!' I said, astonished.

'To be sure, now we have nothing to do but go down.'

'Oh, if that is all, you are quite right; but after all, when we have gone down, we shall have to get up again, I suppose?'

'Oh I don't trouble myself about that. Come, there's no time to lose; I am going to the library. Perhaps there is some manuscript of Saknussemm's there, and I should be glad to consult it.'

'Well, while you are there I will go into the town. Won't you?'

'Oh, that is very uninteresting to me. It is not what is upon this island, but what is underneath, that interests me.'

I went out, and wandered wherever chance took me.

It would not be easy to lose your way in Rejkiavik. I was therefore under no necessity to inquire the road, which exposes one to mistakes when the only medium of intercourse is gesture.

The town extends along a low and marshy level, between two hills. An immense bed of lava bounds it on one side, and falls gently towards the sea. On the other extends the vast bay of Faxa, shut in at the north by the enormous glacier of the Snæfell, and of which the Valkyria was for the time the only occupant. Usually the English and French conservators of fisheries moor in this bay, but just then they were cruising about the western coasts of the island.

The longest of the only two streets that Rejkiavik possesses was parallel with the beach. Here live the merchants and traders, in wooden cabins made of red planks set horizontally; the other street, running west, ends at the little lake between the house of the bishop and other non-commercial people.

I had soon explored these melancholy ways; here and there I got a glimpse of faded turf, looking like a worn-out bit of carpet, or some appearance of a kitchen garden, the sparse vegetables of which (potatoes, cabbages, and lettuces), would have figured appropriately upon a Lilliputian table. A few sickly wallflowers were trying to enjoy the air and sunshine.

About the middle of the tin-commercial street I found the public cemetery, inclosed with a mud wall, and where there seemed plenty of room.

Then a few steps brought me to the Governor's house, a but compared with the town hall of Hamburg, a palace in comparison with the cabins of the Icelandic population.

Between the little lake and the town the church is built in the Protestant style, of calcined stones extracted out of the volcanoes by their own labour and at their own expense; in high westerly winds it was manifest that the red tiles of the roof would be scattered in the air, to the great danger of the faithful worshippers.

On a neighbouring hill I perceived the national school, where, as I was informed later by our host, were taught Hebrew, English, French, and Danish, four languages of which, with shame I confess it, I don't know a single word; after an examination I should have had to stand last of the forty scholars educated at this little college, and I should have been held unworthy to sleep along with them in one of those little double closets, where more delicate youths would have died of suffocation the very first night.

In three hours I had seen not only the town but its environs. The general aspect was wonderfully dull. No trees, and scarcely any vegetation. Everywhere bare rocks, signs of volcanic action. The Icelandic buts are made of earth and turf, and the walls slope inward; they rather resemble roofs placed on the ground. But then these roofs are meadows of comparative fertility. Thanks to the internal heat, the grass grows on them to some degree of perfection. It is carefully mown in the hay season; if it were not, the horses would come to pasture on these green abodes.

In my excursion I met but few people. On returning to the main street I found the greater part of the population busied in drying, salting, and putting on board codfish, their chief export. The men looked like robust but heavy, blond Germans with pensive eyes, conscious of being far removed from their fellow creatures, poor exiles relegated to this land of ice, poor creatures who should have been Esquimaux, since nature had condemned them to live only just outside the arctic circle! In vain did I try to detect a smile upon their lips; sometimes by a spasmodic and involuntary contraction of the muscles they seemed to laugh, but they never smiled.

Their costume consisted of a coarse jacket of black woollen cloth called in Scandinavian lands a 'vadmel,' a hat with a very broad brim, trousers with a narrow edge of red, and a bit of leather rolled round the foot for shoes.

The women looked as sad and as resigned as the men; their faces were agreeable but expressionless, and they wore gowns and petticoats of dark 'vadmel'; as maidens, they wore over their braided hair a little knitted brown cap; when married, they put around their heads a coloured handkerchief, crowned with a peak of white linen.

After a good walk I returned to M. Fridrikssen's house, where I found my uncle already in his host's company.

TEN

INTERESTING CONVERSATIONS WITH ICELANDIC SAVANTS

Dinner was ready. Professor Liedenbrock devoured his portion voraciously, for his compulsory fast on board had converted his stomach into a vast unfathomable gulf. There was nothing remarkable in the meal itself; but the hospitality of our host, more Danish than Icelandic, reminded me of the heroes of old. It was evident that we were more at home than he was himself.

The conversation was carried on in the vernacular tongue, which my uncle mixed with German and M. Fridrikssen with Latin for my benefit. It turned upon scientific questions as befits philosophers; but Professor Liedenbrock was excessively reserved, and at every sentence spoke to me with his eyes, enjoining the most absolute silence upon our plans.

In the first place M. Fridrikssen wanted to know what success my uncle had had at the library.

'Your library! why there is nothing but a few tattered books upon almost deserted shelves.'

'Indeed!' replied M. Fridrikssen, 'why we possess eight thousand volumes, many of them valuable and scarce, works in the old Scandinavian language, and we have all the novelties that Copenhagen sends us every year.'

'Where do you keep your eight thousand volumes? For my part—'

'Oh, M. Liedenbrock, they are all over the country. In this icy region we are fond of study. There is not a farmer nor a fisherman that cannot read and does not read. Our principle is, that books, instead of growing mouldy behind an iron grating, should be worn out under the eyes of many readers. Therefore, these volumes are passed from one to another, read over and over, referred to again and again; and it often happens that they find their way back to their shelves only after an absence of a year or two.'

'And in the meantime,' said my uncle rather spitefully, 'strangers—'

'Well, what would you have? Foreigners have their libraries at home, and the first essential for labouring people is that they should be educated. I repeat to you the love of reading runs in Icelandic blood. In 1816 we founded a prosperous literary society; learned strangers think themselves honoured in becoming members of it. It publishes books which educate our fellow-countrymen, and do the country great service. If you will consent to be a corresponding member, Herr Liedenbrock, you will be giving us great pleasure.'

My uncle, who had already joined about a hundred learned societies, accepted with a grace which evidently touched M. Fridrikssen.

'Now,' said he, 'will you be kind enough to tell me what books you hoped to find in our library and I may perhaps enable you to consult them?'

My uncle's eyes and mine met. He hesitated. This direct question went to the root of the matter. But after a moment's reflection he decided on speaking.

'Monsieur Fridrikssen, I wished to know if amongst your ancient books you possessed any of the works of Arne Saknussemm?'

'Arne Saknussemm!' replied the Rejkiavik professor. 'You mean that learned sixteenth century savant, a naturalist, a chemist, and a traveller?'

'Just so!'

'One of the glories of Icelandic literature and science?'

'That's the man.'

'An illustrious man anywhere!'

'Quite so.'

'And whose courage was equal to his genius!'

'I see that you know him well.'

My uncle was bathed in delight at hearing his hero thus described. He feasted his eyes upon M. Fridrikssen's face.

'Well,' he cried, 'where are his works?'

'His works, we have them not.'

'What—not in Iceland?'

'They are neither in Iceland nor anywhere else.'

'Why is that?'

'Because Arne Saknussemm was persecuted for heresy, and in 1573 his books were burned by the hands of the common hangman.'

'Very good! Excellent!' cried my uncle, to the great scandal of the professor of natural history.

'What!' he cried.

'Yes, yes; now it is all clear, now it is all unravelled; and I see why Saknussemm, put into the Index Expurgatorius, and compelled to hide the discoveries made by his genius, was obliged to bury in an incomprehensible cryptogram the secret—'

'What secret?' asked M. Fridrikssen, starting.

'Oh, just a secret which—' my uncle stammered.

'Have you some private document in your possession?' asked our host.

'No; I was only supposing a case.'

'Oh, very well,' answered M. Fridrikssen, who was kind enough not to pursue the subject when he had noticed the embarrassment of his friend. 'I hope you will not leave our island until you have seen some of its mineralogical wealth.'

'Certainly,' replied my uncle; 'but I am rather late; or have not others been here before me?'

'Yes, Herr Liedenbrock; the labours of MM. Olafsen and Povelsen, pursued by order of the king, the researches of Troïl the scientific mission of MM. Gaimard and Robert on the

French *corvette La Recherche*,[1] and lately the observations of scientific men who came in the Reine Hortense, have added materially to our knowledge of Iceland. But I assure you there is plenty left.'

'Do you think so?' said my uncle, pretending to look very modest, and trying to hide the curiosity was flashing out of his eyes.

'Oh, yes; how many mountains, glaciers, and volcanoes there are to study, which are as yet but imperfectly known! Then, without going any further, that mountain in the horizon. That is Snæfell.'

'Ah!' said my uncle, as coolly as he was able, 'is that Snæfell?'

'Yes; one of the most curious volcanoes, and the crater of which has scarcely ever been visited.'

'Is it extinct?'

'Oh, yes; more than five hundred years.'

'Well,' replied my uncle, who was frantically locking his legs together to keep himself from jumping up in the air, 'that is where I mean to begin my geological studies, there on that Seffel—Fessel—what do you call it?'

'Snæfell,' replied the excellent M. Fridrikssen.

This part of the conversation was in Latin; I had understood every word of it, and I could hardly conceal my amusement at seeing my uncle trying to keep down the excitement and satisfaction which were brimming over in every limb and every feature. He tried hard to put on an innocent little expression of simplicity; but it looked like a diabolical grin.

'Yes,' said he, 'your words decide me. We will try to scale that Snæfell; perhaps even we may pursue our studies in its crater!'

1. Recherche was sent out in 1835 by Admiral Duperré to learn the fate of the lost expedition of M. de Blosseville in the Lilloise which has never been heard of.

'I am very sorry,' said M. Fridrikssen, 'that my engagements will not allow me to absent myself, or I would have accompanied you myself with both pleasure and profit.'

'Oh, no, no!' replied my uncle with great animation, 'we would not disturb any one for the world, M. Fridrikssen. Still, I thank you with all my heart: the company of such a talented man would have been very serviceable, but the duties of your profession—'

I am glad to think that our host, in the innocence of his Icelandic soul, was blind to the transparent artifices of my uncle.

'I very much approve of your beginning with that volcano, M. Liedenbrock. You will gather a harvest of interesting observations. But, tell me, how do you expect to get to the peninsula of Snæfell?'

'By sea, crossing the bay. That's the most direct way.'

'No doubt; but it is impossible.'

'Why?'

'Because we don't possess a single boat at Rejkiavik.'

'You don't mean to say so?'

'You will have to go by land, following the shore. It will be longer, but more interesting.'

'Very well, then; and now I shall have to see about a guide.'

'I have one to offer you.'

'A safe, intelligent man.'

'Yes; an inhabitant of that peninsula He is an eiderdown hunter, and very clever. He speaks Danish perfectly.'

'When can I see him?'

'Tomorrow, if you like.'

'Why not Today?'

'Because he won't be here till Tomorrow.'

'Tomorrow, then,' added my uncle with a sigh.

This momentous conversation ended in a few minutes with warm acknowledgments paid by the German to the Icelandic

Professor. At this dinner my uncle had just elicited important facts, amongst others, the history of Saknussemm, the reason of the mysterious document, that his host would not accompany him in his expedition, and that the very next day a guide would be waiting upon him.

ELEVEN

A GUIDE FOUND TO THE CENTRE OF THE EARTH

In the evening I took a short walk on the beach and returned at night to my plank-bed, where I slept soundly all night.

When I awoke I heard my uncle talking at a great rate in the next room. I immediately dressed and joined him.

He was conversing in the Danish language with a tall man, of robust build. This fine fellow must have been possessed of great strength. His eyes, set in a large and ingenuous face, seemed to me very intelligent; they were of a dreamy sea-blue. Long hair, which would have been called red even in England, fell in long meshes upon his broad shoulders. The movements of this native were lithe and supple; but he made little use of his arms in speaking, like a man who knew nothing or cared nothing about the language of gestures. His whole appearance bespoke perfect calmness and self-possession, not indolence but tranquillity. It was felt at once that he would be beholden to nobody, that he worked for his own convenience, and that nothing in this world could astonish or disturb his philosophic calmness.

I caught the shades of this Icelander's character by the way in which he listened to the impassioned flow of words which fell from the Professor. He stood with arms crossed, perfectly unmoved by my uncle's incessant gesticulations. A negative was expressed by a slow movement of the head from left to right, an affirmative by a slight bend, so slight that his long hair scarcely moved. He carried economy of motion even to parsimony.

Certainly I should never have dreamt in looking at this man that he was a hunter; he did not look likely to frighten his game, nor did he seem as if he would even get near it. But the mystery was explained when M. Fridrikssen informed me that this tranquil personage was only a hunter of the eider duck, whose under plumage constitutes the chief wealth of the island. This is the celebrated eider down, and it requires no great rapidity of movement to get it.

Early in summer the female, a very pretty bird, goes to build her nest among the rocks of the fiords with which the coast is fringed. After building the nest she feathers it with down plucked from her own breast. Immediately the hunter, or rather the trader, comes and robs the nest, and the female recommences her work. This goes on as long as she has any down left. When she has stripped herself bare the male takes his turn to pluck himself. But as the coarse and hard plumage of the male has no commercial value, the hunter does not take the trouble to rob the nest of this; the female therefore lays her eggs in the spoils of her mate, the young are hatched, and next year the harvest begins again.

Now, as the eider duck does not select steep cliffs for her nest, but rather the smooth terraced rocks which slope to the sea, the Icelandic hunter might exercise his calling without any inconvenient exertion. He was a farmer who was not obliged either to sow or reap his harvest, but merely to gather it in.

This grave, phlegmatic, and silent individual was called Hans Bjelke; and he came recommended by M. Fridrikssen. He was our future guide. His manners were a singular contrast with my uncle's.

Nevertheless, they soon came to understand each other. Neither looked at the amount of the payment: the one was ready to accept whatever was offered; the other was ready to give whatever was demanded. Never was bargain more readily concluded.

The result of the treaty was, that Hans engaged on his part to conduct us to the village of Stapi, on the south shore of the Snæfell peninsula, at the very foot of the volcano. By land this would be about twenty-two miles, to be done, said my uncle, in two days.

But when he learnt that the Danish mile was 24,000 feet long, he was obliged to modify his calculations and allow seven or eight days for the march.

Four horses were to be placed at our disposal—two to carry him and me, two for the baggage. Hams, as was his custom, would go on foot. He knew all that part of the coast perfectly, and promised to take us the shortest way.

His engagement was not to terminate with our arrival at Stapi; he was to continue in my uncle's service for the whole period of his scientific researches, for the remuneration of three rixdales a week (about twelve shillings), but it was an express article of the covenant that his wages should be counted out to him every Saturday at six o'clock in the evening, which, according to him, was one indispensable part of the engagement.

The start was fixed for the 16th of June. My uncle wanted to pay the hunter a portion in advance, but he refused with one word:

'Efter,' said he.

'After,' said the Professor for my edification.

The treaty concluded, Hans silently withdrew.

'A famous fellow,' cried my uncle; 'but he little thinks of the marvellous part he has to play in the future.'

'So he is to go with us as far as—'

'As far as the centre of the earth, Axel.'

Forty-eight hours were left before our departure; to my great regret I had to employ them in preparations; for all our ingenuity was required to pack every article to the best advantage; instruments here, arms there, tools in this package, provisions in that: four sets of packages in all.

The instruments were:

1. An Eigel's centigrade thermometer, graduated up to 150 degrees (302 degrees Fahr.), which seemed to me too much or too little. Too much if the internal heat was to rise so high, for in this case we should be baked, not enough to measure the temperature of springs or any matter in a state of fusion.

2. An aneroid barometer, to indicate extreme pressures of the atmosphere. An ordinary barometer would not have answered the purpose, as the pressure would increase during our descent to a point which the mercurial barometer[1] would not register.

3. A chronometer, made by Boissonnas, jun., of Geneva, accurately set to the meridian of Hamburg.

4. Two compasses, viz., a common compass and a dipping needle.

5. A night glass.

6. Two of Ruhmkorff's apparatus, which, by means of an

1. In M. Verne's book a 'manometer' is the instrument used, of which very little is known. In a complete list of philosophical instruments the translator cannot find the name. As he is assured by a first-rate instrument maker, Chadburn, of Liverpool, that an aneroid can be constructed to measure any depth, he has thought it best to furnish the adventurous professor with this more familiar instrument. The 'manometer' is generally known as a pressure gauge.—(Tr.)

2. Ruhmkorff's apparatus consists of a Bunsen pile worked with bichromate of potash, which makes no smell; an induction coil carries the electricity generated by the pile into communication with a lantern of peculiar construction; in this lantern there is a spiral glass tube from which the air has been excluded, and in which remains only a residuum of carbonic acid gas or of nitrogen. When the apparatus is put in action this gas becomes luminous, producing a white steady light. The pile and coil are placed in a leathern bag which the traveller carries over his shoulders; the lantern outside of the bag throws sufficient light into deep darkness; it enables one to venture without fear of explosions into the midst of the most inflammable gases, and is not extinguished even in the deepest waters. M. Ruhmkorff is a learned and most ingenious man of science; his great discovery is his induction coil, which produces a powerful stream of electricity. He obtained in 1864 the quinquennial prize of 50,000 franc reserved by the French government for the most ingenious application of electricity.

electric current, supplied a safe and handy portable light[2]

The arms consisted of two of Purdy's rifles and two brace of pistols. But what did we want arms for? We had neither savages nor wild beasts to fear, I supposed. But my uncle seemed to believe in his arsenal as in his instruments, and more especially in a considerable quantity of gun cotton, which is unaffected by moisture, and the explosive force of which exceeds that of gunpowder.

The tools comprised two pickaxes, two spades, a silk ropeladder, three iron-tipped sticks, a hatchet, a hammer, a dozen wedges and iron spikes, and a long knotted rope. Now this was a large load, for the ladder was 300 feet long.

And there were provisions too: this was not a large parcel, but it was comforting to know that of essence of beef and biscuits there were six months' consumption. Spirits were the only liquid, and of water we took none; but we had flasks, and my uncle depended on springs from which to fill them. Whatever objections I hazarded as to their quality, temperature, and even absence, remained ineffectual.

To complete the exact inventory of all our travelling accompaniments, I must not forget a pocket medicine chest, containing blunt scissors, splints for broken limbs, a piece of tape of unbleached linen, bandages and compresses, lint, a lancet for bleeding, all dreadful articles to take with one. Then there was a row of phials containing dextrine, alcoholic ether, liquid acetate of lead, vinegar, and ammonia drugs which afforded me no comfort. Finally, all the articles needful to supply Ruhmkorff's apparatus.

My uncle did not forget- a supply of tobacco, coarse grained powder, and amadou, nor a leathern belt in which he carried a sufficient quantity of gold, silver, and paper money. Six pairs of boots and shoes, made waterproof with a composition of indiarubber and naphtha, were packed amongst the tools.

'Clothed, shod, and equipped like this,' said my uncle, 'there is no telling how far we may go.'

The 14th was wholly spent in arranging all our different articles. In the evening we dined with Baron Tramps; the mayor of Rejkiavik, and Dr. Hyaltalin, the first medical man of the place, being of the party. M. Fridrikssen was not there. I learned afterwards that he and the Governor disagreed upon some question of administration, and did not speak to each other. I therefore knew not a single word of all that was said at this semi-official dinner; but I could not help noticing that my uncle talked the whole time.

On the 15th our preparations were all made. Our host gave the Professor very great pleasure by presenting him with a map of Iceland far more complete than that of Hendersen. It was the map of M. Olaf Nikolas Olsen, in the proportion of 1 to 480,000 of the actual size of the island, and published by the Icelandic Literary Society. It was a precious document for a mineralogist.

Our last evening was spent in intimate conversation with M. Fridrikssen, with whom I felt the liveliest sympathy; then, after the talk, succeeded, for me, at any rate, a disturbed and restless night.

At five in the morning I was awoke by the neighing and pawing of four horses under my window. I dressed hastily and came down into the street. Hans was finishing our packing, almost as it were without moving a limb; and yet he did his work cleverly. My uncle made more noise than execution, and the guide seemed to pay very little attention to his energetic directions.

At six o'clock our preparations were over. M. Fridrikssen shook hands with us. My uncle thanked him heartily for his extreme kindness. I constructed a few fine Latin sentences to express my cordial farewell. Then we bestrode our steeds and with his last adieu M. Fridrikssen treated me to a line of Virgil eminently applicable to such uncertain wanderers as we were likely to be:

'Et quacumque viam dedent fortuna sequamur.'
'Therever fortune clears a way,
Thither our ready footsteps stray.'

TWELVE

A BARREN LAND

We had started under a sky overcast but calm. There was no fear of heat, none of disastrous rain. It was just the weather for tourists.

The pleasure of riding on horseback over an unknown country made me easy to be pleased at our first start. I threw myself wholly into the pleasure of the trip, and enjoyed the feeling of freedom and satisfied desire. I was beginning to take a real share in the enterprise.

'Besides,' I said to myself, 'where's the risk? Here we are travelling all through a most interesting country! We are about to climb a very remarkable mountain; at the worst we are going to scramble down an extinct crater. It is evident that Saknussemm did nothing more than this. As for a passage leading to the centre of the globe, it is mere rubbish! perfectly impossible! Very well, then; let us get all the good we can out of this expedition, and don't let us haggle about the chances.'

This reasoning having settled my mind, we got out of Rejkiavik.

Hans moved steadily on, keeping ahead of us at an even, smooth, and rapid pace. The baggage horses followed him without giving any trouble. Then came my uncle and myself, looking not so very ill-mounted on our small but hardy animals.

Iceland is one of the largest islands in Europe. Its surface is 14,000 square miles, and it contains but 16,000 inhabitants. Geographers have divided it into four quarters, and we were crossing diagonally the south-west quarter, called the 'Sudvester Fjordungr.'

On leaving Rejkiavik Hans took us by the seashore. We passed lean pastures which were trying very hard, but in vain, to look green; yellow came out best. The rugged peaks of the trachyte rocks presented faint outlines on the eastern horizon; at times a few patches of snow, concentrating the vague light, glittered upon the slopes of the distant mountains; certain peaks, boldly uprising, passed through the grey clouds, and reappeared above the moving mists, like breakers emerging in the heavens.

Often these chains of barren rocks made a dip towards the sea, and encroached upon the scanty pasturage: but there was always enough room to pass. Besides, our horses instinctively chose the easiest places without ever slackening their pace. My uncle was refused even the satisfaction of stirring up his beast with whip or voice. He had no excuse for being impatient. I could not help smiling to see so tall a man on so small a pony, and as his long legs nearly touched the ground he looked like a six-legged centaur.

'Good horse! good horse!' he kept saying. 'You will see, Axel, that there is no more sagacious animal than the Icelandic horse. He is stopped by neither snow, nor storm, nor impassable roads, nor rocks, glaciers, or anything. He is courageous, sober, and surefooted. He never makes a false step, never shies. If there is a river or fiord to cross (and we shall meet with many) you will see him plunge in at once, just as if he were amphibious, and gain the opposite bank. But we must not hurry him; we must let him have his way, and we shall get on at the rate of thirty miles a day.'

'We may; but how about our guide?'

'Oh, never mind him. People like him get over the ground without a thought. There is so little action in this man that he will never get tired; and besides, if he wants it, he shall have my horse. I shall get cramped if I don't have a little action. The arms are all right, but the legs want exercise.'

We were advancing at a rapid pace. The country was already

almost a desert. Here and there was a lonely farm, called a boër built either of wood, or of sods, or of pieces of lava, looking like a poor beggar by the wayside. These ruinous huts seemed to solicit charity from passers-by; and on very small provocation we should have given alms for the relief of the poor inmates. In this country there were no roads and paths, and the poor vegetation, however slow, would soon efface the rare travellers' footsteps.

Yet this part of the province, at a very small distance from the capital, is reckoned among the inhabited and cultivated portions of Iceland. What, then, must other tracts be, more desert than this desert? In the first half mile we had not seen one farmer standing before his cabin door, nor one shepherd tending a flock less wild than himself, nothing but a few cows and sheep left to themselves. What then would be those convulsed regions upon which we were advancing, regions subject to the dire phenomena of eruptions, the offspring of volcanic explosions and subterranean convulsions?

We were to know them before long, but on consulting Olsen's map, I saw that they would be avoided by winding along the seashore. In fact, the great plutonic action is confined to the central portion of the island; there, rocks of the trappean and volcanic class, including trachyte, basalt, and tuffs and agglomerates associated with streams of lava, have made this a land of supernatural horrors. I had no idea of the spectacle which was awaiting us in the peninsula of Snæfell, where these ruins of a fiery nature have formed a frightful chaos.

In two hours from Rejkiavik we arrived at the burgh of Gufunes, called Aolkirkja, or principal church. There was nothing remarkable here but a few houses, scarcely enough for a German hamlet.

Hans stopped here half an hour. He shared with us our frugal breakfast; answering my uncle's questions about the road and our resting place that night with merely yes or no, except when he said 'Gardär.'

I consulted the map to see where Gardär was. I saw there was a small town of that name on the banks of the Hvalfiord, four miles from Rejkiavik. I showed it to my uncle.

'Four miles only!' he exclaimed; 'four miles out of twenty-eight. What a nice little walk!'

He was about to make an observation to the guide, who without answering resumed his place at the head, and went on his way.

Three hours later, still treading on the colourless grass of the pasture land, we had to work round the Kolla fiord, a longer way but an easier one than across that inlet. We soon entered into a 'pingstar' or parish called Ejulberg, from whose steeple twelve o'clock would have struck, if Icelandic churches were rich enough to possess clocks. But they are like the parishioners who have no watches and do without.

There our horses were baited; then taking the narrow path to left between a chain of hills and the sea, they carried us to our next stage, the aolkirkja of Brantär and one mile farther on, to Saurboër 'Annexia,' a chapel of ease built on the south shore of the Hvalfiord.

It was now four o'clock, and we had gone four Icelandic miles, or twenty-four English miles.

In that place the fiord was at least three English miles wide; the waves rolled with a rushing din upon the sharp-pointed rocks; this inlet was confined between walls of rock, precipices crowned by sharp peaks 2,000 feet high, and remarkable for the brown strata which separated the beds of reddish tuff. However much I might respect the intelligence of our quadrupeds, I hardly cared to put it to the test by trusting myself to it on horseback across an arm of the sea.

If they are as intelligent as they are said to be, I thought, they won't try it. In any case, I will tax my intelligence to direct theirs.

But my uncle would not wait. He spurred on to the edge. His steed lowered his head to examine the nearest waves and stopped. My uncle, who had an instinct of his own, too, applied pressure, and was again refused by the animal significantly shaking his head. Then followed strong language, and the whip; but the brute answered these arguments with kicks and endeavours to throw his rider. At last the clever little pony, with a bend of his knees, started from under the Professor's legs, and left him standing upon two boulders on the shore just like the colossus of Rhodes.

'Confounded brute!' cried the unhorsed horseman, suddenly degraded into a pedestrian, just as ashamed as a cavalry officer degraded to a foot soldier.

'Färja,' said the guide, touching his shoulder.

'What! a boat?'

'Der,' replied Hans, pointing to one.

'Yes,' I cried; 'there is a boat.'

'Why did not you say so then? Well, let us go on.'

'Tidvatten,' said the guide.

'What is he saying?'

'He says tide,' said my uncle, translating the Danish word.

'No doubt we must wait for the tide.'

'Förbida,' said my uncle.

'Ja,' replied Hans.

My uncle stamped with his foot, while the horses went on to the boat.

I perfectly understood the necessity of abiding a particular moment of the tide to undertake the crossing of the fiord, when, the sea having reached its greatest height, it should be slack water. Then the ebb and flow have no sensible effect, and the boat does not risk being carried either to the bottom or out to sea.

That favourable moment arrived only with six o'clock; when my uncle, myself, the guide, two other passengers and the four horses, trusted ourselves to a somewhat fragile raft. Accustomed as I was to the swift and sure steamers on the Elbe, I found the oars of the rowers rather a slow means of propulsion. It took us more than an hour to cross the fiord; but the passage was effected without any mishap.

In another half hour we had reached the aolkirkja of Gardär.

THIRTEEN

HOSPITALITY UNDER THE ARCTIC CIRCLE

It ought to have been night-time, but under the 65th parallel there was nothing surprising in the nocturnal polar light. In Iceland during the months of June and July the sun does not set.

But the temperature was much lower. I was cold and more hungry than cold. Welcome was the sight of the boër which was hospitably opened to receive us.

It was a peasant's house, but in point of hospitality it was equal to a king's. On our arrival the master came with outstretched hands, and without more ceremony he beckoned us to follow him.

To accompany him down the long, narrow, dark passage, would have been impossible. Therefore, we followed, as he bid us. The building was constructed of roughly squared timbers, with rooms on both sides, four in number, all opening out into the one passage: these were the kitchen, the weaving shop, the badstofa, or family sleeping-room, and the visitors' room, which was the best of all. My uncle, whose height had not been thought of in building the house, of course hit his head several times against the beams that projected from the ceilings.

We were introduced into our apartment, a large room with a floor of earth stamped hard down, and lighted by a window, the panes of which were formed of sheep's bladder, not admitting too much light. The sleeping accommodation consisted of dry litter, thrown into two wooden frames painted red, and ornamented with Icelandic sentences. I was hardly expecting so much comfort; the only discomfort proceeded from the strong odour of dried fish, hung meat, and sour milk, of which my nose made bitter complaints.

When we had laid aside our travelling wraps the voice of the host was heard inviting us to the kitchen, the only room where a fire was lighted even in the severest cold.

My uncle lost no time in obeying the friendly call, nor was I slack in following.

The kitchen chimney was constructed on the ancient pattern; in the middle of the room was a stone for a hearth, over it in the roof a hole to let the smoke escape. The kitchen was also a dining-room.

At our entrance the host, as if he had never seen us, greeted us with the word *'Sællvertu,'* which means 'be happy,' and came and kissed us on the cheek.

After him his wife pronounced the same words, accompanied with the same ceremonial; then the two placing their hands upon their hearts, inclined profoundly before us.

I hasten to inform the reader that this Icelandic lady was the mother of nineteen children, all, big and little, swarming in the midst of the dense wreaths of smoke with which the fire on the hearth filled the chamber. Every moment I noticed a fair-haired and rather melancholy face peeping out of the rolling volumes of smoke—they were a perfect cluster of unwashed angels.

My uncle and I treated this little tribe with kindness; and in a very short time we each had three or four of these brats on our shoulders, as many on our laps, and the rest between our knees. Those who could speak kept repeating *'Sællvertu,'* in every conceivable tone; those that could not speak made up for that want by shrill cries.

This concert was brought to a close by the announcement of dinner. At that moment our hunter returned, who had been seeing his horses provided for; that is to say, he had economically let them loose in the fields, where the poor beasts had to content themselves with the scanty moss they could pull off the rocks and a few meagre sea weeds, and the next day they would not fail to come of themselves and resume the labours of the previous day.

'*Sællvertu,*' said Hans.

Then calmly, automatically, and dispassionately he kissed the host, the hostess, and their nineteen children.

This ceremony over, we sat at table, twenty-four in number, and therefore one upon another. The luckiest had only two urchins upon their knees.

But silence reigned in all this little world at the arrival of the soup, and the national taciturnity resumed its empire even over the children. The host served out to us a soup made of lichen and by no means unpleasant, then an immense piece of dried fish floating in butter rancid with twenty years' keeping, and, therefore, according to Icelandic gastronomy, much preferable to fresh butter. Along with this, we had 'skye,' a sort of clotted milk, with biscuits, and a liquid prepared from juniper berries; for beverage we had a thin milk mixed with water, called in this country 'blanda.' It is not for me to decide whether this diet is wholesome or not; all I can say is, that I was desperately hungry, and that at dessert I swallowed to the very last gulp of a thick broth made from buckwheat.

As soon as the meal was over the children disappeared, and their elders gathered round the peat fire, which also burnt such miscellaneous fuel as briars, cow-dung, and fishbones. After this little pinch of warmth the different groups retired to their respective rooms. Our hostess hospitably offered us her assistance in undressing, according to Icelandic usage; but on our gracefully declining, she insisted no longer, and I was able at last to curl myself up in my mossy bed.

At five next morning we bade our host farewell, my uncle with difficulty persuading him to accept a proper remuneration; and Hans signalled the start.

At a hundred yards from Gardär the soil began to change its aspect; it became boggy and less favourable to progress. On our right the chain of mountains was indefinitely prolonged like an immense system of natural fortifications, of which we were following the counter-scarp or lesser steep; often we were met by streams, which we had to ford with great care, not to wet our packages.

The desert became wider and more hideous; yet from time to time we seemed to descry a human figure that fled at our approach, sometimes a sharp turn would bring us suddenly within a short distance of one of these spectres, and I was filled with loathing at the sight of a huge deformed head, the skin shining and hairless, and repulsive sores visible through the gaps in the poor creature's wretched rags.

The unhappy being forbore to approach us and offer his misshapen hand. He fled away, but not before Hans had saluted him with the customary *'Sællvertu.'*

'Spetelsk,' said he.

'A leper!' my uncle repeated.

This word produced a repulsive effect. The horrible disease of leprosy is too common in Iceland; it is not contagious, but hereditary, and lepers are forbidden to marry.

These apparitions were not cheerful, and did not throw any charm over the less and less attractive landscapes. The last tufts of grass had disappeared from beneath our feet. Not a tree was to be seen, unless we except a few dwarf birches as low as brushwood. Not an animal but a few wandering ponies that their owners would not feed. Sometimes we could see a hawk balancing himself on his wings under the grey cloud, and then darting away south with rapid flight. I felt melancholy under this savage aspect of nature, and my thoughts went away to the cheerful scenes I had left in the far south.

We had to cross a few narrow fiords, and at last quite a wide gulf; the tide, then high, allowed us to pass over without delay, and to reach the hamlet of Alftanes, one mile beyond.

That evening, after having forded two rivers full of trout and pike, called Alfa and Heta, we were obliged to spend the night in a deserted building worthy to be haunted by all the elfins of Scandinavia. The ice king certainly held court here, and gave us all night long samples of what he could do.

No particular event marked the next day. Bogs, dead levels, melancholy desert tracks, wherever we travelled. By nightfall we had accomplished half our journey, and we lay at Krösolbt.

On the 19th of June, for about a mile, that is an Icelandic mile, we walked upon hardened lava; this ground is called in the country 'hraun'; the writhen surface presented the appearance of distorted, twisted cables, sometimes stretched in length, sometimes contorted together; an immense torrent, once liquid, now solid, ran from the nearest mountains, now extinct volcanoes, but the ruins around revealed the violence of the past eruptions. Yet here and there were a few jets of steam from hot springs.

We had no time to watch these phenomena; we had to proceed on our way. Soon at the foot of the mountains the boggy land reappeared, intersected by little lakes. Our route now lay westward; we had turned the great bay of Faxa, and the twin peaks of Snæfell rose white into the cloudy sky at the distance of at least five miles.

The horses did their duty well, no difficulties stopped them in their steady career. I was getting tired; but my uncle was as firm and straight as he was at our first start. I could not help admiring his persistency, as well as the hunter's, who treated our expedition like a mere promenade.

June 20. At six p.m. we reached Büdir, a village on the sea shore; and the guide there claiming his due, my uncle settled with him. It was Hans' own family, that is, his uncles and cousins, who gave us hospitality; we were kindly received, and without taxing too much the goodness of these folks, I would willingly have tarried here to recruit after my fatigues. But my uncle, who wanted no recruiting, would not hear of it, and the next morning we had to bestride our beasts again.

The soil told of the neighbourhood of the mountain, whose granite foundations rose from the earth like the knotted roots of some huge oak. We were rounding the immense base of the volcano. The Professor hardly took his eyes off it. He tossed up his arms and seemed to defy it, and to declare, 'There stands the giant that I shall conquer.' After about four hours' walking the horses stopped of their own accord at the door of the priest's house at Stapi.

FOURTEEN

BUT ARCTICS CAN BE INHOSPITABLE, TOO

Stapi is a village consisting of about thirty huts, built of lava, at the south side of the base of the volcano. It extends along the inner edge of a small fiord, inclosed between basaltic walls of the strangest construction.

Basalt is a brownish rock of igneous origin. It assumes regular forms, the arrangement of which is often very surprising. Here nature had done her work geometrically, with square and compass and plummet. Everywhere else her art consists alone in throwing down huge masses together in disorder. You see cones imperfectly formed, irregular pyramids, with a fantastic disarrangement of lines; but here, as if to exhibit an example of regularity, though in advance of the very earliest architects, she has created a severely simple order of architecture, never surpassed either by the splendours of Babylon or the wonders of Greece.

I had heard of the Giant's Causeway in Ireland, and Fingal's Cave in Staffa, one of the Hebrides; but I had never yet seen a basaltic formation.

At Stapi I beheld this phenomenon in all its beauty.

The wall that confined the fiord, like all the coast of the peninsula, was composed of a series of vertical columns thirty feet high. These straight shafts, of fair proportions, supported an architrave of horizontal slabs, the overhanging portion of which formed a semi-arch over the sea. At. intervals, under this natural shelter, there spread out vaulted entrances in beautiful curves, into which the waves came dashing with foam and spray. A few shafts of basalt, torn from their hold by the fury of tempests, lay along the soil like remains of an ancient temple, in ruins for ever fresh, and over which centuries passed without leaving a trace of age upon them.

This was our last stage upon the earth. Hans had exhibited great intelligence, and it gave me some little comfort to think then that he was not going to leave us.

On arriving at the door of the rector's house, which was not different from the others, I saw a man shoeing a horse, hammer in hand, and with a leathern apron on.

'*Sællvertu,*' said the hunter.

'*God dag,*' said the blacksmith in good Danish.

'*Kyrkoherde,*' said Hans, turning round to my uncle.

'The rector,' repeated the Professor. 'It seems, Axel, that this good man is the rector.'

Our guide in the meanwhile was making the '*kyrkoherde*' aware of the position of things; when the latter, suspending his labours for a moment, uttered a sound no doubt understood between horses and farriers, and immediately a tall and ugly hag appeared from the hut. She must have been six feet at the least. I was in great alarm lest she should treat me to the Icelandic kiss; but there was no occasion to fear, nor did she do the honours at all too gracefully.

The visitors' room seemed to me the worst in the whole cabin. It was close, dirty, and evil smelling. But we had to be content. The rector did not to go in for antique hospitality. Very far from it. Before the day was over I saw that we had to do with a blacksmith, a fisherman, a hunter, a joiner, but not at all with a minister of the Gospel. To be sure, it was a week-day; perhaps on a Sunday he made amends.

I don't mean to say anything against these poor priests, who after all are very wretched. They receive from the Danish Government a ridiculously small pittance, and they get from the parish the fourth part of the tithe, which does not come to sixty marks a year (about £4). Hence the necessity to work for their livelihood; but after fishing, hunting, and shoeing horses for any length of time, one soon gets into the ways and manners of fishermen, hunters, and farriers, and other rather rude and uncultivated people; and that evening I found out that temperance was not among the virtues that distinguished my host.

My uncle soon discovered what sort of a man he had to do with; instead of a good and learned man he found a rude and coarse peasant. He therefore resolved to commence the grand expedition at once, and to leave this inhospitable parsonage. He cared nothing about fatigue, and resolved to spend some days upon the mountain.

The preparations for our departure were therefore made the very day after our arrival at Stapi. Hans hired the services of three Icelanders to do the duty of the horses in the transport of the burdens; but as soon as we had arrived at the crater these natives were to turn back and leave us to our own devices. This was to be clearly understood.

My uncle now took the opportunity to explain to Hans that it was his intention to explore the interior of the volcano to its farthest limits.

Hans merely nodded. There or elsewhere, down in the bowels of the earth, or anywhere on the surface, all was alike to him. For my own part the incidents of the journey had hitherto kept me amused, and made me forgetful of coming evils; but now my fears again were beginning to get the better of me. But what could I do? The place to resist the Professor would have been Hamburg, not the foot of Snæfell.

One thought, above all others, harassed and alarmed me; it was one calculated to shake firmer nerves than mine.

Now, thought I, here we are, about to climb Snæfell. Very good. We will explore the crater. Very good, too, others have done as much without dying for it. But that is not all. If there is a way to penetrate into the very bowels of the island, if that ill-advised Saknussemm has told a true tale, we shall lose our way amidst the deep subterranean passages of this volcano. Now, there is no proof that Snæfell is extinct. Who can assure us that an eruption is not brewing at this very moment? Does it follow that because the monster has slept since 1229 he must therefore never awake again? And if he wakes up presently, where shall we be?

It was worth while debating this question, and I did debate it. I could not sleep for dreaming about eruptions. Now, the part of ejected scoriae and ashes seemed to my mind a very rough one to act.

So, at last, when I could hold out no longer, I resolved to lay the case before my uncle, as prudently and as cautiously as possible, just under the form of an almost impossible hypothesis.

I went to him. I communicated my fears to him, and drew back a step to give him room for the explosion which I knew must follow. But I was mistaken.

'I was thinking of that,' he replied with great simplicity.

What could those words mean?—Was he actually going to listen to reason? Was he contemplating the abandonment of his plans? This was too good to be true.

After a few moments' silence, during which I dared not question him, he resumed:

'I was thinking of that. Ever since we arrived at Stapi I have been occupied with the important question you have just opened, for we must not be guilty of imprudence.'

'No, indeed!' I replied with forcible emphasis.

'For six hundred years Snæfell has been dumb; but he may speak again. Now, eruptions are always preceded by certain well-known phenomena. I have therefore examined the natives, I have studied external appearances, and I can assure you, Axel, that there will be no eruption.'

At this positive affirmation I stood amazed and speechless.

'You don't doubt my word?' said my uncle. 'Well, follow me.'

I obeyed like an automaton. Coming out from the priest's house, the Professor took a straight road, which, through an opening in the basaltic wall, led away from the sea. We were soon in the open country, if one may give that name to a vast extent of mounds of volcanic products. This tract seemed crushed under a rain of enormous ejected rocks of trap, basalt, granite, and all kinds of igneous rocks.

Here and there I could see puffs and jets of steam curling up into the air, called in Icelandic 'reykir,' issuing from thermal springs, and indicating by their motion the volcanic energy underneath. This seemed to justify my fears: But I fell from the height of my new-born hopes when my uncle said:

'You see all these volumes of steam, Axel; well, they demonstrate that we have nothing to fear from the fury of a volcanic eruption.'

'Am I to believe that?' I cried.

'Understand this clearly,' added the Professor. 'At the approach of an eruption these jets would redouble their activity, but disappear altogether during the period of the eruption. For the elastic fluids, being no longer under pressure, go off by way of the crater instead of escaping by their usual passages through the fissures in the soil. Therefore, if these vapours remain in their usual condition, if they display no augmentation of force, and if you add to this the observation that the wind and rain are not ceasing and being replaced by a still and heavy atmosphere, then you may affirm that no eruption is preparing.'

'But—'

'No more; that is sufficient. When science has uttered her voice, let babblers hold their peace.'

I returned to the parsonage, very crestfallen. My uncle had beaten me with the weapons of science. Still I had one hope left, and this was, that when we had reached the bottom of the crater it would be impossible, for want of a passage, to go deeper, in spite of all the Saknussemm's in Iceland.

I spent that whole night in one constant nightmare; in the heart of a volcano, and from the deepest depths of the earth I saw myself tossed up amongst the interplanetary spaces under the form of an eruptive rock.

The next day, June 23, Hans was awaiting us with his companions carrying provisions, tools, and instruments; two iron pointed sticks, two rifles, and two shot belts were for my uncle and myself. Hans, as a cautious man, had added to our luggage a leathern bottle full of water, which, with that in our flasks, would ensure us a supply of water for eight days.

It was nine in the morning. The priest and his tall Megæra were awaiting us at the door. We supposed they were standing there to bid us a kind farewell. But the farewell was put in the unexpected form of a heavy bill, in which everything was charged, even to the very air we breathed in the pastoral house, infected as it was. This worthy couple were fleecing us just as a Swiss innkeeper might have done, and estimated their imperfect hospitality at the highest price.

My uncle paid without a remark: a man who is starting for the centre of the earth need not be particular about a few rix dollars.

This point being settled, Hans gave the signal, and we soon left Stapi behind us.

FIFTEEN

SNÆFELL AT LAST

Snæfell is 5,000 feet high. Its double cone forms the limit of a trachytic belt which stands out distinctly in the mountain system of the island. From our starting point we could see the two peaks boldly projected against the dark grey sky; I could see an enormous cap of snow coming low down upon the giant's brow.

We walked in single file, headed by the hunter, who ascended by narrow tracks, where two could not have gone abreast. There was therefore no room for conversation.

After we had passed the basaltic wall of the fiord of Stapi we passed over a vegetable fibrous peat bog, left from the ancient vegetation of this peninsula. The vast quantity of this unworked fuel would be sufficient to warm the whole population of Iceland for a century; this vast turbary measured in certain ravines had in many places a depth of seventy feet, and presented layers of carbonized remains of vegetation alternating with thinner layers of tufaceous pumice.

As a true nephew of the Professor Liedenbrock, and in spite of my dismal prospects, I could not help observing with interest the mineralogical curiosities which lay about me as in a vast museum, and I constructed for myself a complete geological account of Iceland.

This most curious island has evidently been projected from the bottom of the sea at a comparatively recent date. Possibly, it may still be subject to gradual elevation. If this is the case, its origin may well be attributed to subterranean fires. Therefore, in this case, the theory of Sir Humphry Davy, Saknussemm's document, and my uncle's theories would all go off in smoke.

This hypothesis led me to examine with more attention the appearance of the surface, and I soon arrived at a conclusion as to the nature of the forces which presided at its birth.

Iceland, which is entirely devoid of alluvial soil, is wholly composed of volcanic tufa, that is to say, an agglomeration of porous rocks and stones. Before the volcanoes broke out it consisted of trap rocks slowly upraised to the level of the sea by the action of central forces. The internal fires had not yet forced their way through.

But at a later period a wide chasm formed diagonally from south-west to north-east, through which was gradually forced out the trachyte which was to form a mountain chain. No violence accompanied this change; the matter thrown out was in vast quantities, and the liquid material oozing out from the abysses of the earth slowly spread in extensive plains or in hillocky masses. To this period belong the felspar, syenites, and porphyries.

But with the help of this outflow the thickness of the crust of the island increased materially, and therefore also its powers of resistance. It may easily be conceived what vast quantities of elastic gases, what masses of molten matter accumulated beneath its solid surface whilst no exit was practicable after the cooling of the trachytic crust. Therefore a time would come when the elastic and explosive forces of the imprisoned gases would upheave this ponderous cover and drive out for themselves openings through tall chimneys. Hence then the volcano would distend and lift up the crust, and then burst through a crater suddenly formed at the summit or thinnest part of the volcano.

To the eruption succeeded other volcanic phenomena. Through the outlets now made first escaped the ejected basalt of which the plain we had just left presented such marvellous specimens. We were moving over grey rocks of dense and massive formation, which in cooling had formed into hexagonal prisms. Everywhere around us we saw truncated cones, formerly so many fiery mouths.

After the exhaustion of the basalt, the volcano, the power of which grew by the extinction of the lesser craters, supplied an egress to lava, ashes, and scoriae, of which I could see lengthened screes streaming down the sides of the mountain like flowing hair.

Such was the succession of phenomena which produced Iceland, all arising from the action of internal fire; and to suppose that the mass within did not still exist in a state of liquid incandescence was absurd; and nothing could surpass the absurdity of fancying that it was possible to reach the earth's centre.

So I felt a little comforted as we advanced to the assault of Snæfell.

The way was growing more and more arduous, the ascent steeper and steeper; the loose fragments of rock trembled beneath us, and the utmost care was needed to avoid dangerous falls.

Hans went on as quietly as if he were on level ground; sometimes he disappeared altogether behind the huge blocks, then a shrill whistle would direct us on our way to him. Sometimes he would halt, pick up a few bits of stone, build them up into a recognisable form, and thus made landmarks to guide us in our way back. A very wise precaution in itself, but, as things turned out, quite useless.

Three hours' fatiguing march had only brought us to the base of the mountain. There Hans bid us come to a halt, and a hasty breakfast was served out. My uncle swallowed two mouthfuls at a time to get on faster. But, whether he liked it or not, this was a rest as well as a breakfast hour and he had to wait till it pleased our guide to move on, which came to pass in an hour. The three Icelanders, just as taciturn as their comrade the hunted, never spoke, and ate their breakfasts in silence.

We were now beginning to scale the steep sides of Snæfell.

Its snowy summit, by an optical illusion not unfrequent in mountains, seemed close to us, and yet how many weary hours it took to reach it! The stones, adhering by no soil or fibrous roots of vegetation, rolled away from under our feet, and rushed down the precipice below with the swiftness of an avalanche.

At some places the flanks of the mountain formed an angle with the horizon of at least 36 degrees; it was impossible to climb them, and these stony cliffs had to be tacked round, not without great difficulty. Then we helped each other with our sticks.

I must admit that my uncle kept as close to me as he could; he never lost sight of me, and in many straits his arm furnished me with a powerful support. He himself seemed to possess an instinct for equilibrium, for he never stumbled. The Icelanders, though burdened with our loads, climbed with the agility of mountaineers.

To judge by the distant appearance of the summit of Snæfell, it would have seemed too steep to ascend on our side. Fortunately, after an hour of fatigue and athletic exercises, in the midst of the vast surface of snow presented by the hollow between the two peaks, a kind of staircase appeared unexpectedly which greatly facilitated our ascent. It was formed by one of those torrents of stones flung up by the eruptions, called 'sting' by the Icelanders. If this torrent had not been arrested in its fall by the formation of the sides of the mountain, it would have gone on to the sea and formed more islands.

Such as it was, it did us good service. The steepness increased, but these stone steps allowed us to rise with facility, and even with such rapidity that, having rested for a moment while my companions continued their ascent, I perceived them already reduced by distance to microscopic dimensions.

At seven we had ascended the two thousand steps of this grand staircase, and we had attained a bulge in the mountain, a kind of bed on which rested the cone proper of the crater.

Three thousand two hundred feet below us stretched the sea. We had passed the limit of perpetual snow, which, on account of the moisture of the climate, is at a greater elevation in Iceland than the high latitude would give reason to suppose. The cold was excessively keen. The wind was blowing violently. I was exhausted. The Professor saw that my limbs were refusing to perform their office, and in spite of his impatience he decided on stopping. He therefore spoke to the hunter, who shook his head, saying:

'Ofvanför.'

'It seems we must go higher,' said my uncle.

Then he asked Hans for his reason.

'Mistour,' replied the guide.

'Ja Mistour,' said one of the Icelanders in a tone of alarm.

'What does that word mean?' I asked uneasily.

'Look!' said my uncle.

I looked down upon the plain. An immense column of pulverized pumice, sand and dust was rising with a whirling circular motion like a waterspout; the wind was lashing it on to that side of Snæfell where we were holding on; this dense veil, hung across the sun, threw a deep shadow over the mountain. If that huge revolving pillar sloped down, it would involve us in its whirling eddies. This phenomenon, which is not unfrequent when the wind blows from the glaciers, is called in Icelandic 'mistour.'

'Hastigt! hastigt!' cried our guide.

Without knowing Danish I understood at once that we must follow Hans at the top of our speed. He began to circle round the cone of the crater, but in a diagonal direction so as to facilitate our progress. Presently the dust storm fell upon the mountain, which quivered under the shock; the loose stones, caught with the irresistible blasts of wind, flew about in a perfect hail as in an eruption. Happily we were on the opposite side, and sheltered from all harm. But for the precaution of our guide, our mangled bodies, torn and pounded into fragments, would have been carried afar like the ruins hurled along by some unknown meteor.

Yet Hans did not think it prudent to spend the night upon the sides of the cone. We continued our zigzag climb. The fifteen hundred remaining feet took us five hours to clear; the circuitous route, the diagonal and the counter marches, must have measured at least three leagues. I could stand it no longer. I was yielding to the effects of hunger and cold. The rarefied air scarcely gave play to the action of my lungs.

At last, at eleven in the sunlight night, the summit of Snæfell was reached, and before going in for shelter into the crater I had time to observe the midnight sun, at his lowest point, gilding with his pale rays the island that slept at my feet.

SIXTEEN

BOLDLY DOWN THE CRATER

Supper was rapidly devoured, and the little company housed themselves as best they could. The bed was hard, the shelter not very substantial, and our position an anxious one, at five thousand feet above the sea level. Yet I slept particularly well; it was one of the best nights I had ever had, and I did not even dream.

Next morning we awoke half frozen by the sharp keen air, but with the light of a splendid sun. I rose from my granite bed and went out to enjoy the magnificent spectacle that lay unrolled before me.

I stood on the very summit of the southernmost of Snæfell's peaks. The range of the eye extended over the whole island. By an optical law which obtains at all great heights, the shores seemed raised and the centre depressed. It seemed as if one of Helbesmer's raised maps lay at my feet. I could see deep valleys intersecting each other in every direction, precipices like low walls, lakes reduced to ponds, rivers abbreviated into streams. On my right were numberless glaciers and innumerable peaks, some plumed with feathery clouds of smoke. The undulating surface of these endless mountains, crested with sheets of snow, reminded one of a stormy sea. If I looked westward, there the ocean lay spread out in all its magnificence, like a mere continuation of those flock-like summits. The eye could hardly tell where the snowy ridges ended and the foaming waves began.

I was thus steeped in the marvellous ecstasy which all high summits develop in the mind; and now without giddiness, for I was beginning to be accustomed to these sublime aspects of nature. My dazzled eyes were bathed in the bright flood of the solar rays. I was forgetting where and who I was, to live the life of elves and sylphs, the fanciful creation of Scandinavian superstitions. I felt intoxicated with the sublime pleasure of lofty elevations without thinking of the profound abysses into which I was shortly to be plunged. But I was brought back to the realities of things by the arrival of Hans and the Professor, who joined me on the summit.

My uncle pointed out to me in the far west a light steam or mist, a semblance of land, which bounded the distant horizon of waters.

'Greenland!' said he.

'Greenland?' I cried.

'Yes; we are only thirty-five leagues from it; and during thaws the white bears, borne by the ice fields from the north, are carried even into Iceland. But never mind that. Here we are at the top of Snæfell and here are two peaks, one north and one south. Hans will tell us the name of that on which we are now standing.'

The question being put, Hans replied:

'*Scartaris.*'

My uncle shot a triumphant glance at me.

'Now for the crater!' he cried.

The crater of Snæfell resembled an inverted cone, the openingof which might be half a league in diameter. Its depth appeared to be about two thousand feet. Imagine the aspect of such a reservoir, brim full and running over with liquid fire amid the rolling thunder. The bottom of the funnel was about 250 feet in circuit, so that the gentle slope allowed its lower brim to be reached without much difficulty. Involuntarily I compared the whole crater to an enormous erected mortar, and the comparison put me in a terrible fright.

'What madness,' I thought, 'to go down into a mortar, perhaps a loaded mortar, to be shot up into the air at a moment's notice!'

But I did not try to back out of it. Hans with perfect coolness resumed the lead, and I followed him without a word.

In order to facilitate the descent, Hans wound his way down the cone by a spiral path. Our route lay amidst eruptive rocks, some of which, shaken out of their loosened beds, rushed bounding down the abyss, and in their fall awoke echoes remarkable for their loud and well-defined sharpness.

In certain parts of the cone there were glaciers. Here Hans advanced only with extreme precaution, sounding his way with his iron-pointed pole, to discover any crevasses in it. At particularly dubious passages we were obliged to connect ourselves with each other by a long cord, in order that any man who missed his footing might be held up by his companions. This solid formation was prudent, but did not remove all danger.

Yet, notwithstanding the difficulties of the descent, down steeps unknown to the guide, the journey was accomplished without accidents, except the loss of a coil of rope, which escaped from the hands of an Icelander, and took the shortest way to the bottom of the abyss.

At mid-day we arrived. I raised my head and saw straight above me the upper aperture of the cone, framing a bit of sky of very small circumference, but almost perfectly round. Just upon the edge appeared the snowy peak of Saris, standing out sharp and clear against endless space.

At the bottom of the crater were three chimneys, through which, in its eruptions, Snæfell had driven forth fire and lava from its central furnace. Each of these chimneys was a hundred feet in diameter. They gaped before us right in our path. I had not the courage to look down either of them. But Professor Liedenbrock had hastily surveyed all three; he was panting, running from one to the other, gesticulating, and uttering incoherent expressions. Hans and his comrades, seated upon loose lava rocks, looked at him with asmuch wonder as they knew how to express, and perhaps taking him for an escaped lunatic.

Suddenly my uncle uttered a cry. I thought his foot must have slipped and that he had fallen down one of the holes. But, no; I saw him, with arms outstretched and legs straddling wide apart, erect before a granite rock that stood in the centre of the crater, just like a pedestal made ready to receive a statue of Pluto. He stood like a man stupefied, but the stupefaction soon gave way to delirious rapture.

'Axel, Axel,' he cried. 'Come, come!'

I ran. Hans and the Icelanders never stirred.

'Look!' cried the Professor.

And, sharing his astonishment, but I think not his joy, I read on the western face of the block, in Runic characters, half mouldered away with lapse of ages, this thrice-accursed name:

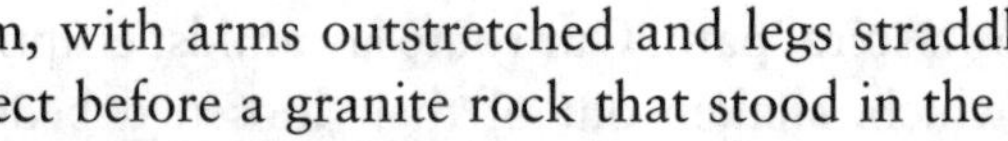

'Arne Saknussemm!' replied my uncle. 'Do you yet doubt?'

I made no answer; and I returned in silence to my lava seat in a state of utter speechless consternation. Here was crushing evidence.

How long I remained plunged in agonizing reflections I

cannot tell; all that I know is, that on raising my head again, I saw only my uncle and Hans at the bottom of the crater. The Icelanders had been dismissed, and they were now descending the outer slopes of Snæfell to return to Stapi.

Hans slept peaceably at the foot of a rock, in a lava bed, where he had found a suitable couch for himself; but my uncle was pacing around the bottom of the crater like a wild beast in a cage. I had neither the wish nor the strength to rise, and following the guide's example I went off into an unhappy slumber, fancying I could hear ominous noises or feel tremblings within the recesses of the mountain.

Thus the first night in the crater passed away.

The next morning, a grey, heavy, cloudy sky seemed to droop over the summit of the cone. I did not know this first from the appearances of nature, but I found it out by my uncle's impetuous wrath.

I soon found out the cause, and hope dawned again in my heart. For this reason.

Of the three ways open before us, one had been taken by Saknussemm. The indications of the learned Icelander hinted at in the cryptogram, pointed to this fact that the shadow of Scartaris came to touch that particular way during the latter days of the month of June.

That sharp peak might hence be considered as the gnomon of a vast sun dial, the shadow projected from which on a certain day would point out the road to the centre of the earth.

Now, no sun no shadow, and therefore no guide. Here was June 25. If the sun was clouded for six days we must postpone our visit till next year.

My limited powers of description would fail, were I to attempt a picture of the Professor's angry impatience. The day wore on, and no shadow came to lay itself along the bottom of the crater. Hans did not move from the spot he had selected; yet he must be asking himself what were we waiting for, if he asked himself anything at all. My uncle spoke not a word to me. His gaze, ever directed upwards, was lost in the grey and misty space beyond.

On the 26th nothing yet. Rain mingled with snow was falling all day long. Hans built a but of pieces of lava. I felt a malicious pleasure in watching the thousand rills and cascades that came tumbling down the sides of the cone, and the deafening continuous din awaked by every stone against which they bounded.

My uncle's rage knew no bounds. It was enough to irritate a meeker man than he; for it was foundering almost within the port.

But Heaven never sends unmixed grief, and for Professor Liedenbrock there was a satisfaction in store proportioned to his desperate anxieties.

The next day the sky was again overcast; but on the 29th of June, the last day but one of the month, with the change of the moon came a change of weather. The sun poured a flood of light down the crater. Every hillock, every rock and stone, every projecting surface, had its share of the beaming torrent, and threw its shadow on the ground. Amongst them all, Scartaris laid down his sharp-pointed angular shadow which began to move slowly in the opposite direction to that of the radiant orb.

My uncle turned too, and followed it.

At noon, being at its least extent, it came and softly fell upon the edge of the middle chimney.

'There it is! there it is!' shouted the Professor.

'Now for the centre of the globe!' he added in Danish.

I looked at Hans, to hear what he would say.

'Forüt!' was his tranquil answer.

'Forward!' replied my uncle.

It was thirteen minutes past one.

SEVENTEEN

VERTICAL DESCENT

Now began our real journey. Hitherto our toil had overcome all difficulties, now difficulties would spring up at every step.

I had not yet ventured to look down the bottomless pit into which I was about to take a plunge The supreme hour had come. I might now either share in the enterprise or refuse to move forward. But I was ashamed to recoil in the presence of the hunter. Hans accepted the enterprise with such calmness, such indifference, such perfect disregard of any possible danger that I blushed at the idea of being less brave than he. If I had been alone I might have once more tried the effect of argument; but in the presence of the guide I held my peace; my heart flew back to my sweet Virlandaise, and I approached the central chimney.

I have already mentioned that it was a hundred feet in diameter, and three hundred feet round. I bent over a projecting rock and gazed down. My hair stood on end with terror. The bewildering feeling of vacuity laid hold upon me. I felt my centre of gravity shifting its place, and giddiness mounting into my brain like drunkenness. There is nothing more treacherous than this attraction down deep abysses. I was just about to drop down, when a hand laid hold of me. It was that of Hans. I suppose I had not taken as many lessons on gulf exploration as I ought to have done in the Frelsers Kirk at Copenhagen.

But, however short was my examination of this well, I had taken some account of its conformation. Its almost perpendicular walls were bristling with innumerable projections which would facilitate the descent. But if there was no want of steps, still there was no rail. A rope fastened to the edge of the aperture might have helped us down. But how were we to unfasten it, when arrived at the other end?

My uncle employed a very simple expedient to obviate this difficulty. He uncoiled a cord of the thickness of a finger, and four hundred feet long; first he dropped half of it down, then he passed it round a lava block that projected conveniently, and threw the other half down the chimney. Each of us could then descend by holding with the hand both halves of the rope, which would not be able to unroll itself from its hold; when two hundred feet down, it would be easy to get possession of the whole of the rope by letting one end go and pulling down by the other. Then the exercise would go on again ad infinitum.

'Now,' said my uncle, after having completed these preparations, 'now let us look to our loads. I will divide them into three lots; each of us will strap one upon his back. I mean only fragile articles.'

Of course, we were not included under that head.

'Hans,' said he, 'will take charge of the tools and a portion of the provisions; you, Axel, will take another third of the provisions, and the arms; and I will take the rest of the provisions and the delicate instruments.'

'But,' said I, 'the clothes, and that mass of ladders and ropes, what is to become of them?'

'They will go down by themselves.'

'How so?' I asked.

'You will see presently.'

My uncle was always willing to employ magnificent resources. Obeying orders, Hans tied all the non-fragile articles in one bundle, corded them firmly, and sent them bodily down the gulf before us.

I listened to the dull thuds of the descending bale. My uncle, leaning over the abyss, followed the descent of the luggage with a satisfied nod, and only rose erect when he had quite lost sight of it.

'Very well, now it is our turn.'

Now I ask any sensible man if it was possible to hear those words without a shudder.

The Professor fastened his package of instruments upon his shoulders; Hans took the tools; I took the arms: and the descent commenced in the following order; Hans, my uncle, and myself. It was effected in profound silence, broken only by the descent of loosened stones down the dark gulf.

I dropped as it were, frantically clutching the double cord with one hand and buttressing myself from the wall with the other by means of my stick. One idea overpowered me almost, fear lest the rock should give way from which I was hanging. This cord seemed a fragile thing for three persons to be suspended from. I made as little use of it as possible, performing wonderful feats of equilibrium upon the lava projections which my foot seemed to catch hold of like a hand.

When one of these slippery steps shook under the heavier form of Hans, he said in his tranquil voice:

'Gif akt!'

'Attention!' repeated my uncle.

In half an hour we were standing upon the surface of a rock jammed in across the chimney from one side to the other.

Hans pulled the rope by one of its ends, the other rose in the air; after passing the higher rock it came down again, bringing with it a rather dangerous shower of bits of stone and lava.

Leaning over the edge of our narrow standing ground, I observed that the bottom of the hole was still invisible.

The same manœuvre was repeated with the cord, and half an hour after we had descended another two hundred feet.

I don't suppose the maddest geologist under such circumstances would have studied the nature of the rocks that we were passing. I am sure I did trouble my head about them. Pliocene, miocene, eocene, cretaceous, jurassic, triassic, permian, carboniferous, devonian, silurian, or primitive was all one to me. But the Professor, no doubt, was pursuing his observations or taking notes, for in one of our halts he said to me:

'The farther I go the more confidence I feel. The order of these volcanic formations affords the strongest confirmation to the theories of Davy. We are now among the primitive rocks, upon which the chemical operations took place which are produced by the contact of elementary bases of metals with water. I repudiate the notion of central heat altogether. We shall see further proof of that very soon.'

No variation, always the same conclusion. Of course, I was not inclined to argue. My silence was taken for consent and the descent went on.

Another three hours, and I saw no bottom to the chimney yet. When I lifted my head I perceived the gradual contraction of its aperture. Its walls, by a gentle incline, were drawing closer to each other, and it was beginning to grow darker.

Still we kept descending. It seemed to me that the falling stones were meeting with an earlier resistance, and that the concussion gave a more abrupt and deadened sound.

As I had taken care to keep an exact account of our manœuvres with the rope, which I knew that we had repeated fourteen times, each descent occupying half an hour, the conclusion was easy that we had been seven hours, plus fourteen quarters of rest, making ten hours and a half. We had started at one, it must therefore now be eleven o'clock; and the depth to which we had descended was fourteen times 200 feet, or 2,800 feet.

At this moment I heard the voice of Hans.

'Halt!' he cried.

I stopped short just as I was going to place my feet upon my uncle's head.

'We are there,' he cried.

'Where?' said I, stepping near to him.

'At the bottom of the perpendicular chimney,' he answered.

'Is there no way farther?'

'Yes; there is a sort of passage which inclines to the right. We will see about that Tomorrow. Let us have our supper, and go to sleep.'

The darkness was not yet complete. The provision case was opened; we refreshed ourselves, and went to sleep as well as we could upon a bed of stones and lava fragments.

When lying on my back, I opened my eyes and saw a bright sparkling point of light at the extremity of the gigantic tube 3,000 feet long, now a vast telescope.

It was a star which, seen from this depth, had lost all scintillation, and which by my computation should be ß *Ursa minor*. Then I fell fast asleep.

EIGHTEEN

THE WONDERS OF TERRESTRIAL DEPTHS

At eight in the morning a ray of daylight came to wake us up. The thousand shining surfaces of lava on the walls received it on its passage, and scattered it like a shower of sparks.

There was light enough to distinguish surrounding objects.

'Well, Axel, what do you say to it?' cried my uncle, rubbing his hands. 'Did you ever spend a quieter night in our little house at Königsberg? No noise of cart wheels, no cries of basket women, no boatmen shouting!'

'No doubt it is very quiet at the bottom of this well, but there is something alarming in the quietness itself.'

'Now come!' my uncle cried; 'if you are frightened already, what will you be by and by? We have not gone a single inch yet into the bowels of the earth.'

'What do you mean?'

'I mean that we have only reached the level of the island. long vertical tube, which terminates at the mouth of the crater, has its lower end only at the level of the sea.'

'Are you sure of that?'

'Quite sure. Consult the barometer.'

In fact, the mercury, which had risen in the instrument as fast as we descended, had stopped at twenty-nine inches.

'You see,' said the Professor, 'we have now only the pressure of our atmosphere, and I shall be glad when the aneroid takes the place of the barometer.'

And in truth this instrument would become useless as soon as the weight of the atmosphere should exceed the pressure ascertained at the level of the sea.

'But,' I said, 'is there not reason to fear that this ever-increasing pressure will become at last very painful to bear?'

'No; we shall descend at a slow rate, and our lungs will become inured to a denser atmosphere. Æronauts find the want of air as they rise to high elevations, but we shall perhaps have too much: of the two, this is what I should prefer. Don't let us lose a moment. Where is the bundle we sent down before us?'

I then remembered that we had searched for it in vain the evening before. My uncle questioned Hans, who, after having examined attentively with the eye of a huntsman, replied:

'Der huppe!'

'Up there.'

And so it was. The bundle had been caught by a projection a hundred feet above us. Immediately the Icelander climbed up like a cat, and in a few minutes the package was in our possession.

'Now,' said my uncle, 'let us breakfast; but we must lay in a good stock, for we don't know how long we may have to go on.'

The biscuit and extract of meat were washed down with a draught of water mingled with a little gin.

Breakfast over, my uncle drew from his pocket a small notebook, intended for scientific observations. He consulted his instruments, and recorded:

'Monday, July 1.

'Chronometer, 8.17 a.m.; barometer, 297 in.; thermometer, 6° (43° F.). Direction, E.S.E.'

This last observation applied to the dark gallery, and was indicated by the compass.

'Now, Axel,' cried the Professor with enthusiasm, 'now we are really going into the interior of the earth. At this precise moment the journey commences.'

So saying, my uncle took in one hand Ruhmkorff's apparatus, which was hanging from his neck; and with the other he formed an electric communication with the coil in the lantern, and a sufficiently bright light dispersed the darkness of the passage.

Hans carried the other apparatus, which was also put into action. This ingenious application of electricity would enable us to go on for a long time by creating an artificial light even in the midst of the most inflammable gases.

'Now, march!' cried my uncle.

Each shouldered his package. Hans drove before him the load of cords and clothes; and, myself walking last, we entered the gallery.

At the moment of becoming engulfed in this dark gallery, I raised my head, and saw for the last time through the length of that vast tube the sky of Iceland, which I was never to behold again.

The lava, in the last eruption of 1229, had forced a passage through this tunnel. It still lined the walls with a thick and glistening coat. The electric light was here intensified a hundredfold by reflection.

The only difficulty in proceeding lay in not sliding too fast down an incline of about forty-five degrees; happily certain asperities and a few blisterings here and there formed steps, and we descended, letting our baggage slip before us from the end of a long rope.

But that which formed steps under our feet became stalactites overhead. The lava, which was porous in many places, had formed a surface covered with small rounded blisters; crystals of opaque quartz, set with limpid tears of glass, and hanging like clustered chandeliers from the vaulted roof, seemed as it were to kindle and form a sudden illumination as we passed on our way. It seemed as if the genii of the depths were lighting up their palace to receive their terrestrial guests.

'It is magnificent!' I cried spontaneously. 'My uncle, what a sight! Don't you admire those blending hues of lava, passing from reddish brown to bright yellow by imperceptible shades? And these crystals are just like globes of light.'

'Ali, you think so, do you, Axel, my boy? Well, you will see greater splendours than these, I hope. Now let us march: march!'

He had better have said slide, for we did nothing but drop down the steep inclines. It was the facifs descensus Averni of Virgil. The compass, which I consulted frequently, gave our direction as southeast with inflexible steadiness. This lava stream deviated neither to the right nor to the left.

Yet there was no sensible increase of temperature. This justified Davy's theory, and more than once I consulted the thermometer with surprise. Two hours after our departure it only marked 10° (50° Fahr.), an increase of only 4°. This gave reason for believing that our descent was more horizontal than vertical. As for the exact depth reached, it was very easy to ascertain that; the Professor measured accurately the angles of deviation and inclination on the road, but he kept the results to himself.

About eight in the evening he signalled to stop. Hans sat down at once. The lamps were hung upon a projection in the lava; we were in a sort of cavern where there was plenty of air. Certain puffs of air reached us. What atmospheric disturbance was the cause of them? I could not answer that question at the moment. Hunger and fatigue made me incapable of reasoning.

A descent of seven hours consecutively is not made without considerable expenditure of strength. I was exhausted. The order to 'halt' therefore gave me pleasure. Hans laid our provisions upon a block of lava, and we ate with a good appetite. But one thing troubled me, our supply of water was half consumed. My uncle reckoned upon a fresh supply from subterranean sources, but hitherto we had met with none. I could not help drawing his attention to this circumstance.

'Are you surprised at this want of springs?' he said.

'More than that, I am anxious about it; we have only water enough for five days.'

'Don't be uneasy, Axel, we shall find more than we want.'

'When?'

'When we have left this bed of lava behind us. How could springs break through such walls as these?'

'But perhaps this passage runs to a very great depth. It seems to me that we have made no great progress vertically.'

'Why do you suppose that?'

'Because if we had gone deep into the crust of earth, we should have encountered greater heat.'

'According to your system,' said my uncle. 'But what does the thermometer say?'

'Hardly fifteen degrees (59° Fahr), nine degrees only since our departure.'

'Well, what is your conclusion?'

'This is my conclusion. According to exact observations, the increase of temperature in the interior of the globe advances at the rate of one degree (1 4/5° Fahr.) for every hundred feet. But certain local conditions may modify this rate. Thus at Yakoutsk in Siberia the increase of a degree is ascertained to be reached every 36 feet. This difference depends upon the heat-conducting power of the rocks. Moreover, in the neighbourhood of an extinct volcano, through gneiss, it has been observed that the increase of a degree is only attained at every 125 feet. Let us therefore assume this last hypothesis as the most suitable to our situation, and calculate.'

'Well, do calculate, my boy.'

'Nothing is easier,' said I, putting down figures in my note book. 'Nine times a hundred and twenty-five feet gives a depth of eleven hundred and twenty-five feet.'

'Very accurate indeed.'

'Well?'

'By my observation we are at 10,000 feet below the level of the sea.'

'Is that possible?'

'Yes, or figures are of no use.'

The Professor's calculations were quite correct. We had already attained a depth of six thousand feet beyond that hitherto reached by the foot of man, such as the mines of Kitz Bahl in Tyrol, and those of Wuttembourg in Bohemia.

The temperature, which ought to have been 81° (178° Fahr.) was scarcely 15° (59° Fahr.). Here was cause for reflection.

NINETEEN

GEOLOGICAL STUDIES IN SITU

Next day, Tuesday, June 30, at 6 a.m., the descent began again.

We were still following the gallery of lava, a real natural staircase, and as gently sloping as those inclined planes which in some old houses are still found instead of flights of steps. And so we went on until 12.17, the, precise moment when we overtook Hans, who had stopped.

'Ah! here we are,' exclaimed my uncle, 'at the very end of the chimney.'

I looked around me. We were standing at the intersection of two roads, both dark and narrow. Which were we to take?

This was a difficulty.

Still my uncle refused to admit an appearance of hesitation, either before me or the guide; he pointed out the Eastern tunnel, and we were soon all three in it.

Besides there would have been interminable hesitation before this choice of roads; for since there was no indication whatever to guide our choice, we were obliged to trust to chance.

The slope of this gallery was scarcely perceptible, and its sections very unequal. Sometimes we passed a series of arches succeeding each other like the majestic arcades of a gothic cathedral. Here the architects of the middle ages might have found studies for every form of the sacred art which sprang from the development of the pointed arch. A mile farther we had to bow or heads under corniced elliptic arches in the romanesque style; and massive pillars standing out from the wall bent under the spring of the vault that rested heavily upon them. In other places this magnificence gave way to narrow channels between low structures which looked like beaver's huts, and we had to creep along through extremely narrow passages.

The heat was perfectly bearable. Involuntarily I began to think of its heat when the lava thrown out by Snæfell was boiling and working through this now silent road. I imagined the torrents of fire hurled back at every angle in the gallery, and the accumulation of intensely heated vapours in the midst of this confined channel.

I only hope, thought I, that this so-called extinct volcano won't take a fancy in his old age to begin his sports again!

I abstained from communicating these fears to Professor Liedenbrock. He would never have understood them at all. He had but one idea—forward! He walked, he slid, he scrambled, he tumbled, with a persistency which one could not but admire.

By six in the evening, after a not very fatiguing walk, we had gone two leagues south, but scarcely a quarter of a mile down.

My uncle said it was time to go to sleep. We ate without talking, and went to sleep without reflection.

Our arrangements for the night were very simple; a railway rug each, into which we rolled ourselves, was our sole covering. We had neither cold nor intrusive visits to fear. Travellers who penetrate into the wilds of central Africa, and into the pathless forests of the New World, are obliged to watch over each other by night. But we enjoyed absolute safety and utter seclusion; no savages or wild beasts infested these silent depths.

Next morning, we awoke fresh and in good spirits. The road was resumed. As the day before, we followed the path of the lava. It was impossible to tell what rocks we were passing: the tunnel, instead of tending lower, approached more and more nearly to a horizontal direction, I even fancied a slight rise. But about ten this upward tendency became so evident, and therefore so fatiguing, that I was obliged to slacken my pace.

'Well, Axel?' demanded the Professor impatiently.

'Well, I cannot stand it any longer,' I replied.

'What! after three hours' walk over such easy ground.'

'It may be easy, but it is tiring all the same.'

'What, when we have nothing to do but keep going down!'

'Going up, if you please.'

'Going up!' said my uncle, with a shrug.

'No doubt, for the last half-hour the inclines have gone the other way, and at this rate we shall soon arrive upon the level soil of Iceland.'

The Professor nodded slowly and uneasily like a man that declines to be convinced. I tried to resume the conversation. He answered not a word, and gave the signal for a start. I saw that his silence was nothing but ill-humour.

Still I had courageously shouldered my burden again, and

was rapidly following Hans, whom my uncle preceded. I was anxious not to be left behind. My greatest care was not to lose sight of my companions. I shuddered at the thought of being lost in the mazes of this vast subterranean labyrinth.

Besides, if the ascending road did become steeper, I was comforted with the thought that it was bringing us nearer to the surface. There was hope in this. Every step confirmed me in it, and I was rejoicing at the thought of meeting my little Gräuben again.

By midday there was a change in the appearance of this wall of the gallery. I noticed it by a diminution of the amount of light reflected from the sides; solid rock was appearing in the place of the lava coating. The mass was composed of inclined and sometimes vertical strata. We were passing through rocks of the transition or silurian[1] system.

'It is evident,' I cried, 'the marine deposits formed in the second period, these shales, limestones, and sandstones. We are turning away from the primary granite. We are just as if we were people of Hamburg going to Lubeck by way of Hanover!'

I had better have kept my observations to myself. But my geological instinct was stronger than my prudence, and uncle Liedenbrock heard my exclamation.

'What's that you are saying?' he asked.

'See,' I said, pointing to the varied series of sandstones and limestones, and the first indication of slate.

'Well?'

'We are at the period when the first plants and animals appeared.'

1. The name given by Sir Roderick Murchison to a vast series of fossiliferous strata, which lies between the non-fossiliferous slaty schists below and the old red sandstone above. The system is well developed in the region of Shropshire, etc., once inhabited by the Silures under Caractacus, or Caradoc. (Tr.)

'Do you think so?'

'Look close, and examine.'

I obliged the Professor to move his lamp over the walls of the gallery. I expected some signs of astonishment; but he spoke not a word, and went on.

Had he understood me or not? Did he refuse to admit, out of self-love as an uncle and a philosopher, that he had mistaken his way when he chose the eastern tunnel? or was he determined to examine this passage to its farthest extremity? It was evident that we had left the lava path, and that this road could not possibly lead to the extinct furnace of Snæfell.

Yet I asked myself if I was not depending too much on this change in the rock. Might I not myself be mistaken? Were we really crossing the layers of rock which overlie the granite foundation?

If I am right, I thought, I must soon find some fossil remains of primitive life; and then we must yield to evidence. I will look.

I had not gone a hundred paces before incontestable proofs presented themselves. It could not be otherwise, for in the Silurian age the seas contained at least fifteen hundred vegetable and animal species. My feet, which had become accustomed to the indurated lava floor, suddenly rested upon a dust composed of the debris of plants and shells. In the walls were distinct impressions of fucoids and lycopodites.

Professor Liedenbrock could not be mistaken, I thought, and yet he pushed on, with, I suppose, his eyes resolutely shut.

This was only invincible obstinacy. I could hold out no longer. I picked up a perfectly formed shell, which had belonged to an animal not unlike the woodlouse: then, joining my uncle, I said:

'Look at this!'

'Very well,' said he quietly, 'it is the shell of a crustacean, of an extinct species called a trilobite. Nothing more.'

'But don't you conclude—?'

'Just what you conclude yourself. Yes; I do, perfectly. We have left the granite and the lava. It is possible that I may be mistaken. But I cannot be sure of that until I have reached the very end of this gallery.'

'You are right in doing this, my uncle, and I should quite approve of your determination, if there were not a danger threatening us nearer and nearer.'

'What danger?'

'The want of water.'

'Well, Axel, we will put ourselves upon rations.'

TWENTY

THE FIRST SIGNS OF DISTRESS

In fact, we had to ration ourselves. Our provision of water could not last more than three days. I found that out for certain when supper-time came. And, to our sorrow, we had little reason to expect to find a spring in these transition beds.

The whole of the next day the gallery opened before us its endless arcades. We moved on almost without a word. Hans' silence seemed to be infecting us.

The road was now not ascending, at least not perceptibly. Sometimes, even, it seemed to have a slight fall. But this tendency, which was very trifling, could not do anything to reassure the Professor; for there was no change in the beds, and the transitional characteristics became more and more decided.

The electric light was reflected in sparkling splendour from the schist, limestone, and old red sandstone of the walls. It might have been thought that we were passing through a section of Wales, of which an ancient people gave its name to this system. Specimens of magnificent marbles clothed the walls, some of a greyish agate fantastically veined with white, others of rich crimson or yellow dashed with splotches of red; then came dark cherry-coloured marbles relieved by the lighter tints of limestone.

The greater part of these bore impressions of primitive organisms. Creation had evidently advanced since the day before. Instead of rudimentary trilobites, I noticed remains of a more perfect order of beings, amongst others ganoid fishes and some of those sauroids in which palaeontologists have discovered the earliest reptile forms. The Devonian seas were peopled by animals of these species, and deposited them by thousands in the rocks of the newer formation.

It was evident that we were ascending that scale of animal life in which man fills the highest place. But Professor Liedenbrock seemed not to notice it.

He was awaiting one of two events, either the appearance of a vertical well opening before his feet, down which our descent might be resumed, or that of some obstacle which should effectually turn us back on our own footsteps. But evening came and neither wish was gratified.

On Friday, after a night during which I felt pangs of thirst, our little troop again plunged into the winding passages of the gallery.

After ten hours' walking I observed a singular deadening of the reflection of our lamps from the side walls. The marble, the schist, the limestone, and the sandstone were giving way to a dark and lustreless lining. At one moment, the tunnel becoming very narrow, I leaned against the wall.

When I removed my hand it was black. I looked nearer, and found we were in a coal formation.

'A coal mine!' I cried.

'A mine without miners,' my uncle replied.

'Who knows?' I asked.

'I know,' the Professor pronounced decidedly, 'I am certain that this gallery driven through beds of coal was never pierced by the hand of man. But whether it be the hand of nature or not does not matter. Supper time is come; let us sup.'

Hans prepared some food. I scarcely ate, and I swallowed down the few drops of water rationed out to me. One flask half full was all we had left to slake the thirst of three men.

After their meal my two companions laid themselves down upon their rugs, and found in sleep a solace for their fatigue. But I could not sleep, and I counted every hour until morning.

On Saturday, at six, we started afresh. In twenty minutes we reached a vast open space; I then knew that the hand of man had not hollowed out this mine; the vaults would have been shored up, and, as it was, they seemed to be held up by a miracle of equilibrium.

This cavern was about a hundred feet wide and a hundred and fifty in height. A large mass had been rent asunder by a subterranean disturbance. Yielding to some vast power from below it had broken asunder, leaving this great hollow into which human beings were now penetrating for the first time.

The whole history of the carboniferous period was written upon these gloomy walls, and a geologist might with ease trace all its diverse phases. The beds of coal were separated by strata of sandstone or compact clays, and appeared crushed under the weight of overlying strata.

At the age of the world which preceded the secondary period, the earth was clothed with immense vegetable forms, the product of the double influence of tropical heat and constant moisture; a vapoury atmosphere surrounded the earth, still veiling the direct rays of the sun.

Thence arises the conclusion that the high temperature then existing was due to some other source than the heat of the sun. Perhaps even the orb of day may not have been ready yet to play the splendid part he now acts. There were no &8216;climates&8217; as yet, and a torrid heat, equal from pole to equator, was spread over the whole surface of the globe.

Whence this heat? Was it from the interior of the earth?

Notwithstanding the theories of Professor Liedenbrock, a violent heat did at that time brood within the body of the spheroid. Its action was felt to the very last coats of the terrestrial crust; the plants, unacquainted with the beneficent influences of the sun, yielded neither flowers nor scent. But their roots drew vigorous life from the burning soil of the early days of this planet.

There were but few trees. Herbaceous plants alone existed. There were tall grasses, ferns, lycopods, besides sigillaria, asterophyllites, now scarce plants, but then the species might be counted by thousands.

The coal measures owe their origin to this period of profuse vegetation. The yet elastic and yielding crust of the earth obeyed the fluid forces beneath. Thence innumerable fissures and depressions. The plants, sunk underneath the waters, formed by degrees into vast accumulated masses.

Then came the chemical action of nature; in the depths of the seas the vegetable accumulations first became peat; then, acted upon by generated gases and the heat of fermentation, they underwent a process of complete mineralization.

Thus were formed those immense coalfields, which nevertheless, are not inexhaustible, and which three centuries at the present accelerated rate of consumption will exhaust unless the industrial world will devise a remedy.

These reflections came into my mind whilst I was contemplating the mineral wealth stored up in this portion of the globe. These no doubt, I thought, will never be discovered; the working of such deep mines would involve too large an outlay, and where would be the use as long as coal is yet spread far and wide near the surface? Such as my eyes behold these virgin stores, such they will be when this world comes to an end.

But still we marched on, and I alone was forgetting the length of the way by losing myself in the midst of geological contemplations. The temperature remained what it had been during our passage through the lava and schists. Only my sense of smell was forcibly affected by an odour of protocarburet of hydrogen. I immediately recognised in this gallery the presence of a considerable quantity of the dangerous gas called by miners firedamp, the explosion of which has often occasioned such dreadful catastrophes.

Happily, our light was from Ruhmkorff's ingenious apparatus. If unfortunately we had explored this gallery with torches, a terrible explosion would have put an end to travelling and travellers at one stroke.

This excursion through the coal mine lasted till night. My uncle scarcely could restrain his impatience at the horizontal road. The darkness, always deep twenty yards before us, prevented us from estimating the length of the gallery; and I was beginning to think it must be endless, when suddenly at six o'clock a wall very unexpectedly stood before us. Right or left, top or bottom, there was no road farther; we were at the end of a blind alley. 'Very well, it's all right!' cried my uncle, 'now, at any rate, we shall know what we are about. We are not in Saknussemm's road, and all we have to do is to go back. Let us take a night's rest, and in three days we shall get to the fork in the road.' 'Yes,' said I, 'if we have any strength left.' 'Why not?' 'Because Tomorrow we shall have no water.' 'Nor courage either?' asked my uncle severely. I dared make no answer.

TWENTY ONE

COMPASSION FUSES THE PROFESSOR'S HEART

Next day we started early. We had to hasten forward. It was a three days' march to the cross roads.

I will not speak of the sufferings we endured in our return. My uncle bore them with the angry impatience of a man obliged to own his weakness; Hans with the resignation of his passive nature; I, I confess, with complaints and expressions of despair. I had no spirit to oppose this ill fortune.

As I had foretold, the water failed entirely by the end of the first day's retrograde march. Our fluid aliment was now nothing but gin; but this infernal fluid burned my throat, and I could not even endure the sight of it. I found the temperature and the air stifling. Fatigue paralysed my limbs. More than once I dropped down motionless. Then there was a halt; and my uncle and the Icelander did their best to restore me. But I saw that the former was struggling painfully against excessive fatigue and the tortures of thirst.

At last, on Tuesday, July 8, we arrived on our hands and knees, and half dead, at the junction of the two roads. There I dropped like a lifeless lump, extended on the lava soil. It was ten in the morning.

Hans and my uncle, clinging to the wall, tried to nibble a few bits of biscuit. Long moans escaped from my swollen lips.

After some time my uncle approached me and raised me in his arms.

'Poor boy!' said he, in genuine tones of compassion.

I was touched with these words, not being accustomed to see the excitable Professor in a softened mood. I grasped his trembling hands in mine. He let me hold them and looked at me. His eyes were moistened.

Then I saw him take the flask that was hanging at his side. To my amazement he placed it on my lips.

'Drink!' said he.

Had I heard him? Was my uncle beside himself? I stared at, him stupidly, and felt as if I could not understand him.

'Drink!' he said again.

And raising his flask he emptied it every drop between my lips.

Oh! infinite pleasure! a slender sip of water came to moisten my burning mouth. It was but one sip but it was enough to recall my ebbing life.

I thanked my uncle with clasped hands.

'Yes,' he said, 'a draught of water; but it is the very last - you hear! - the last. I had kept it as a precious treasure at the bottom of my flask. Twenty times, nay, a hundred times, have I fought against a frightful impulse to drink it off. But no, Axel, I kept it for you.'

'My dear uncle,' I said, whilst hot tears trickled down my face.

'Yes, my poor boy, I knew that as soon as you arrived at these cross roads you would drop half dead, and I kept my last drop of water to reanimate you.'

'Thank you, thank you,' I said. Although my thirst was only partially quenched, yet some strength had returned. The muscles of my throat, until then contracted, now relaxed again; and the inflammation of my lips abated somewhat; and I was now able to speak. .

'Let us see,' I said, 'we have now but one thing to do. We have no water; we must go back.'

While I spoke my uncle avoided looking at me; he hung his head down; his eyes avoided mine.

'We must return,' I exclaimed vehemently; 'we must go back on our way to Snæfell. May God give us strength to climb up the crater again!'

'Return!' said my uncle, as if he was rather answering himself than me.

'Yes, return, without the loss of a minute.'

A long silence followed.

'So then, Axel,' replied the Professor ironically, 'you have found no courage or energy in these few drops of water?'

'Courage?'

'I see you just as feeble-minded as you were before, and still expressing only despair!'

What sort of a man was this I had to do with, and what schemes was he now revolving in his fearless mind?

'What! you won't go back?'

'Should I renounce this expedition just when we have the fairest chance of success! Never!'

'Then must we resign ourselves to destruction?'

'No, Axel, no; go back. Hans will go with you. Leave me to myself!'

'Leave you here!'

'Leave me, I tell you. I have undertaken this expedition. I will carry it out to the end, and I will not return. Go, Axel, go!'

My uncle was in high state of excitement. His voice, which had for a moment been tender and gentle, had now become hard and threatening. He was struggling with gloomy resolutions against impossibilities. I would not leave him in this bottomless abyss, and on the other hand the instinct of self-preservation prompted me to fly.

The guide watched this scene with his usual phlegmatic unconcern. Yet he understood perfectly well what was going on between his two companions. The gestures themselves were sufficient to show that we were each bent on taking a different road; but Hans seemed to take no part in a question upon which depended his life. He was ready to start at a given signal, or to stay, if his master so willed it.

How I wished at this moment I could have made him understand me. My words, my complaints, my sorrow would have had some influence over that frigid nature. Those dangers which our guide could not understand I could have demonstrated and proved to him. Together we might have over-ruled the obstinate Professor; if it were needed, we might perhaps have compelled him to regain the heights of Snæfell.

I drew near to Hans. I placed my hand upon his. He made no movement. My parted lips sufficiently revealed my sufferings. The Icelander slowly moved his head, and calmly pointing to my uncle said:

'Master.'

'Master!' I shouted; 'you madman! no, he is not the master

of our life; we must fly, we must drag him. Do you hear me? Do you understand?'

I had seized Hans by the arm. I wished to oblige him to rise. I strove with him. My uncle interposed.

'Be calm, Axel! you will get nothing from that immovable servant. Therefore, listen to my proposal.'

I crossed my arms, and confronted my uncle boldly.

'The want of water,' he said, 'is the only obstacle in our way. In this eastern gallery made up of lavas, schists, and coal, we have not met with a single particle of moisture. Perhaps we shall be more fortunate if we follow the western tunnel.'

I shook my head incredulously.

'Hear me to the end,' the Professor went on with a firm voice. 'Whilst you were lying there motionless, I went to examine the conformation of that gallery. It penetrates directly downward, and in a few hours it will bring us to the granite rocks. There we must meet with abundant springs. The nature of the rock assures me of this, and instinct agrees with logic to support my conviction. Now, this is my proposal. When Columbus asked of his ships' crews for three days more to discover a new world, those crews, disheartened and sick as they were, recognised the justice of the claim, and he discovered America. I am the Columbus of this nether world, and I only ask for one more day. If in a single day I have not met with the water that we want, I swear to you we will return to the surface of the earth.'

In spite of my irritation I was moved with these words, as well as with the violence my uncle was doing to his own wishes in making so hazardous a proposal.

'Well,' I said, 'do as you will, and God reward your superhuman energy. You have now but a few hours to tempt fortune. Let us start!'

TWENTY TWO

TOTAL FAILURE OF WATER

This time the descent commenced by the new gallery. Hans walked first as was his custom.

We had not gone a hundred yards when the Professor, moving his lantern along the walls, cried:

'Here are primitive rocks. Now we are in the right way. Forward!'

When in its early stages the earth was slowly cooling, its contraction gave rise in its crust to disruptions, distortions, fissures, and chasms. The passage through which we were moving was such a fissure, through which at one time granite poured out in a molten state. Its thousands of windings formed an inextricable labyrinth through the primeval mass.

As fast as we descended, the succession of beds forming the primitive foundation came out with increasing distinctness. Geologists consider this primitive matter to be the base of the mineral crust of the earth, and have ascertained it to be composed of three different formations, schist, gneiss, and mica schist, resting upon that unchangeable foundation, the granite.

Never had mineralogists found themselves in so marvellous a situation to study nature in situ. What the boring machine, an insensible, inert instrument, was unable to bring to the surface of the inner structure of the globe, we were able to peruse with our own eyes and handle with our own hands.

Through the beds of schist, coloured with delicate shades of green, ran in winding course threads of copper and manganese, with traces of platinum and gold. I thought, what riches are here buried at an unapproachable depth in the earth, hidden for ever from the covetous eyes of the human race! These treasures have been buried at such a profound depth by the convulsions of primeval times that they run no chance of ever being molested by the pickaxe or the spade.

To the schists succeeded gneiss, partially stratified, remarkable for the parallelism and regularity of its lamina, then mica schists, laid in large plates or flakes, revealing their lamellated structure by the sparkle of the white shining mica.

The light from our apparatus, reflected from the small facets of quartz, shot sparkling rays at every angle, and I seemed to be moving through a diamond, within which the quickly darting rays broke across each other in a thousand flashing coruscations.

About six o'clock this brilliant fete of illuminations underwent a sensible abatement of splendour, then almost ceased. The walls assumed a crystallised though sombre appearance; mica was more closely mingled with the feldspar and quartz to form the proper rocky foundations of the earth, which bears without distortion or crushing the weight of the four terrestrial systems. We were immured within prison walls of granite.

It was eight in the evening. No signs of water had yet appeared. I was suffering horribly. My uncle strode on. He refused to stop. He was listening anxiously for the murmur of distant springs. But, no, there was dead silence.

And now my limbs were failing beneath me. I resisted pain and torture, that I might not stop my uncle, which would have driven him to despair, for the day was drawing near to its end, and it was his last.

At last I failed utterly; I uttered a cry and fell.

'Come to me, I am dying.'

My uncle retraced his steps. He gazed upon me with his arms crossed; then these muttered words passed his lips:

'It's all over!'

The last thing I saw was a fearful gesture of rage, and my

eyes closed.

When I reopened them I saw my two companions motionless and rolled up in their coverings. Were they asleep? As for me, I could not get one moment's sleep. I was suffering too keenly, and what embittered my thoughts was that there was no remedy. My uncle's last words echoed painfully in my ears: 'it's all over!' For in such a fearful state of debility it was madness to think of ever reaching the upper world again.

We had above us a league and a half of terrestrial crust. The weight of it seemed to be crushing down upon my shoulders. I felt weighed down, and I exhausted myself with imaginary violent exertions to turn round upon my granite couch.

A few hours passed away. A deep silence reigned around us, the silence of the grave. No sound could reach us through walls, the thinnest of which were five miles thick.

Yet in the midst of my stupefaction I seemed to be aware of a noise. It was dark down the tunnel, but I seemed to see the Icelander vanishing from our sight with the lamp in his hand.

Why was he leaving us? Was Hans going to forsake us? My uncle was fast asleep. I wanted to shout, but my voice died upon my parched and swollen lips. The darkness became deeper, and the last sound died away in the far distance.

'Hans has abandoned us,' I cried. 'Hans! Hans!'

But these words were only spoken within me. They went no farther. Yet after the first moment of terror I felt ashamed of suspecting a man of such extraordinary faithfulness. Instead of ascending he was descending the gallery. An evil design would have taken him up not down. This reflection restored me to calmness, and I turned to other thoughts. None but some weighty motive could have induced so quiet a man to forfeit his sleep. Was he on a journey of discovery? Had he during the silence of the night caught a sound, a murmuring of something in the distance, which had failed to affect my hearing?

TWENTY THREE

WATER DISCOVERED

For a whole hour I was trying to work out in my delirious brain the reasons which might have influenced this seemingly tranquil huntsman. The absurdest notions ran in utter confusion through my mind. I thought madness was coming on!

But at last a noise of footsteps was heard in the dark abyss. Hans was approaching. A flickering light was beginning to glimmer on the wall of our darksome prison; then it came out full at the mouth of the gallery. Hans appeared.

He drew close to my uncle, laid his hand upon his shoulder, and gently woke him. My uncle rose up.

'What is the matter?' he asked.

'Watten!' replied the huntsman.

No doubt under the inspiration of intense pain everybody becomes endowed with the gift of divers tongues. I did not know a word of Danish, yet instinctively I understood the word he had uttered.

'Water! water!' I cried, clapping my hands and gesticulating like a madman.

'Water!' repeated my uncle. 'Hvar?' he asked, in Icelandic.

'Nedat,' replied Hans.

'Where? Down below!' I understood it all. I seized the hunter's hands, and pressed them while he looked on me without moving a muscle of his countenance.

The preparations for our departure were not long in making, and we were soon on our way down a passage inclining two feet in seven. In an hour we had gone a mile and a quarter, and descended two thousand feet.

Then I began to hear distinctly quite a new sound of

something running within the thickness of the granite wall, a kind of dull, dead rumbling, like distant thunder. During the first part of our walk, not meeting with the promised spring, I felt my agony returning; but then my uncle acquainted me with the cause of the strange noise.

'Hans was not mistaken,' he said. 'What you hear is the rushing of a torrent.'

'A torrent?' I exclaimed.

'There can be no doubt; a subterranean river is flowing around us.'

We hurried forward in the greatest excitement. I was no longer sensible of my fatigue. This murmuring of waters close at hand was already refreshing me. It was audibly increasing. The torrent, after having for some time flowed over our heads, was now running within the left wall, roaring and rushing. Frequently I touched the wall, hoping to feel some indications of moisture: But there was no hope here.

Yet another half hour, another half league was passed.

Then it became clear that the hunter had gone no farther. Guided by an instinct peculiar to mountaineers he had as it were felt this torrent through the rock; but he had certainly seen none of the precious liquid; he had drunk nothing himself.

Soon it became evident that if we continued our walk we should widen the distance between ourselves and the stream, the noise of which was becoming fainter.

We returned. Hans stopped where the torrent seemed closest. I sat near the wall, while the waters were flowing past me at a distance of two feet with extreme violence. But there was a thick granite wall between us and the object of our desires.

Without reflection, without asking if there were any means of procuring the water, I gave way to a movement of despair.

Hans glanced at me with, I thought, a smile of compassion.

He rose and took the lamp. I followed him. He moved towards the wall. I looked on. He applied his ear against the dry stone, and moved it slowly to and fro, listening intently. I perceived at once that he was examining to find the exact place where the torrent could be heard the loudest. He met with that point on the left side of the tunnel, at three feet from the ground.

I was stirred up with excitement. I hardly dared guess what the hunter was about to do. But I could not but understand, and applaud and cheer him on, when I saw him lay hold of the pickaxe to make an attack upon the rock.

'We are saved!' I cried.

'Yes,' cried my uncle, almost frantic with excitement. 'Hans is right. Capital fellow! Who but he would have thought of it?'

Yes; who but he? Such an expedient, however simple, would never have entered into our minds. True, it seemed most hazardous to strike a blow of the hammer in this part of the earth's structure. Suppose some displacement should occur and crush us all! Suppose the torrent, bursting through, should drown us in a sudden flood! There was nothing vain in these fancies. But still no fears of falling rocks or rushing floods could stay us now; and our thirst was so intense that, to satisfy it, we would have dared the waves of the north Atlantic.

Hans set about the task which my uncle and I together could not have accomplished. If our impatience had armed our hands with power, we should have shattered the rock into a thousand fragments. Not so Hans. Full of self possession, he calmly wore his way through the rock with a steady succession of light and skilful strokes, working through an aperture six inches wide at the outside. I could hear a louder noise of flowing waters, and I fancied I could feel the delicious fluid refreshing my parched lips.

The pick had soon penetrated two feet into the granite partition, and our man had worked for above an hour. I was in an agony of impatience. My uncle wanted to employ stronger measures, and I had some difficulty in dissuading him; still he had just taken a pickaxe in his hand, when a sudden hissing was heard, and a jet of water spurted out with violence against the opposite wall.

Hans, almost thrown off his feet by the violence of the shock, uttered a cry of grief and disappointment, of which I soon under-. stood the cause, when plunging my hands into the spouting torrent, I withdrew them in haste, for the water was scalding hot.

'The water is at the boiling point,' I cried.

'Well, never mind, let it cool,' my uncle replied.

The tunnel was filling with steam, whilst a stream was forming, which by degrees wandered away into subterranean windings, and soon we had the satisfaction of swallowing our first draught.

Could anything be more delicious than the sensation that our burning intolerable thirst was passing away, and leaving us to enjoy comfort and pleasure? But where was this water from? No matter. It was water; and though still warm, it brought life back to the dying. I kept drinking without stopping, and almost without tasting.

At last after a most delightful time of reviving energy, I cried, 'Why, this is a chalybeate spring!'

'Nothing could be better for the digestion,' said my uncle. 'It is highly impregnated with iron. It will be as good for us as going to the Spa, or to Töplitz.'

'Well, it is delicious!'

'Of course it is, water should be, found six miles underground. It has an inky flavour, which is not at all unpleasant. What a capital source of strength Hans has found for us here. We will call it after his name.'

'Agreed,' I cried.

And Hansbach it was from that moment.

Hans was none the prouder. After a moderate draught, he went quietly into a corner to rest.

'Now,' I said, 'we must not lose this water.'

'What is the use of troubling ourselves?' my uncle, replied.

'I fancy it will never fail.'

'Never mind, we cannot be sure; let us fill the water bottle and our flasks, and then stop up the opening.'

My advice was followed so far as getting in a supply; but the stopping up of the hole was not so easy to accomplish. It was in vain that we took up fragments of granite, and stuffed them in with tow, we only scalded our hands without succeeding. The pressure was too great, and our efforts were fruitless.

'It is quite plain,' said I, 'that the higher body of this water is at a considerable elevation. The force of the jet shows that.'

'No doubt,' answered my uncle. 'If this column of water is 32,000 feet high?that is, from the surface of the earth, it is equal to the weight of a thousand atmospheres. But I have got an idea.'

'Well?'

'Why should we trouble ourselves to stop the stream from coming out at all?'

'Because --' Well, I could not assign a reason.

'When our flasks are empty, where shall we fill them again? Can we tell that?'

No; there was no certainty.

'Well, let us allow the water to run on. It will flow down, and will both guide and refresh us.'

'That is well planned,' I cried. 'With this stream for our guide, there is no reason why we should not succeed in our undertaking.'

'Ah, my boy! you agree with me now,' cried the Professor, laughing.

'I agree with you most heartily.'

'Well, let us rest awhile; and then we will start again.'

I was forgetting that it was night. The chronometer soon informed me of that fact; and in a very short time, refreshed and thankful, we all three fell into a sound sleep.

TWENTY FOUR

WELL SAID, OLD MOLE! CANST THOU WORK I' THE GROUND SO FAST?

By the next day we had forgotten all our sufferings. At first, I was wondering that I was no longer thirsty, and I was for asking for the reason. The answer came in the murmuring of the stream at my feet.

We breakfasted, and drank of this excellent chalybeate water. I felt wonderfully stronger, and quite decided upon pushing on. Why should not so firmly convinced a man as my uncle, furnished with so industrious a guide as Hans, and accompanied by so determined a nephew as myself, go on to final success? Such were the magnificent plans which struggled for mastery within me. If it had been proposed to me to return to the summit of Snæfell, I should have indignantly declined.

Most fortunately, all we had to do was to descend.

'Let us start!' I cried, awakening by my shouts the echoes of the vaulted hollows of the earth.

On Thursday, at 8 a.m., we started afresh. The granite tunnel winding from side to side, earned us past unexpected turns, and seemed almost to form a labyrinth; but, on the whole, its direction seemed to be south-easterly. My uncle never ceased to consult his compass, to keep account of the ground gone over.

The gallery dipped down a very little way from the horizontal, scarcely more than two inches in a fathom, and the stream ran gently murmuring at our feet. I compared it to a friendly genius guiding us underground, and caressed with my hand the soft naiad, whose comforting voice accompanied our steps. With my reviving spirits these mythological notions seemed to come unbidden.

As for my uncle, he was beginning to storm against the horizontal road. He loved nothing better than a vertical path; but this way seemed indefinitely prolonged, and instead of sliding along the hypothenuse as we were now doing, he would willingly have dropped down the terrestrial radius. But there was no help for it, and as long as we were approaching the centre at all we felt that we must not complain.

From time to time, a steeper path appeared; our naiad then began to tumble before us with a hoarser murmur, and we went down with her to a greater depth.

On the whole, that day and the next we made considerable way horizontally, very little vertically.

On Friday evening, the 10th of July, according to our calculations, we were thirty leagues south-east of Rejkiavik, and at a depth of two leagues and a half.

At our feet there now opened a frightful abyss. My uncle, however, was not to be daunted, and he clapped his hands at the steepness of the descent.

'This will take us a long way,' he cried, 'and without much difficulty; for the projections in the rock form quite a staircase.'

The ropes were so fastened by Hans as to guard against accident, and the descent commenced. I can hardly call it perilous, for I was beginning to be familiar with this kind of exercise.

This well, or abyss, was a narrow cleft in the mass of the granite, called by geologists a 'fault,' and caused by the unequal cooling of the globe of the earth. If it had at one time been a passage for eruptive matter thrown out by Snæfell, I still could not understand why no trace was left of its passage. We kept going down a kind of winding staircase, which seemed almost to have been made by the hand of man.

Every quarter of an hour we were obliged to halt, to take a little necessary repose and restore the action of our limbs. We then sat down upon a fragment of rock, and we talked as we ate and drank from the stream.

Of course, down this fault the Hansbach fell in a cascade, and lost some of its volume; but there was enough and to spare to slake our thirst. Besides, when the incline became more gentle, it would of course resume its peaceable course. At this moment it reminded me of my worthy uncle, in his frequent fits of impatience and anger, while below it ran with the calmness of the Icelandic hunter.

On the 6th and 7th of July we kept following the spiral curves of this singular well, penetrating in actual distance no more than two leagues; but being carried to a depth of five leagues below the level of the sea. But on the 8th, about noon, the fault took, towards the south-east, a much gentler slope, one of about forty-five degrees.

Then the road became monotonously easy. It could not be otherwise, for there was no landscape to vary the stages of our journey.

On Wednesday, the 15th, we were seven leagues underground, and had travelled fifty leagues away from Snæfell. Although we were tired, our health was perfect, and the medicine chest had not yet had occasion to be opened.

My uncle noted every hour the indications of the compass, the chronometer, the aneroid, and the thermometer the very same which he has published in his scientific report of our journey. It was therefore not difficult to know exactly our whereabouts. When he told me that we had gone fifty leagues horizontally, I could not repress an exclamation of astonishment, at the thought that we had now long left Iceland behind us.

'What is the matter?' he cried.

'I was reflecting that if your calculations are correct we are no longer under Iceland.'

'Do you think so?'

'I am not mistaken,' I said, and examining the map, I added, 'We have passed Cape Portland, and those fifty leagues bring us under the wide expanse of ocean.'

'Under the sea,' my uncle repeated, rubbing his hands with

delight.

'Can it be?' I said. 'Is the ocean spread above our heads?'

'Of course, Axel. What can be more natural? At Newcastle are there not coal mines extending far under the sea?'

It was all very well for the Professor to call this so simple, but I could not feel quite easy at the thought that the boundless ocean was rolling over my head. And yet it really mattered very little whether it was the plains and mountains that covered our heads, or the Atlantic waves, as long as we were arched over by solid granite. And, besides, I was getting used to this idea; for the tunnel, now running straight, now winding as capriciously in its inclines as in its turnings, but constantly preserving its south-easterly direction, and always running deeper, was gradually carrying us to very great depths indeed.

Four days later, Saturday, the 18th of July, in the evening, we arrived at a kind of vast grotto; and here my uncle paid Hans his weekly wages, and it was settled that the next day, Sunday, should be a day of rest.

TWENTY FIVE

DE PROFUNDIS

I therefore awoke next day relieved from the preoccupation of an immediate start. Although we were in the very deepest of known depths, there was something not unpleasant about it. And, besides, we were beginning to get accustomed to this troglodyte[1] life. I no longer thought of sun, moon, and stars, trees, houses, and towns, nor of any of those terrestrial superfluities which are necessaries of men who live upon the earth's surface. Being fossils, we looked upon all those things

1. The name of an Ethiopian tribe who lived in caves and holes.

as mere jokes.

The grotto was an immense apartment. Along its granite floor ran our faithful stream. At this distance from its spring the water was scarcely tepid, and we drank of it with pleasure.

After breakfast the Professor gave a few hours to the arrangement of his daily notes.

'First,' said he, 'I will make a calculation to ascertain our exact position. I hope, after our return, to draw a map of our journey, which will be in reality a vertical section of the globe, containing the track of our expedition.'

'That will be curious, uncle; but are your observations sufficiently accurate to enable you to do this correctly?'

'Yes; I have everywhere observed the angles and the inclines. I am sure there is no error. Let us see where we are now. Take your compass, and note the direction.'

I looked, and replied carefully:

'South-east by east.'

'Well,' answered the Professor, after a rapid calculation, 'I infer that we have gone eighty-five leagues since we started.!'

'Therefore we are under mid-Atlantic?'

'To be sure we are.'

'And perhaps at this very moment there is a storm above, and ships over our heads are being rudely tossed by the tempest.'

'Quite probable.'

'And whales are lashing the roof of our prison with their tails?'

'It may be, Axel, but they won't shake us here. But let us go back to our calculation. Here we are eighty-five leagues south-east of Snæfell, and I reckon that we are at a depth of sixteen leagues.'

'Sixteen leagues?' I cried.

'No doubt.'

'Why, this is the very limit assigned by science to the thickness of the crust of the earth.'

'I don't deny it.'

'And here, according to the law of increasing temperature, there ought to be a heat of 2,732° Fahr.!'

'So there should, my lad.'

'And all this solid granite ought to be running in fusion.'

'You see that it is not so, and that, as so often happens, facts come to overthrow theories.'

'I am obliged to agree; but, after all, it is surprising.'

'What does the thermometer say?'

'Twenty-seven, six tenths (82° Fahr.).'

'Therefore the savants are wrong by 2,705°, and the proportional increase is a mistake. Therefore Humphry Davy was right, and I am not wrong in following him. What do you say now?'

'Nothing.'

In truth, I had a good deal to say. I gave way in no respect to Davy's theory. I still held to the central heat, although I did not feel its effects. I preferred to admit in truth, that this chimney of an extinct volcano, lined with lavas, which are non-conductors of heat, did not suffer the heat to pass through its walls.

But without stopping to look up new arguments I simply took up our situation such as it was.

'Well, admitting all your calculations to be quite correct, you must allow me to draw one rigid result therefrom.'

'What is it. Speak freely.!'

'At the latitude of Iceland, where we now are, the radius of the earth, the distance from the centre to the surface is about 1,583 leagues; let us say in round numbers 1,600 leagues, or 4,800 miles. Out of 1,600 leagues we have gone twelve!'

'So you say.'

'And these twelve at a cost of 85 leagues diagonally?'

'Exactly so.'

'In twenty days?'

'Yes.'

'Now, sixteen leagues are the hundredth part of the earth's

radius. At this rate we shall be two thousand days, or nearly five years and a half, in getting to the centre.'

No answer was vouchsafed to this rational conclusion. 'Without reckoning, too, that if a vertical depth of sixteen leagues can be attained only by a diagonal descent of eighty-four, it follows that we must go eight thousand miles in a south-easterly direction; so that we shall emerge from some point in the earth's circumference instead of getting to the centre!'

'Confusion to all your figures, and all your hypotheses besides,' shouted my uncle in a sudden rage. 'What is the basis of them all? How do you know that this passage does not run straight to our destination? Besides, there is a precedent. What one man has done, another may do.'

'I hope so; but, still, I may be permitted—'

'You shall have my leave to hold your tongue, Axel, but not to talk in that irrational way.'

I could see the awful Professor bursting through my uncle's skin, and I took timely warning.

'Now look at your aneroid. What does that say?'

'It says we are under considerable pressure.'

'Very good; so you see that by going gradually down, and getting accustomed to the density of the atmosphere, we don't suffer at all.'

'Nothing, except a little pain in the ears.'

'That's nothing, and you may get rid of even that by quick breathing whenever you feel the pain.'

'Exactly so,' I said, determined not to say a word that might cross my uncle's prejudices. 'There is even positive pleasure in living in this dense atmosphere. Have you observed how intense sound is down here?'

'No doubt it is. A deaf man would soon learn to hear perfectly.'

'But won't this density augment?'

'Yes; according to a rather obscure law. It is well known that the weight of bodies diminishes as fast as we descend. You know that it is at the surface of the globe that weight is most sensibly felt, and that at the centre there is no weight at all.'

'I am aware of that; but, tell me, will not air at last acquire the density of water?'

'Of course, under a pressure of seven hundred and ten atmospheres.'

'And how, lower down still?'

'Lower down the density will still increase.'

'But how shall we go down then.'

'Why, we must fill our pockets with stones.'

'Well, indeed, my worthy uncle, you are never at a loss for an answer.'

I dared venture no farther into the region of probabilities, for I might presently have stumbled upon an impossibility, which would have brought the Professor on the scene when he was not wanted.

Still, it was evident that the air, under a pressure which might reach that of thousands of atmospheres, would at last reach the solid state, and then, even if our bodies could resist the strain, we should be stopped, and no reasonings would be able to get us on any farther.

But I did not advance this argument. My uncle would have met it with his inevitable Saknussemm, a precedent which possessed no weight with me; for even if the journey of the learned Icelander were really attested, there was one very simple answer, that in the sixteenth century there was neither barometer or aneroid and therefore Saknussemm could not tell how far he had gone.

But I kept this objection to myself, and waited the course of events.

The rest of the day was passed in calculations and in conversations. I remained a steadfast adherent of the opinions of Professor Liedenbrock, and I envied the stolid indifference of Hans, who, without going into causes and effects, went on with his eyes shut wherever his destiny guided him.

TWENTY SIX

THE WORST PERIL OF ALL

It must be confessed that hitherto things had not gone on so badly, and that I had small reason to complain. If our difficulties became no worse, we might hope to reach our end. And to what a height of scientific glory we should then attain! I had become quite a Liedenbrock in my reasonings; seriously I had. But would this state of things last in the strange place we had come to? Perhaps it might.

For several days steeper inclines, some even frightfully near to the perpendicular, brought us deeper and deeper into the mass of the interior of the earth. Some days we advanced nearer to the centre by a league and a half, or nearly two leagues. These were perilous descents, in which the skill and marvellous coolness of Hans were invaluable to us. That unimpassioned Icelander devoted himself with incomprehensible deliberation; and, thanks to him, we crossed many a dangerous spot which we should never have cleared alone.

But his habit of silence gained upon him day by day, and was infecting us. External objects produce decided effects upon the brain. A man shut up between four walls soon loses the power to associate words and ideas together. How many prisoners in solitary confinement become idiots, if not mad, for want of exercise for the thinking faculty!

During the fortnight following our last conversation, no incident occurred worthy of being recorded. But I have good reason for remembering one very serious event which took place at this time, and of which I could scarcely now forget the smallest details.

By the 7th of August our successive descents had brought us

to a depth of thirty leagues; that is, that for a space of thirty leagues there were over our heads solid beds of rock, ocean, continents, and towns. We must have been two hundred leagues from Iceland.

On that day the tunnel went down a gentle slope. I was ahead of the others. My uncle was carrying one of Ruhmkorff's lamps and I the. other. I was examining the beds of granite.

Suddenly turning round I observed that I was alone.

Well, well, I thought; I have been going too fast, or Hans and my uncle have stopped on the way. Come, this won't do; I must join them. Fortunately there is not much of an ascent.

I retraced my steps. I walked for a quarter of an hour. I gazed into the darkness. I shouted. No reply: my voice was lost in the midst of the cavernous echoes which alone replied to my call.

I began to feel uneasy. A shudder ran through me.

'Calmly!' I said aloud to myself, 'I am sure to find my companions again. There are not two roads. I was too far ahead. I will return!'

For half an hour I climbed up. I listened for a call, and in that dense atmosphere a voice could reach very far. But there was a dreary silence in all that long gallery. I stopped. I could not believe that I was lost. I was only bewildered for a time, not lost. I was sure I should find my way again.

'Come,' I repeated, 'since there is but one road, and they are on it, I must find them again. I have but to ascend still. Unless, indeed, missing me, and supposing me to be behind, they too should have gone back. But even in this case I have only to make the greater haste. I shall find them, I am sure.'

I repeated these words in the fainter tones of a half-convinced man. Besides, to associate even such simple ideas with words, and reason with them, was a work of time.

A doubt then seized upon me. Was I indeed in advance when we became separated? Yes, to be sure I was. Hans was after me, preceding my uncle. He had even stopped for a while to strap his baggage better over his shoulders. I could remember this little incident. It was at that very moment that I must have gone on.

Besides, I thought, have not I a guarantee that I shall not lose my way, a clue in the labyrinth, that cannot be broken, my faithful stream? I have but to trace it back, and I must come upon them.

This conclusion revived my spirits, and I resolved to resume my march without loss of time.

How I then blessed my uncle's foresight in preventing the hunter from stopping up the hole in the granite. This beneficent spring, after having satisfied our thirst on the road, would now be my guide among the windings of the terrestrial crust.

Before starting afresh I thought a wash would do me good. I stooped to bathe my face in the Hansbach.

To my stupefaction and utter dismay my feet trod only—the rough dry granite. The stream was no longer at my feet.

TWENTY SEVEN

LOST IN THE BOWELS OF THE EARTH

To describe my despair would be impossible. No words could tell it. I was buried alive, with the prospect before me of dying of hunger and thirst.

Mechanically I swept the ground with my hands. How dry and hard the rock seemed to me!

But how had I left the course of the stream? For it was a terrible fact that it no longer ran at my side. Then I understood the reason of that fearful, silence, when for the last time I listened to hear if any sound from my companions could reach my ears. At the moment when I left the right road I had not noticed the absence of the stream. It is evident that at that moment a deviation had presented itself before me, whilst the Hansbach, following the caprice of another incline, had gone with my companions away into unknown depths.

How was I to return? There was not a trace of their footsteps or of my own, for the foot left no mark upon the granite floor. I racked my brain for a solution of this impracticable problem. One word described my position. Lost!

Lost at an immeasurable depth! Thirty leagues of rock seemed to weigh upon my shoulders with a dreadful pressure. I felt crushed.

I tried to carry back my ideas to things on the surface of the earth. I could scarcely succeed. Hamburg, the house in the Königstrasse, my poor Gräuben, all that busy world underneath which I was wandering about, was passing in rapid confusion before my terrified memory. I could revive with vivid reality all the incidents of our voyage, Iceland, M. Fridrikssen, Snæfell. I said to myself that if, in such a position as I was now in, I was fool enough to cling to one glimpse of hope, it would be madness, and that the best thing I could do was to despair.

What human power could restore me to the light of the sun by rending asunder the huge arches of rock which united over my head, buttressing each other with impregnable strength? Who could place my feet on the right path, and bring me back to my company?

'Oh, my uncle!' burst from my lips in the tone of despair.

It was my only word of reproach, for I knew how much he must be suffering in seeking me, wherever he might be.

When I saw myself thus far removed from all earthly help I had recourse to heavenly succour. The remembrance of my childhood, the recollection of my mother, whom I had only known in my tender early years, came back to me, and I knelt in prayer imploring for the Divine help of which I was so little worthy.

This return of trust in God's providence allayed the

turbulence of my fears, and I was enabled to concentrate upon my situation all the force of my intelligence.

I had three days' provisions with me and my flask was full. But I could not remain alone for long. Should I go up or down?

Up, of course; up continually.

I must thus arrive at the point where I had left the stream, that fatal turn in the road. With the stream at my feet, I might hope to regain the summit of Snæfell.

Why had I not thought of that sooner? Here was evidently a chance of safety. The most pressing duty was to find out again the course of the Hansbach. I rose, and leaning upon my iron-pointed stick I ascended the gallery. The slope was rather steep. I walked on without hope but without indecision, like a man who has made up his mind.

For half an hour I met with no obstacle. I tried to recognise my way by the form of the tunnel, by the projections of certain rocks, by the disposition of the fractures. But no particular sign appeared, and I soon saw that this gallery could not bring me back to the turning point. It came to an abrupt end. I struck against an impenetrable wall, and fell down upon the rock.

Unspeakable despair then seized upon me. I lay overwhelmed, aghast! My last hope was shattered against this granite wall.

Lost in this labyrinth, whose windings crossed each other in all directions, it was no use to think of flight any longer. Here I must die the most dreadful of deaths. And, strange to say, the thought came across me that when some day my petrified remains should be found thirty leagues below the surface in the bowels of the earth, the discovery might lead to grave scientific discussions.

I tried to speak aloud, but hoarse sounds alone passed my dry lips. I panted for breath.

In the midst of my agony a new terror laid hold of me. In falling my lamp had got wrong. I could not set it right, and its light was paling and would soon disappear altogether.

I gazed painfully upon the luminous current growing weaker and weaker in the wire coil. A dim procession of moving shadows seemed slowly unfolding down the darkening walls. I scarcely dared to shut my eyes for one moment, for fear of losing the least glimmer of this precious light. Every instant it seemed about to vanish and the dense blackness to come rolling in palpably upon me.

One last trembling glimmer shot feebly up. I watched it in trembling and anxiety; I drank it in as if I could preserve it, concentrating upon it the full power of my eyes, as upon the very last sensation of light which they were ever to experience, and the next moment I lay in the heavy gloom of deep, thick, unfathomable darkness.

A terrible cry of anguish burst from me. Upon earth, in the midst of the darkest night, light never abdicates its functions altogether. It is still subtle and diffusive, but whatever little there may be, the eye still catches that little. Here there was not an atom; the total darkness made me totally blind.

Then I began to lose my head. I arose with my arms stretched out before me, attempting painfully to feel my way. I began to run wildly, hurrying through the inextricable maze, still descending, still running through the substance of the earth's thick crust, a struggling denizen of geological 'faults,' crying, shouting, yelling, soon bruised by contact with the jagged rock, falling and rising again bleeding, trying to drink the blood which covered my face, and even waiting for some rock to shatter my skull against.

I shall never know whither my mad career took me. After the lapse of some hours, no doubt exhausted, I fell like a lifeless lump at the foot of the wall, and lost all consciousness.

TWENTY EIGHT

THE RESCUE IN THE WHISPERING GALLERY

When I returned to partial life my face was wet with tears. How long that state of insensibility had lasted I cannot say. I had no means now of taking account of time. Never was solitude equal to this, never had any living being been so utterly forsaken.

After my fall I had lost a good deal of blood. I felt it flowing over me. Ah! how happy I should have been could I have died, and if death were not yet to be gone through. I would think no longer. I drove away every idea, and, conquered by my grief, I rolled myself to the foot of the opposite wall.

Already I was feeling the approach of another faint, and was hoping for complete annihilation, when a loud noise reached me. It was like the distant rumble of continuous thunder, and I could hear its sounding undulations rolling far away into the remote recesses of the abyss.

Whence could this noise proceed? It must be from some phenomenon proceeding in the great depths amidst which I lay helpless. Was it an explosion of gas? Was it the fall of some mighty pillar of the globe?

I listened still. I wanted to know if the noise would be repeated. A quarter of an hour passed away. Silence reigned in this gallery. I could not hear even the beating of my heart.

Suddenly my ear, resting by chance against the wall, caught, or seemed to catch, certain vague, indescribable, distant, articulate sounds, as of words.

'This is a delusion,' I thought.

But it was not. Listening more attentively, I heard in reality a murmuring of voices. But my weakness prevented me from understanding what the voices said. Yet it was language, I was sure of it.

For a moment I feared the words might be my own, brought back by the echo. Perhaps I had been crying out unknown to myself. I closed my lips firmly, and laid my ear against the wall again.

'Yes, truly, some one is speaking; those are words!'

Even a few feet from the wall I could hear distinctly. I succeeded in catching uncertain, strange, undistinguishable words. They came as if pronounced in low murmured whispers. The word *'forlorad'* was several times repeated in a tone of sympathy and sorrow.

'Help!' I cried with all my might. 'Help!'

I listened, I watched in the darkness for an answer, a cry, a mere breath of sound, but nothing came. Some minutes passed. A whole world of ideas had opened in my mind. I thought that my weakened voice could never penetrate to my companions.

'It is they,' I repeated. 'What other men can be thirty leagues under ground?'

I again began to listen. Passing my ear over the wall from one place to another, I found the point where the voices seemed to be best heard. The word *'forlorad'* again returned; then the rolling of thunder which had roused me from my lethargy.

'No,' I said, 'no; it is not through such a mass that a voice can be heard. I am surrounded by granite walls, and the loudest explosion could never be heard here! This noise comes along the gallery. There must be here some remarkable exercise of acoustic laws!'

I listened again, and this time, yes this time, I did distinctly hear my name pronounced across the wide interval.

It was my uncle's own voice! He was talking to the guide. And *'forlorad'* is a Danish word.

Then I understood it all. To make myself heard, I must speak along this wall, which would conduct the sound of my voice just as wire conducts electricity.

But there was no time to lose. If my companions moved but a few steps away, the acoustic phenomenon would cease. I therefore approached the wall, and pronounced these words as clearly as possible:

'Uncle Liedenbrock!'

I waited with the deepest anxiety. Sound does not travel with great velocity. Even increased density air has no effect upon its rate of travelling; it merely augments its intensity. Seconds, which seemed ages, passed away, and at last these words reached me:

'Axel! Axel! is it you?'

. . . .

'Yes, yes,' I replied.

. . . .

'My boy, where are you?'

. . . .

'Lost, in the deepest darkness.'

. . . .

'Where is your lamp?'

. . . .

'It is out.'

. . . .

'And the stream?'

. . . .

'Disappeared.'

. . . .

'Axel, Axel, take courage!'

. . . .

'Wait! I am exhausted! I can't answer. Speak to me!'

. . . .

'Courage,' resumed my uncle. 'Don't speak. Listen to me. We have looked for you up the gallery and down the gallery. Could not find you. I wept for you, my poor boy. At last, supposing you were still on the Hansbach, we fired our guns.

Our voices are audible to each other, but our hands cannot touch. But don't despair, Axel! It is a great thing that we can hear each other.'

. . . .

During this time I had been reflecting. A vague hope was returning to my heart. There was one thing I must know to begin with. I placed my lips close to the wall, saying:

'My uncle!'

. . . .

'My boy!' came to me after a few seconds.

. . . .

'We must know how far we are apart.'

. . . .

'That is easy.'

. . . .

'You have your chronometer?'

. . .

'Yes.'

. . . .

'Well, take it. Pronounce my name, noting exactly the second when you speak. I will repeat it as soon as it shall come to me, and you will observe the exact moment when you get my answer.'

'Yes; and half the time between my call and your answer will exactly indicate that which my voice will take in coming to you.'

. . . .

'Just so, my uncle.'

. . . .

'Are you ready?'

. . . .

'Yes.'

. . . . . .

'Now, attention. I am going to call your name.'

. . . .

I put my ear to the wall, and as soon as the name 'Axel' came I immediately replied 'Axel,' then waited.

. . . .

'Forty seconds,' said my uncle. 'Forty seconds between the two words; so the sound takes twenty seconds in coming. Now, at the rate of 1,120 feet in a second, this is 22,400 feet, or four miles and a quarter, nearly.'

. . . .

'Four miles and a quarter!' I murmured.

. . . .

'It will soon be over, Axel.'

. . . .

'Must I go up or down?'

. . . .

'Down—for this reason: We are in a vast chamber, with endless galleries. Yours must lead into it, for it seems as if all the clefts and fractures of the globe radiated round this vast cavern. So get up, and begin walking. Walk on, drag yourself along, if necessary slide down the steep places, and at the end you will find us ready to receive you. Now begin moving.'

. . . .

These words cheered me up.

'Good bye, uncle.' I cried. 'I am going. There will be no more voices heard when once I have started. So good bye!'

. . . .

'Good bye, Axel, au revoir!'

. . . .

These were the last words I heard.

This wonderful underground conversation, carried on with a distance of four miles and a quarter between us, concluded with these words of hope. I thanked God from my heart, for it was He who had conducted me through those vast solitudes to the point where, alone of all others perhaps, the voices of my companions could have reached me.

This acoustic effect is easily explained on scientific

grounds. It arose from the concave form of the gallery and the conducting power of the rock. There are many examples of this propagation of sounds which remain unheard in the intermediate space. I remember that a similar phenomenon has been observed in many places; amongst others on the internal surface of the gallery of the dome of St. Paul's in London, and especially in the midst of the curious caverns among the quarries near Syracuse, the most wonderful of which is called Dionysius' Ear.

These remembrances came into my mind, and I clearly saw that since my uncle's voice really reached me, there could be no obstacle between us. Following the direction by which the sound came, of course I should arrive in his presence, if my strength did not fail me.

I therefore rose; I rather dragged myself than walked. The slope was rapid, and I slid down.

Soon the swiftness of the descent increased horribly, and threatened to become a fall. I no longer had the strength to stop myself.

Suddenly there was no ground under me. I felt myself revolving in air, striking and rebounding against the craggy projections of a vertical gallery, quite a well; my head struck against a sharp corner of the rock, and I became unconscious.

TWENTY NINE

THALATTA! THALATTA!

When I came to myself, I was stretched in half darkness, covered with thick coats and blankets. My uncle was watching over me, to discover the least sign of life. At my first sigh he took my hand; when I opened my eyes he uttered a cry of joy.

'He lives! he lives!' he cried.

'Yes, I am still alive,' I answered feebly.

'My dear nephew,' said my uncle, pressing me to his breast, 'you are saved.'

I was deeply touched with the tenderness of his manner as he uttered these words, and still more with the care with which he watched over me. But such trials were wanted to bring out the Professor's tenderer qualities.

At this moment Hans came, he saw my hand in my uncle's, and I may safely say that there was joy in his countenance.

'*God dag,*' said he.

'How do you do, Hans? How are you? And now, uncle, tell me where we are at the present moment?'

'Tomorrow, Axel, Tomorrow. Now you are too faint and weak. I have bandaged your head with compresses which must not be disturbed. Sleep now, and Tomorrow I will tell you all.'

'But do tell me what time it is, and what day.'

'It is Sunday, the 8th of August, and it is ten at night. You must ask me no more questions until the 10th.'

In truth I was very weak, and my eyes involuntarily closed. I wanted a good night's rest; and I therefore went off to sleep, with the knowledge that I had been four long days alone in the heart of the earth.

Next morning, on awakening, I looked round me. My couch, made up of all our travelling gear, was in a charming grotto, adorned with splendid stalactites, and the soil of which was a fine sand. It was half light. There was no torch, no lamp, yet certain mysterious glimpses of light came from without through a narrow opening in the grotto. I heard too a vague and indistinct noise, something like the murmuring of waves breaking upon a shingly shore, and at times I seemed to hear the whistling of wind.

I wondered whether I was awake, whether I dreaming, whether my brain, crazed by my fall, was not affected by imaginary noises. Yet neither eyes, nor ears could be so utterly deceived.

It is a ray of daylight, I thought, sliding in through this cleft in the rock! That is indeed the murmuring of waves! That is the rustling noise of wind. Am I quite mistaken, or have we returned to the surface of the earth? Has my uncle given up the expedition, or is it happily terminated?

I was asking myself these unanswerable questions when the Professor entered.

'Good morning, Axel,' he cried cheerily. 'I feel sure you are better.'

'Yes, I am indeed,' said I, sitting up on my couch.

'You can hardly fail to be better, for you have slept quietly. Hans and I watched you by turns, and we have noticed you were evidently recovering.'

'Indeed, I do feel a great deal better, and I will give you a proof of that presently if you will let me have my breakfast.'

'You shall eat, lad. The fever has left you. Hans rubbed your wounds with some ointment or other of which the Icelanders keep the secret, and they have healed marvellously. Our hunter is a splendid fellow!'

Whilst he went on talking, my uncle prepared a few provisions, which I devoured eagerly, notwithstanding his advice to the contrary. All the while I was overwhelming him with questions which he answered readily.

I then learnt that my providential fall had brought me exactly to the extremity of an almost perpendicular shaft; and as I had landed in the midst of an accompanying torrent of stones, the least of which would have been enough to crush me, the conclusion was that a loose portion of the rock had come down with me. This frightful conveyance had thus carried me into the arms of my uncle, where I fell bruised, bleeding, and insensible.

'Truly it is wonderful that you have not been killed a hundred times over. But, for the love of God, don't let us ever separate again, or we many never see each other more.'

'Not separate! Is the journey not over, then?' I opened a pair of astonished eyes, which immediately called for the question:

'What is the matter, Axel?'

'I have a question to ask you. You say that I am safe and sound?'

'No doubt you are.'

'And all my limbs unbroken?'

'Certainly.'

'And my head?'

'Your head, except for a few bruises, is all right; and it is on your shoulders, where it ought to be.'

'Well, I am afraid my brain is affected.'

'Your mind affected!'

'Yes, I fear so. Are we again on the surface of the globe?'

'No, certainly not.'

'Then I must be mad; for don't I see the light of day, and don't I hear the wind blowing, and the sea breaking on the shore?'

'Ah! is that all?'

'Do tell me all about it.'

'I can't explain the inexplicable, but you will soon see and understand that geology has not yet learnt all it has to learn.'

'Then let us go,' I answered quickly.

'No, Axel; the open air might be bad for you.'

'Open air?'

'Yes; the wind is rather strong. You must not expose yourself.'

'But I assure you I am perfectly well.'

'A little patience, my nephew. A relapse might get us into trouble, and we have no time to lose, for the voyage may be a long one.'

'The voyage!'

'Yes, rest Today, and Tomorrow we will set sail.'

'Set sail!'—and I almost leaped up.

What did it all mean? Had we a river, a lake, a sea to depend upon? Was there a ship at our disposal in some underground harbour?

My curiosity was highly excited, my uncle vainly tried to restrain me. When he saw that my impatience was doing me harm, he yielded.

I dressed in haste. For greater safety I wrapped myself in a blanket, and came out of the grotto.

THIRTY

A NEW MARE INTERNUM

At first I could hardly see anything. My eyes, unaccustomed to the light, quickly closed. When I was able to reopen them, I stood more stupefied even than surprised.

'The sea!' I cried.

'Yes,' my uncle replied, 'the Liedenbrock Sea; and I don't suppose any other discoverer will ever dispute my claim to name it after myself as its first discoverer.'

A vast sheet of water, the commencement of a lake or an ocean, spread far away beyond the range of the eye, reminding me forcibly of that open sea which drew from Xenophon's ten thousand Greeks, after their long retreat, the simultaneous cry, 'Thalatta! thalatta!' the sea! the sea! The deeply indented shore was lined with a breadth of fine shining sand, softly lapped by the waves, and strewn with the small shells which had been inhabited by the first of created beings. The waves broke on this shore with the hollow echoing murmur peculiar to vast inclosed spaces. A light foam flew over the waves before the breath of a moderate breeze, and some of the spray fell upon my face. On this slightly inclining shore, about a hundred fathoms from the limit of the waves, came down the foot of a huge wall of vast cliffs, which rose majestically to an enormous height. Some of these, dividing the beach with their sharp spurs, formed capes and promontories, worn away by the ceaseless action of the surf. Farther on the eye discerned their massive outline sharply defined against the hazy distant horizon.

It was quite an ocean, with the irregular shores of earth, but desert and frightfully wild in appearance.

If my eyes were able to range afar over this great sea, it was because a peculiar light brought to view every detail of it. It was not the light of the sun, with his dazzling shafts of brightness and the splendour of his rays; nor was it the pale and uncertain shimmer of the moonbeams, the dim reflection of a nobler body of light. No; the illuminating power of this light, its trembling diffusiveness, its bright, clear whiteness, and its low temperature, showed that it must be of electric origin. It was like an aurora borealis, a continuous cosmical phenomenon, filling a cavern of sufficient extent to contain an ocean.

The vault that spanned the space above, the sky, if it could be called so, seemed composed of vast plains of cloud, shifting and variable vapours, which by their condensation must at certain times fall in torrents of rain. I should have thought that under so powerful a pressure of the atmosphere there could be no evaporation; and yet, under a law unknown to me, there were broad tracts of vapour suspended in the air. But then 'the weather was fine.' The play of the electric light produced singular effects upon the upper strata of cloud. Deep shadows reposed upon their lower wreaths; and often, between two separated fields of cloud, there glided down a ray of unspeakable lustre. But it was not solar light, and there was no heat. The general effect was sad, supremely melancholy. Instead of the shining firmament, spangled with its innumerable stars, shining singly or in clusters, I felt that all these subdued and shaded fights were ribbed in by vast walls of granite, which seemed to overpower me with their weight, and that all this space, great as it was, would not be enough for the march of the humblest of satellites.

Then I remembered the theory of an English captain, who likened the earth to a vast hollow sphere, in the interior of which the air became luminous because of the vast pressure that weighed upon it; while two stars, Pluto and Proserpine, rolled within upon the circuit of their mysterious orbits.

We were in reality shut up inside an immeasurable excavation. Its width could not be estimated, since the shore ran widening as far as eye could reach, nor could its length, for the dim horizon bounded the new. As for its height, it must have been several leagues. Where this vault rested upon its granite base no eye could tell; but there was a cloud hanging far above, the height of which we estimated at 12,000 feet, a greater height than that of any terrestrial vapour, and no doubt due to the great density of the air.

The word cavern does not convey any idea of this immense space; words of human tongue are inadequate to describe the discoveries of him who ventures into the deep abysses of earth.

Besides I could not tell upon what geological theory to account for the existence of such an excavation. Had the cooling of the globe produced it? I knew of celebrated caverns from the descriptions of travellers, but had never heard of any of such dimensions as this.

If the grotto of Guachara, in Colombia, visited by Humboldt, had not given up the whole of the secret of its depth to the philosopher, who investigated it to the depth of 2,500 feet, it probably did not extend much farther. The immense mammoth cave in Kentucky is of gigantic proportions, since its vaulted roof rises five hundred feet[1] above the level of an unfathomable lake and travellers have explored its ramifications to the extent of forty miles. But what were these cavities compared to that

1. One hundred and twenty. (Tr.)

in which I stood with wonder and admiration, with its sky of luminous vapours, its bursts of electric light, and a vast sea filling its bed? My imagination fell powerless before such immensity.

I gazed upon these wonders in silence. Words failed me to express my feelings. I felt as if I was in some distant planet Uranus or Neptune—and in the presence of phenomena of which my terrestrial experience gave me no cognisance. For such novel sensations, new words were wanted; and my imagination failed to supply them. I gazed, I thought, I admired, with a stupefaction mingled with a certain amount of fear.

The unforeseen nature of this spectacle brought back the colour to my cheeks. I was under a new course of treatment with the aid of astonishment, and my convalescence was promoted by this novel system of therapeutics; besides, the dense and breezy air invigorated me, supplying more oxygen to my lungs.

It will be easily conceived that after an imprisonment of forty seven days in a narrow gallery it was the height of physical enjoyment to breathe a moist air impregnated with saline particles.

I was delighted to leave my dark grotto. My uncle, already familiar with these wonders, had ceased to feel surprise.

'You feel strong enough to walk a little way now?' he asked.

'Yes, certainly; and nothing could be more delightful.'

'Well, take my arm, Axel, and let us follow the windings of the shore.'

I eagerly accepted, and we began to coast along this new sea. On the left huge pyramids of rock, piled one upon another, produced a prodigious titanic effect. Down their sides flowed numberless waterfalls, which went on their way in brawling but pellucid streams. A few light vapours, leaping from rock to rock, denoted the place of hot springs; and streams flowed softly down to the common basin, gliding down the gentle slopes with a softer murmur.

Amongst these streams I recognised our faithful travelling companion, the Hansbach, coming to lose its little volume quietly in the mighty sea, just as if it had done nothing else since the beginning of the world.

'We shall see it no more,' I said, with a sigh.

'What matters,' replied the philosopher, 'whether this or another serves to guide us?'

I thought him rather ungrateful.

But at that moment my attention was drawn to an unexpected sight. At a distance of five hundred paces, at the turn of a high promontory, appeared a high, tufted, dense forest. It was composed of trees of moderate height, formed like umbrellas, with exact geometrical outlines. The currents of wind seemed to have had no effect upon their shape, and in the midst of the windy blasts they stood unmoved and firm, just like a clump of petrified cedars.

I hastened forward. I could not give any name to these singular creations. Were they some of the two hundred thousand species of vegetables known hitherto, and did they claim a place of their own in the lacustrine flora? No; when we arrived under their shade my surprise turned into admiration. There stood before me productions of earth, but of gigantic stature, which my uncle immediately named.

'It is only a forest of mushrooms,' said he.

And he was right. Imagine the large development attained by these plants, which prefer a warm, moist climate. I knew that the Lycopodon giganteum attains, according to Bulliard, a circumference of eight or nine feet; but here were pale mushrooms, thirty to forty feet high, and crowned with a cap of equal diameter. There they stood in thousands. No light could penetrate between their huge cones, and complete darkness reigned beneath those giants; they formed settlements of domes placed in close array like the round, thatched roofs of a central African city.

Yet I wanted to penetrate farther underneath, though a chill fell upon me as soon as I came under those cellular vaults. For half an hour we wandered from side to side in the damp shades, and it was a comfortable and pleasant change to arrive once more upon the sea shore.

But the subterranean vegetation was not confined to these fungi. Farther on rose groups of tall trees of colourless foliage and easy to recognise. They were lowly shrubs of earth, here attaining gigantic size; lycopodiums, a hundred feet high; the huge sigillaria, found in our coal mines; tree ferns, as tall as our fir-trees in northern latitudes; lepidodendra, with cylindrical forked stems, terminated by long leaves, and bristling with rough hairs like those of the cactus.

'Wonderful, magnificent, splendid!' cried my uncle. 'Here is the entire flora of the second period of the world—the transition period. These, humble garden plants with us, were tall trees in the early ages. Look, Axel, and admire it all. Never had botanist such a feast as this!'

'You are right, my uncle. Providence seems to have preserved in this immense conservatory the antediluvian plants which the wisdom of philosophers has so sagaciously put together again.'

'It is a conservatory, Axel; but is it not also a menagerie?'

'Surely not a menagerie!'

'Yes; no doubt of it. Look at that dust under your feet; see the bones scattered on the ground.'

'So there are!' I cried; 'bones of extinct animals.'

I had rushed upon these remains, formed of indestructible phosphates of lime, and without hesitation I named these monstrous bones, which lay scattered about like decayed trunks of trees.

'Here is the lower jaw of a mastodon,'[2] I said. 'These are

2. These animals belonged to a late geological period, the Pliocene, just before the glacial epoch, and therefore could have no connection with the carboniferous vegetation. (Tr.)

the molar teeth of the deinotherium; this femur must have belonged to the greatest of those beasts, the megatherium. It certainly is a menagerie, for these remains were not brought here by a deluge. The animals to which they belonged roamed on the shores of this subterranean sea, under the shade of those arborescent trees. Here are entire skeletons. And yet I cannot understand the appearance of these quadrupeds in a granite cavern.'

'Why?'

'Because animal life existed upon the earth only in the secondary period, when a sediment of soil had been deposited by the rivers, and taken the place of the incandescent rocks of the primitive period.'

'Well, Axel, there is a very simple answer to your objection that this soil is alluvial.'

'What! at such a depth below the surface of the earth?'

'No doubt; and there is a geological explanation of the fact. At a certain period the earth consisted only of an elastic crust or bark, alternately acted on by forces from above or below, according to the laws of attraction and gravitation. Probably there were subsidences of the outer crust, when a portion of the sedimentary deposits was carried down sudden openings.'

'That may be,' I replied; 'but if there have been creatures now extinct in these underground regions, why may not some of those monsters be now roaming through these gloomy forests, or hidden behind the steep crags?'

And as this unpleasant notion got hold of me, I surveyed with anxious scrutiny the open spaces before me; but no living creature appeared upon the barren strand.

I felt rather tired, and went to sit down at the end of a promontory, at the foot of which the waves came and beat themselves into spray. Thence my eye could sweep every part of the bay; within its extremity a little harbour was formed between the pyramidal cliffs, where the still waters slept untouched by the boisterous winds. A brig and two or three schooners might have moored within it in safety. I almost fancied I should presently see some ship issue from it, full sail, and take to the open sea under the southern breeze.

But this illusion lasted a very short time. We were the only living creatures in this subterranean world. When the wind lulled, a deeper silence than that of the deserts fell upon the arid, naked rocks, and weighed upon the surface of the ocean. I then desired to pierce the distant haze, and to rend asunder the mysterious curtain that hung across the horizon. Anxious queries arose to my lips. Where did that sea terminate? Where did it lead to? Should we ever know anything about its opposite shores?

My uncle made no doubt about it at all; I both desired and feared.

After spending an hour in the contemplation of this marvellous spectacle, we returned to the shore to regain the grotto, and I fell asleep in the midst of the strangest thoughts.

THIRTY ONE

PREPARATIONS FOR A VOYAGE OF DISCOVERY

The next morning I awoke feeling perfectly well. I thought a bathe would do me good, and I went to plunge for a few minutes into the waters of this mediterranean sea, for assuredly it better deserved this name than any other sea.

I came back to breakfast with a good appetite. Hans was a good caterer for our little household; he had water and fire at his disposal, so that he was able to vary our bill of fare now and then. For dessert he gave us a few cups of coffee, and never was coffee so delicious.

'Now,' said my uncle, 'now is the time for high tide, and we must not lose the opportunity to study this phenomenon.'

'What! the tide!' I cried. 'Can the influence of the sun and moon be felt down here?'

'Why not? Are not all bodies subject throughout their mass to the power of universal attraction? This mass of water cannot escape the general law. And in spite of the heavy atmospheric pressure on the surface, you will see it rise like the Atlantic itself.'

At the same moment we reached the sand on the shore, and the waves were by slow degrees encroaching on the shore.

'Here is the tide rising,' I cried.

'Yes, Axel; and judging by these ridges of foam, you may observe that the sea will rise about twelve feet.'

'This is wonderful,' I said.

'No; it is quite natural.'

'You may say so, uncle; but to me it is most extraordinary, and I can hardly believe my eyes. Who would ever have imagined, under this terrestrial crust, an ocean with ebbing and flowing tides, with winds and storms?'

'Well,' replied my uncle, 'is there any scientific reason against it?'

'No; I see none, as soon as the theory of central heat is given up.' 'So then, thus far,' he answered, 'the theory of Sir Humphry Davy is confirmed.'

'Evidently it is; and now there is no reason why there should not be seas and continents in the interior of the earth.'

'No doubt,' said my uncle; 'and inhabited too.'

'To be sure,' said I; 'and why should not these waters yield to us fishes of unknown species?'

'At any rate,' he replied, 'we have not seen any yet.'

'Well, let us make some lines, and see if the bait will draw here as it does in sublunary regions.'

'We will try, Axel, for we must penetrate all secrets of these newly discovered regions.'

'But where are we, uncle? for I have not yet asked you that question, and your instruments must be able to furnish the answer.'

'Horizontally, three hundred and fifty leagues from Iceland.'

'So much as that?'

'I am sure of not being a mile out of my reckoning.'

'And does the compass still show south-east?'

'Yes; with a westerly deviation of nineteen degrees forty-five minutes, just as above ground. As for its dip, a curious fact is coming to light, which I have observed carefully: that the needle, instead of dipping towards the pole as in the northern hemisphere, on the contrary, rises from it.'

'Would you then conclude,' I said, 'that the magnetic pole is somewhere between the surface of the globe and the point where we are?'

'Exactly so; and it is likely enough that if we were to reach the spot beneath the polar regions, about that seventy-first degree where Sir James Ross has discovered the magnetic pole to be situated, we should see the needle point straight up. Therefore that mysterious centre of attraction is at no great depth.'

I remarked: ' It is so; and here is a fact which science has scarcely suspected.'

'Science, my lad, has been built upon many errors; but they are errors which it was good to fall into, for they led to the truth.'

'What depth have we now reached?'

'We are thirty-five leagues below the surface.'

'So,' I said, examining the map, 'the Highlands of Scotland are over our heads, and the Grampians are raising their rugged summits above us.'

'Yes,' answered the Professor laughing. 'It is rather a heavy weight to bear, but a solid arch spans over our heads. The great Architect has built it of the best materials; and never could man have given it so wide a stretch. What are the finest arches of bridges and the arcades of cathedrals, compared with this far reaching vault, with a radius of three leagues, beneath which a wide and tempest-tossed ocean may flow at its ease?'

'Oh, I am not afraid that it will fall down upon my head. But now what are your plans? Are you not thinking of returning to the surface now?'

'Return! no, indeed! We will continue our journey, everything having gone on well so far.'

'But how are we to get down below this liquid surface?'

'Oh, I am not going to dive head foremost. But if all oceans are properly speaking but lakes, since they are encompassed by land, of course this internal sea will be surrounded by a coast of granite, and on the opposite shores we shall find fresh passages opening.'

'How long do you suppose this sea to be?'

'Thirty or forty leagues; so that we have no time to lose, and we shall set sail Tomorrow.'

I looked about for a ship.

'Set sail, shall we? But I should like to see my boat first.'

'It will not be a boat at all, but a good, well-made raft.'

'Why,' I said, 'a raft would be just as hard to make as a boat, and I don't see—'

'I know you don't see; but you might hear if you would listen. Don't you hear the hammer at work? Hans is already busy at it.'

'What, has he already felled the trees?'

'Oh, the trees were already down. Come, and you will see for yourself.'

After half an hour's walking, on the other side of the promontory which formed the little natural harbour, I perceived Hans at work. In a few more steps I was at his side. To my great surprise a half-finished raft was already lying on the sand, made of a peculiar kind of wood, and a great number of planks, straight and bent, and of frames, were covering the ground, enough almost for a little fleet.

'Uncle, what wood is this?' I cried.

'It is fir, pine, or birch, and other northern coniferae,

mineralised by the action of the sea. It is called surturbrand, a variety of brown coal or lignite, found chiefly in Iceland.'

'But surely, then, like other fossil wood, it must be as hard as stone, and cannot float?'

'Sometimes that may happen; some of these woods become true anthracites; but others, such as this, have only gone through the first stage of fossil transformation. Just look,' added my uncle, throwing into the sea one of those precious waifs.

The bit of wood, after disappearing, returned to the surface and oscillated to and fro with the waves.

'Are you convinced?' said my uncle.

'I am quite convinced, although it is incredible!'

By next evening, thanks to the industry and skill of our guide, the raft was made. It was ten feet by five; the planks of surturbrand, braced strongly together with cords, presented an even surface, and when launched this improvised vessel floated easily upon the waves of the Liedenbrock Sea.

THIRTY TWO

WONDERS OF THE DEEP

On the 13th of August we awoke early. We were now to begin to adopt a mode of travelling both more expeditious and less fatiguing than hitherto.

A mast was made of two poles spliced together, a yard was made of a third, a blanket borrowed from our coverings made a tolerable sail. There was no want of cordage for the rigging, and everything was well and firmly made.

The provisions, the baggage, the instruments, the guns, and a good quantity of fresh water from the rocks around, all found their proper places on board; and at six the Professor gave the signal to embark. Hans had fitted up a rudder to steer his vessel. He took the tiller, and unmoored; the sail was set, and we were soon afloat. At the moment of leaving the harbour, my uncle, who was tenaciously fond of naming his new discoveries, wanted to give it a name, and proposed mine amongst others.

'But I have a better to propose,' I said: 'Grauben. Let it be called Port Gräuben; it will look very well upon the map.'

'Port Gräuben let it be then.'

And so the cherished remembrance of my Virlandaise became associated with our adventurous expedition.

The wind was from the north-west. We went with it at a high rate of speed. The dense atmosphere acted with great force and impelled us swiftly on.

In an hour my uncle had been able to estimate our progress. At this rate, he said, we shall make thirty leagues in twenty-four hours, and we shall soon come in sight of the opposite shore.

I made no answer, but went and sat forward. The northern shore was already beginning to dip under the horizon. The eastern and western strands spread wide as if to bid us farewell. Before our eyes lay far and wide a vast sea; shadows of great clouds swept heavily over its silver-grey surface; the glistening bluish rays of electric light, here and there reflected by the dancing drops of spray, shot out little sheaves of light from the track we left in our rear. Soon we entirely lost sight of land; no object was left for the eye to judge by, and but for the frothy track of the raft, I might have thought we were standing still.

About twelve, immense shoals of seaweeds came in sight. I was aware of the great powers of vegetation that characterise these plants, which grow at a depth of twelve thousand feet, reproduce themselves under a pressure of four hundred atmospheres, and sometimes form barriers strong enough to impede the course of a ship. But never, I think, were such seaweeds as those which we saw floating in immense waving lines upon the sea of Liedenbrock.

Our raft skirted the whole length of the fuci, three or four thousand feet long, undulating like vast serpents beyond the reach of sight; I found some amusement in tracing these endless waves, always thinking I should come to the end of them, and for hours my patience was vying with my surprise.

What natural force could have produced such plants, and what must have been the appearance of the earth in the first ages of its formation, when, under the action of heat and moisture, the vegetable kingdom alone was developing on its surface?

Evening came, and, as on the previous day, I perceived no change in the luminous condition of the air. It was a constant condition, the permanency of which might be relied upon.

After supper I laid myself down at the foot of the mast, and fell asleep in the midst of fantastic reveries.

Hans, keeping fast by the helm, let the raft run on, which, after all, needed no steering, the wind blowing directly aft.

Since our departure from Port Gräuben, Professor Liedenbrock had entrusted the log to my care; I was to register every observation, make entries of interesting phenomena, the direction of the wind, the rate of sailing, the way we made—in a word, every particular of our singular voyage.

I shall therefore reproduce here these daily notes, written, so to speak, as the course of events directed, in order to furnish an exact narrative of our passage.

Friday, August 14.—Wind steady, N.W. The raft makes rapid way in a direct line. Coast thirty leagues to leeward. Nothing in sight before us. Intensity of light the same. Weather fine; that is to say, that the clouds are flying high, are light, and bathed in a white atmosphere resembling silver in a state of fusion. Therm. 89° Fahr.

At noon Hans prepared a hook at the end of a line. He

baited it with a small piece of meat and flung it into the sea. For two hours nothing was caught. Are these waters, then, bare of inhabitants? No, there's a pull at the line. Hans draws it in and brings out a struggling fish.

'A sturgeon,' I cried; 'a small sturgeon.'

The Professor eyes the creature attentively, and his opinion differs from mine.

The head of this fish was flat, but rounded in front, and the anterior part of its body was plated with bony, angular scales; it had no teeth, its pectoral fins were large, and of tail there was none. The animal belonged to the same order as the sturgeon, but differed from that fish in many essential particulars. After a short examination my uncle pronounced his opinion.

'This fish belongs to an extinct family, of which only fossil traces are found in the devonian formations.'

'What!' I cried. 'Have we taken alive an inhabitant of the seas of primitive ages?'

'Yes; and you will observe that these fossil fishes have no identity with any living species. To have in one's possession a living specimen is a happy event for a naturalist.'

'But to what family does it belong?'

'It is of the order of ganoids, of the family of the cephalaspidae; and a species of pterichthys. But this one displays a peculiarity confined to all fishes that inhabit subterranean waters. It is blind, and not only blind, but actually has no eyes at all.'

I looked: nothing could be more certain. But supposing it might be a solitary case, we baited afresh, and threw out our line. Surely this ocean is well peopled with fish, for in another couple of hours we took a large quantity of pterichthydes, as well as of others belonging to the extinct family of the dipterides, but of which my uncle could not tell the species; none had organs of sight. This unhoped-for catch recruited our stock of provisions.

Thus it is evident that this sea contains none but species known to us in their fossil state, in which fishes as well as reptiles are the less perfectly and completely organised the farther back their date of creation.

Perhaps we may yet meet with some of those saurians which science has reconstructed out of a bit of bone or cartilage. I took up the telescope and scanned the whole horizon, and found it everywhere a desert sea. We are far away removed from the shores.

I gaze upward in the air. Why should not some of the strange birds restored by the immortal Cuvier again flap their 'sail-broad vans' in this dense and heavy atmosphere? There are sufficient fish for their support. I survey the whole space that stretches overhead; it is as desert as the shore was.

Still my imagination carried me away amongst the wonderful speculations of palaeontology. Though awake I fell into a dream. I thought I could see floating on the surface of the waters enormous chelonia, preadamite tortoises, resembling floating islands. Over the dimly lighted strand there trod the huge mammals of the first ages of the world, the leptotherium (slender beast), found in the caverns of Brazil; the merycotherium (ruminating beast), found in the 'drift' of iceclad Siberia. Farther on, the pachydermatous lophiodon (crested toothed), a gigantic tapir, hides behind the rocks to dispute its prey with the anoplotherium (unarmed beast), a strange creature, which seemed a compound of horse, rhinoceros, camel, and hippopotamus. The colossal mastodon (nipple-toothed) twists and untwists his trunk, and brays and pounds with his huge tusks the fragments of rock that cover the shore; whilst the megatherium (huge beast), buttressed upon his enormous hinder paws, grubs in the soil, awaking the sonorous echoes of the granite rocks with his tremendous roarings. Higher up, the protopitheca—the first monkey that appeared on the globe—is climbing up the steep ascents. Higher yet, the pterodactyle (wing-fingered) darts in irregular zigzags to and fro in the heavy air. In the uppermost regions of the air immense birds, more powerful than the cassowary, and larger than the ostrich, spread their vast breadth of wings and strike with their heads the granite vault that bounds the sky.

All this fossil world rises to life again in my vivid imagination. I return to the scriptural periods or ages of the world, conventionally called 'days,' long before the appearance of man, when the unfinished world was as yet unfitted for his support. Then mydream backed even farther still into the ages before the creation of living beings. The mammals disappear, then the birds vanish, then the reptiles of the secondary period, and finally the fish, the crustaceans, molluscs, and articulated beings. Then the zoophytes of the transition period also return to nothing. I am the only living thing in the world: all life is concentrated in my beating heart alone. There are no more seasons; climates are no more; the heat of the globe continually increases and neutralises that of the sun. Vegetation becomes accelerated. I glide like a shade amongst arborescent ferns, treading with unsteady feet the coloured marls and the particoloured clays; I lean for support against the trunks of immense conifers; I lie in the shade of sphenophylla (wedge-leaved), asterophylla (star-leaved), and lycopods, a hundred feet high.

Ages seem no more than days! I am passed, against my will, in retrograde order, through the long series of terrestrial changes. Plants disappear; granite rocks soften; intense heat converts solid bodies into thick fluids; the waters again cover the face of the earth; they boil, they rise in whirling eddies of steam; white and ghastly mists wrap round the shifting forms of the earth, which by imperceptible degrees dissolves into a gaseous mass, glowing fiery red and white, as large and as shining as the sun.

And I myself am floating with wild caprice in the midst of this nebulous mass of fourteen hundred thousand times the volume of the earth into which it will one day be condensed, and carried forward amongst the planetary bodies. My body is no longer firm and terrestrial; it is resolved into its constituent atoms, subtilised, volatilised. Sublimed into imponderable vapour, I mingle and am lost in the endless foods of those vast globular volumes of vaporous mists, which roll upon their flaming orbits through infinite space.

But is it not a dream? Whither is it carrying me? My feverish hand has vainly attempted to describe upon paper its strange and wonderful details. I have forgotten everything that surrounds me. The Professor, the guide, the raft—are all gone out of my ken. An illusion has laid hold upon me.

'What is the matter?' my uncle breaks in.

My staring eyes are fixed vacantly upon him.

'Take care, Axel, or you will fall overboard.'

At that moment I felt the sinewy hand of Hans seizing me vigorously. But for him, carried away by my dream, I should have thrown myself into the sea.

'Is he mad?' cried the Professor.

'What is it all about?' at last I cried, returning to myself.

'Do you feel ill?' my uncle asked.

'No; but I have had a strange hallucination; it is over now. Is all going on right?'

'Yes, it is a fair wind and a fine sea; we are sailing rapidly along, and if I am not out in my reckoning, we shall soon land.'

At these words I rose and gazed round upon the horizon, still everywhere bounded by clouds alone.

THIRTY THREE

A BATTLE OF MONSTERS

Saturday, August 15.—The sea unbroken all round. No land in sight. The horizon seems extremely distant.

My head is still stupefied with the vivid reality of my dream.

My uncle has had no dreams, but he is out of temper. He

examines the horizon all round with his glass, and folds his arms with the air of an injured man.

I remark that Professor Liedenbrock has a tendency to relapse into an impatient mood, and I make a note of it in my log. All my danger and sufferings were needed to strike a spark of human. feeling out of him; but now that I am well his nature has resumed its sway. And yet, what cause was there for anger? Is not the voyage prospering as favourably as possible under the circumstances? Is not the raft spinning along with marvellous speed?

'—You seem anxious, my uncle,' I said, seeing him continually with his glass to his eye.

'Anxious! No, not at all.'

'Impatient, then?'

'One might be, with less reason than now.'

'Yet we are going very fast.'

'What does that signify? I am not complaining that the rate is slow, but that the sea is so wide.'

I then remembered that the Professor, before starting, had estimated the length of this underground sea at thirty leagues. Now we had made three times the distance, yet still the southern coast was not in sight.

'We are not descending as we ought to be,' the Professor declares. 'We are losing time, and the fact is, I have not come all this way to take a little sail upon a pond on a raft.'

He called this sea a pond, and our long voyage, taking a little sail!

'But,' I remarked, 'since we have followed the road that Saknussemm has shown us—'

'That is just the question. Have we followed that road? Did Saknussemm meet this sheet of water? Did he cross it? Has not the stream that we followed led us altogether astray?'

'At any rate we cannot feel sorry to have come so far. This prospect is magnificent, and—'

'But I don't care for prospects. I came with an object, and

I mean to attain it. Therefore don't talk to me about views and prospects.'

I take this as my answer, and I leave the Professor to bite his lips with impatience. At six in the evening Hans asks for his wages, and his three rix dollars are counted out to him.

Sunday, August 16.—Nothing new. Weather unchanged. The wind freshens. On awaking, my first thought was to observe the intensity of the light. I was possessed with an apprehension lest the electric light should grow dim, or fail altogether. But there seemed no reason to fear. The shadow of the raft was clearly outlined upon the surface of the waves.

Truly this sea is of infinite width. It must be as wide as the Mediterranean or the Atlantic—and why not?

My uncle took soundings several times. He tied the heaviest of our pickaxes to a long rope which he let down two hundred fathoms. No bottom yet; and we had some difficulty in hauling up our plummet.

But when the pick was shipped again, Hans pointed out on its surface deep prints as if it had been violently compressed between two hard bodies.

I looked at the hunter.

'Tänder,' said he.

I could not understand him, and turned to my uncle who was entirely absorbed in his calculations. I had rather not disturb him while he is quiet. I return to the Icelander. He by a snapping motion of his jaws conveys his ideas to me.

'Teeth!' I cried, considering the iron bar with more attention.

Yes, indeed, those are the marks of teeth imprinted upon the metal! The jaws which they arm must be possessed of amazing strength. Is there some monster beneath us belonging to the extinct races, more voracious than the shark, more fearful in vastness than the whale? I could not take my eyes off this indented iron bar. Surely will my last night's dream be realised?

These thoughts agitated me all day, and my imagination scarcely calmed down after several hours' sleep.

Monday, August 17.—I am trying to recall the peculiar instincts of the monsters of the preadamite world, who, coming next in succession after the molluscs, the crustaceans and le fishes, preceded the animals of mammalian race upon the earth. The world then belonged to reptiles. Those monsters held the mastery in the seas of the secondary period. They possessed a perfect organisation, gigantic proportions, prodigious strength. The saurians of our day, the alligators and the crocodiles, are but feeble reproductions of their forefathers of primitive ages.

I shudder as I recall these monsters to my remembrance. No human eye has ever beheld them living. They burdened this earth a thousand ages before man appeared, but their fossil remains, found in the argillaceous limestone called by the English the lias, have enabled their colossal structure to be perfectly built up again and anatomically ascertained.

I saw at the Hamburg museum the skeleton of one of these creatures thirty feet in length. Am I then fated—I, a denizen of earth—to be placed face to face with these representatives of long extinct families? No; surely it cannot be! Yet the deep marks of conical teeth upon the iron pick are certainly those of the crocodile.

My eyes are fearfully bent upon the sea. I dread to see one of these monsters darting forth from its submarine caverns. I suppose Professor Liedenbrock was of my opinion too, and even shared my fears, for after having examined the pick, his eyes traversed the ocean from side to side. What a very bad notion that was of his, I thought to myself, to take soundings just here! He has disturbed some monstrous beast in its remote den, and if we are not attacked on our voyage—

I look at our guns and see that they are all right. My uncle notices it, and looks on approvingly.

Already widely disturbed regions on the surface of the water indicate some commotion below. The danger is approaching. We must be on the look out.

Tuesday, August 18.—Evening came, or rather the time came when sleep weighs down the weary eyelids, for there is no night here, and the ceaseless light wearies the eyes with its persistency just as if we were sailing under an arctic sun. Hans was at the helm. During his watch I slept.

Two hours afterwards a terrible shock awoke me. The raft was heaved up on a watery mountain and pitched down again, at a distance of twenty fathoms.

'What is the matter?' shouted my uncle. 'Have we struck land?'

Hans pointed with his finger at a dark mass six hundred yards away, rising and falling alternately with heavy plunges. I looked and cried:

'It is an enormous porpoise.'

'Yes,' replied my uncle, 'and there is a sea lizard of vast size.'

'And farther on a monstrous crocodile. Look at its vast jaws and its rows of teeth! It is diving down!'

'There's a whale, a whale!' cried the Professor. 'I can see its great fins. See how he is throwing out air and water through his blowers.'

And in fact two liquid columns were rising to a considerable height above the sea. We stood amazed, thunderstruck, at the presence of such a herd of marine monsters. They were of supernatural dimensions; the smallest of them would have crunched our raft, crew and all, at one snap of its huge jaws.

Hans wants to tack to get away from this dangerous neighbourhood; but he sees on the other hand enemies not less terrible; a tortoise forty feet long, and a serpent of thirty, lifting its fearful head and gleaming eyes above the flood.

Flight was out of the question now. The reptiles rose; they wheeled around our little raft with a rapidity greater than that of express trains. They described around us gradually narrowing circles. I took up my rifle. But what could a ball do against the scaly armour with which these enormous beasts were clad?

We stood dumb with fear. They approach us close: on one side the crocodile, on the other the serpent. The remainder of the sea monsters have disappeared. I prepare to fire. Hans stops me by a gesture. The two monsters pass within a hundred and fifty yards of the raft, and hurl themselves the one upon the other, with a fury which prevents them from seeing us.

At three hundred yards from us the battle was fought. We could distinctly observe the two monsters engaged in deadly conflict. But it now seems to me as if the other animals were taking part in the fray—the porpoise, the whale, the lizard, the tortoise. Every moment I seem to see one or other of them. I point them to the Icelander. He shakes his head negatively.

'Tva,' says he.

'What two? Does he mean that there are only two animals?'

'He is right,' said my uncle, whose glass has never left his eye.

'Surely you must be mistaken,' I cried.

'No: the first of those monsters has a porpoise's snout, a lizard's head, a crocodile's teeth; and hence our mistake. It is the ichthyosaurus (the fish lizard), the most terrible of the ancient monsters of the deep.'

'And the other?'

'The other is a plesiosaurus (almost lizard), a serpent, armoured with the carapace and the paddles of a turtle; he is the dreadful enemy of the other.'

Hans had spoken truly. Two monsters only were creating all this commotion; and before my eyes are two reptiles of the primitive world. I can distinguish the eye of the ichthyosaurus glowing like a red-hot coal, and as large as a man's head. Nature has endowed it with an optical apparatus of extreme power, and capable of resisting the pressure of the great volume of water in the depths it inhabits. It has been appropriately called the saurian whale, for it has both the swiftness and the rapid movements of this monster of our own day. This one is not less than a hundred feet long, and I can judge of its size when it sweeps over the waters the vertical coils of its tail. Its jaw is enormous, and according to naturalists it is armed with no less than one hundred and eighty-two teeth.

The plesiosaurus, a serpent with a cylindrical body and a short tail, has four flappers or paddles to act like oars. Its body is entirely covered with a thick armour of scales, and its neck, as flexible as a swan's, rises thirty feet above the waves.

Those huge creatures attacked each other with the greatest animosity. They heaved around them liquid mountains, which rolled even to our raft and rocked it perilously. Twenty times we were near capsizing. Hissings of prodigious force are heard. The two beasts are fast locked together; I cannot distinguish the one from the other. The probable rage of the conqueror inspires us with intense fear.

One hour, two hours, pass away. The struggle continues with unabated ferocity. The combatants alternately approach and recede from our raft. We remain motionless, ready to fire. Suddenly the ichthyosaurus and the plesiosaurus disappear below, leaving a whirlpool eddying in the water. Several minutes pass by while the fight goes on under water.

All at once an enormous head is darted up, the head of the plesiosaurus. The monster is wounded to death. I no longer see his scaly armour. Only his long neck shoots up, drops again, coils and uncoils, droops, lashes the waters like a gigantic whip, and writhes like a worm that you tread on. The water is splashed for a long way around. The spray almost blinds us. But soon the reptile's agony draws to an end; its movements become fainter, its contortions cease to be so violent, and the long serpentine form lies a lifeless log on the labouring deep.

As for the ichthyosaurus—has he returned to his submarine cavern? or will he reappear on the surface of the sea?

THIRTY FOUR

THE GREAT GEYSER

Wednesday, August 19.—Fortunately the wind blows violently, and has enabled us to flee from the scene of the late terrible struggle. Hans keeps at his post at the helm. My uncle, whom the absorbing incidents of the combat had drawn away from his contemplations, began again to look impatiently around him.

The voyage resumes its uniform tenor, which I don't care to break with a repetition of such events as yesterday's.

Thursday, Aug. 20.—Wind N.N.E., unsteady and fitful. Temperature high. Rate three and a half leagues an hour.

About noon a distant noise is heard. I note the fact without being able to explain it. It is a continuous roar.

'In the distance,' says the Professor, 'there is a rock or islet, against which the sea is breaking.'

Hans climbs up the mast, but sees no breakers. The ocean' is smooth and unbroken to its farthest limit.

Three hours pass away. The roarings seem to proceed from a very distant waterfall.

I remark upon this to my uncle, who replies doubtfully: 'Yes, I am convinced that I am right.' Are we, then, speeding forward to some cataract which will cast us down an abyss? This method of getting on may please the Professor, because it is vertical; but for my part I prefer the more ordinary modes of horizontal progression.

At any rate, some leagues to the windward there must be some noisy phenomenon, for now the roarings are heard with increasing loudness. Do they proceed from the sky or the ocean?

I look up to the atmospheric vapours, and try to fathom their depths. The sky is calm and motionless. The clouds have reached the utmost limit of the lofty vault, and there lie still bathed in the bright glare of the electric light. It is not there that we must seek for the cause of this phenomenon. Then I examine the horizon, which is unbroken and clear of all mist. There is no change in its aspect. But if this noise arises from a fall, a cataract, if all this ocean flows away headlong into a lower basin yet, if that deafening roar is produced by a mass of falling water, the current must needs accelerate, and its increasing speed will give me the measure of the peril that threatens us. I consult the current: there is none. I throw an empty bottle into the sea: it lies still.

About four Hans rises, lays hold of the mast, climbs to its top. Thence his eye sweeps a large area of sea, and it is fixed upon a point. His countenance exhibits no surprise, but his eye is immovably steady.

'He sees something,' says my uncle.

'I believe he does.'

Hans comes down, then stretches his arm to the south, saying:

'Dere nere!'

'Down there?' repeated my uncle.

Then, seizing his glass, he gazes attentively for a minute, which seems to me an age.

'Yes, yes!' he cried. 'I see a vast inverted cone rising from the surface.'

'Is it another sea beast?'

'Perhaps it is.'

'Then let us steer farther westward, for we know something of the danger of coming across monsters of that sort.'

'Let us go straight on,' replied my uncle.

I appealed to Hans. He maintained his course inflexibly.

Yet, if at our present distance from the animal, a distance of twelve leagues at the least, the column of water driven through its blowers may be distinctly seen, it must needs be of vast size. The commonest prudence would counsel immediate flight; but we did not come so far to be prudent.

Imprudently, therefore, we pursue our way. The nearer we approach, the higher mounts the jet of water. What monster can possibly fill itself with such a quantity of water, and spurt it up so continuously?

At eight in the evening we are not two leagues distant from it. Its body—dusky, enormous, hillocky—lies spread upon the sea like an islet. Is it illusion or fear? Its length seems to me a couple of thousand yards. What can be this cetacean, which neither Cuvier nor Blumenbach knew anything about? It lies motionless, as if asleep; the sea seems unable to move it in the least; it is the waves that undulate upon its sides. The column of water thrown up to a height of five hundred feet falls in rain with a deafening uproar. And here are we scudding like lunatics before the wind, to get near to a monster that a hundred whales a day would not satisfy!

Terror seizes upon me. I refuse to go further. I will cut the halliards if necessary! I am in open mutiny against the Professor, who vouchsafes no answer.

Suddenly Hans rises, and pointing with his finger at the menacing object, he says:

'Holm.'

'An island!' cries my uncle.

'That's not an island!' I cried sceptically.

'It's nothing else,' shouted the Professor, with a loud laugh.

'But that column of water?'

'Geyser,' said Hans.

'No doubt it is a geyser, like those in Iceland.'

At first I protest against being so widely mistaken as to have taken an island for a marine monster. But the evidence is against me, and I have to confess my error. It is nothing worse than a natural phenomenon.

As we approach nearer the dimensions of the liquid column

become magnificent. The islet resembles, with a most deceiving likeness, an enormous cetacean, whose head dominates the waves at a height of twenty yards. The geyser, a word meaning 'fury,' rises majestically from its extremity. Deep and heavy explosions are heard from time to time, when the enormous jet, possessed with more furious violence, shakes its plumy crest, and springs with a bound till it reaches the lowest stratum of the clouds. It stands alone. No steam vents, no hot springs surround it, and all the volcanic power of the region is concentrated here. Sparks of electric fire mingle with the dazzling sheaf of lighted fluid, every drop of which refracts the prismatic colours.

'Let us land,' said the Professor.

'But we must carefully avoid this waterspout, which would sink our raft in a moment.'

Hans, steering with his usual skill, brought us to the other extremity of the islet.

I leaped up on the rock; my uncle lightly followed, while our hunter remained at his post, like a man too wise ever to be astonished.

We walked upon granite mingled with siliceous tufa. The soil shivers and shakes under our feet, like the sides of an overheated boiler filled with steam struggling to get loose. We come in sight of a small central basin, out of which the geyser springs. I plunge a register thermometer into the boiling water. It marks an intense heat of 325°, which is far above the boiling point; therefore this water issues from an ardent furnace, which is not at all in harmony with Professor Liedenbrock's theories. I cannot help making the remark.

'Well,' he replied, 'how does that make against my doctrine?'

'Oh, nothing at all,' I said, seeing that I was going in opposition to immovable obstinacy.

Still I am constrained to confess that hitherto we have been wonderfully favoured, and that for some reason unknown to myself we have accomplished our journey under singularly favourable conditions of temperature. But it seems manifest to me that some day we shall reach a region where the central heat attains its highest limits, and goes beyond a point that can be registered by our thermometers.

'That is what we shall see.' So says the Professor, who, having named this volcanic islet after his nephew, gives the signal to embark again.

For some minutes I am still contemplating the geyser. I notice that it throws up its column of water with variable force: sometimes sending it to a great height, then again to a lower, which I attribute to the variable pressure of the steam accumulated in its reservoir.

At last we leave the island, rounding away past the low rocks on its southern shore. Hans has taken advantage of the halt to refit his rudder.

But before going any farther I make a few observations, to calculate the distance we have gone over, and note them in my journal. We have crossed two hundred and seventy leagues of sea since leaving Port Gräuben; and we are six hundred and twenty leagues from Iceland, under England.[1]

THIRTY FIVE

AN ELECTRIC STORM

Friday, August 21.—On the morrow the magnificent geyser has disappeared. The wind has risen, and has rapidly carried us away from Axel Island. The roarings become lost in the distance.

1. This distance carries the travellers as far as under the Pyrenees if the league measures three miles. (Tr.)

The weather—if we may use that term—will change before long. The atmosphere is charged with vapours, pervaded with the electricity generated by the evaporation of saline waters. The clouds are sinking lower, and assume an olive hue. The electric light can scarcely penetrate through the dense curtain which has dropped over the theatre on which the battle of the elements is about to be waged.

I feel peculiar sensations, like many creatures on earth at the approach of violent atmospheric changes. The heavily voluted cumulus clouds lower gloomily and threateningly; they wear that implacable look which I have sometimes noticed at the outbreak of a great storm. The air is heavy; the sea is calm.

In the distance the clouds resemble great bales of cotton, piled up in picturesque disorder. By degrees they dilate, and gain in huge size what they lose in number. Such is their ponderous weight that they cannot rise from the horizon; but, obeying an impulse from higher currents, their dense consistency slowly yields. The gloom upon them deepens; and they soon present to our view a ponderous mass of almost level surface. From time to time a fleecy tuft of mist, with yet some gleaming light left upon it, drops down upon the dense floor of grey, and loses itself in the opaque and impenetrable mass.

The atmosphere is evidently charged and surcharged with electricity. My whole body is saturated; my hair bristles just as when you stand upon an insulated stool under the action of an electrical machine. It seems to me as if my companions, the moment they touched me, would receive a severe shock like that from an electric eel.

At ten in the morning the symptoms of storm become aggravated. The wind never lulls but to acquire increased strength; the vast bank of heavy clouds is a huge reservoir of fearful windy gusts and rushing storms.

I am loth to believe these atmospheric menaces, and yet I cannot help muttering:

'Here's some very bad weather coming on.'

The Professor made no answer. His temper is awful, to judge from the working of his features, as he sees this vast length of ocean unrolling before him to an indefinite extent. He can only spare time to shrug his shoulders viciously.

'There's a heavy storm coming on,' I cried, pointing towards the horizon. 'Those clouds seem as if they were going to crush the sea.'

A deep silence falls on all around. The lately roaring winds are hushed into a dead calm; nature seems to breathe no more, and to be sinking into the stillness of death. On the mast already I see the light play of a lambent St. Elmo's fire; the outstretched sail catches not a breath of wind, and hangs like a sheet of lead. The rudder stands motionless in a sluggish, waveless sea. But if we have now ceased to advance why do we yet leave that sail loose, which at the first shock of the tempest may capsize us in a moment?

'Let us reef the sail and cut the mast down!' I cried. 'That will be safest.'

'No, no! Never!' shouted my impetuous uncle. 'Never! Let the wind catch us if it will! What I want is to get the least glimpse of rock or shore, even if our raft should be smashed into shivers!'

The words were hardly out of his mouth when a sudden change took place in the southern sky. The piled-up vapours condense into water; and the air, put into violent action to supply the vacuum left by the condensation of the mists, rouses itself into a whirlwind. It rushes on from the farthest recesses of the vast cavern. The darkness deepens; scarcely can I jot down a few hurried notes. The helm makes a bound. My uncle falls full length; I creep close to him. He has laid a firm hold upon a rope, and appears to watch with grim satisfaction this awful display of elemental strife.

Hans stirs not. His long hair blown by the pelting storm, and laid flat across his immovable countenance, makes him a strange figure; for the end of each lock of loose flowing hair is tipped with little luminous radiations. This frightful mask of electric sparks suggests to me, even in this dizzy excitement, a comparison with preadamite man, the contemporary of the ichthyosaurus and the megatherium.[1]

The mast yet holds firm. The sail stretches tight like a bubble ready to burst. The raft flies at a rate that I cannot reckon, but not so fast as the foaming clouds of spray which it dashes from side to side in its headlong speed.

'The sail! the sail!' I cry, motioning to lower it.

'No!' replies my uncle.

'Nej!' repeats Hans, leisurely shaking his head.

But now the rain forms a rushing cataract in front of that horizon toward which we are running with such maddening speed. But before it has reached us the rain cloud parts asunder, the sea boils, and the electric fires are brought into violent action by a mighty chemical power that descends from the higher regions. The most vivid flashes of lightning are mingled with the violent crash of continuous thunder. Ceaseless fiery arrows dart in and out amongst the flying thunder-clouds; the vaporous mass soon glows with incandescent heat; hailstones rattle fiercely down, and as they dash upon our iron tools they too emit gleams and flashes of lurid light. The heaving waves resemble fiery volcanic hills, each belching forth its own interior flames, and every crest is plumed with dancing fire. My eyes fail under the dazzling light, my ears are stunned with the incessant crash of thunder. I must be bound to the mast, which bows like a reed before the mighty strength of the storm.

(Here my notes become vague and indistinct. I have only been able to find a few which I seem to have jotted down almost unconsciously. But their very brevity and their obscurity reveal the intensity of the excitement which dominated me, and describe the actual position even better than my memory could do.)

1. Father of the mammoth and the mastodon. (Tr.)

Sunday, 23.—Where are we? Driven forward with a swiftness that cannot be measured.

The night was fearful; no abatement of the storm. The din and uproar are incessant; our ears are bleeding; to exchange a word is impossible.

The lightning flashes with intense brilliancy, and never seems to cease for a moment. Zigzag streams of bluish white fire dash down upon the sea and rebound, and then take an upward flight till they strike the granite vault that overarches our heads. Suppose that solid roof should crumble down upon our heads! Other flashes with incessant play cross their vivid fires, while others again roll themselves into balls of living fire which explode like bombshells, but the music of which scarcely-adds to the din of the battle strife that almost deprives us of our senses of hearing and sight; the limit of intense loudness has been passed within which the human ear can distinguish one sound from another. If all the powder magazines in the world were to explode at once, we should hear no more than we do now.

From the under surface of the clouds there are continual emissions of lurid light; electric matter is in continual evolution from their component molecules; the gaseous elements of the air need to be slaked with moisture; for innumerable columns of water rush upwards into the air and fall back again in white foam.

Whither are we flying? My uncle lies full length across the raft.

The heat increases. I refer to the thermometer; it indicates . . . (the figure is obliterated).

Monday, August 24.—Will there be an end to it? Is the atmospheric condition, having once reached this density, to become final?

We are prostrated and worn out with fatigue. But Hans is as usual. The raft bears on still to the south-east. We have made two hundred leagues since we left Axel Island.

At noon the violence of the storm redoubles. We are obliged to secure as fast as possible every article that belongs to our cargo. Each of us is lashed to some part of the raft. The waves rise above our heads.

For three days we have never been able to make each other hear a word. Our mouths open, our lips move, but not a word can be heard. We cannot even make ourselves heard by approaching our mouth close to the ear.

My uncle has drawn nearer to me. He has uttered a few words. They seem to be 'We are lost'; but I am not sure.

At last I write down the words: 'Let us lower the sail.'

He nods his consent.

Scarcely has he lifted his head again before a ball of fire has bounded over the waves and lighted on board our raft. Mast and sail flew up in an instant together, and I saw them carried up to prodigious height, resembling in appearance a pterodactyle, one of those strong birds of the infant world.

We lay there, our blood running cold with unspeakable terror. The fireball, half of it white, half azure blue, and the size of a ten-inch shell, moved slowly about the raft, but revolving on its own axis with astonishing velocity, as if whipped round by the force of the whirlwind. Here it comes, there it glides, now it is up the ragged stump of the mast, thence it lightly leaps on the provision bag, descends with a light bound, and just skims the powder magazine. Horrible! we shall be blown up; but no, the dazzling disk of mysterious light nimbly leaps aside; it approaches Hans, who fixes his blue eye upon it steadily; it threatens the head of my uncle, who falls upon his knees with his head down to avoid it. And now my turn comes; pale and trembling under the blinding splendour and the melting heat, it drops at my feet, spinning silently round upon the deck; I try to move my foot away, but cannot.

A suffocating smell of nitrogen fills the air, it enters the throat, it fills the lungs. We suffer stifling pains.

Why am I unable to move my foot? Is it riveted to the

planks? Alas! the fall upon our fated raft of this electric globe has magnetised every iron article on board. The instruments, the tools, our guns, are clashing and clanking violently in their collisions with each other; the nails of my boots cling tenaciously to a plate of iron let into the timbers, and I cannot draw my foot away from the spot. At last by a violent effort I release myself at the instant when the ball in its gyrations was about to seize upon it, and carry me off my feet ....

Ah! what a flood of intense and dazzling light! the globe has burst, and we are deluged with tongues of fire!

Then all the light disappears. I could just see my uncle at full length on the raft, and Hans still at his helm and spitting fire under the action of the electricity which has saturated him.

But where are we going to? Where?

Tuesday, August 25.—I recover from a long swoon. The storm continues to roar and rage; the lightnings dash hither and thither, like broods of fiery serpents filling all the air. Are we still under the sea? Yes, we are borne at incalculable speed. We have been carried under England, under the channel, under France, perhaps under the whole of Europe.

A fresh noise is heard! Surely it is the sea breaking upon the rocks! But then . . . .

THIRTY SIX

CALM PHILOSOPHIC DISCUSSIONS

Here I end what I may call my log, happily saved from the wreck, and I resume my narrative as before.

What happened when the raft was dashed upon the rocks is more than I can tell. I felt myself hurled into the waves; and if I escaped from death, and if my body was not torn over the sharp edges of the rocks, it was because the powerful arm of Hans came to my rescue.

The brave Icelander carried me out of the reach of the waves, over a burning sand where I found myself by the side of my uncle.

Then he returned to the rocks, against which the furious waves were beating, to save what he could. I was unable to speak. I was shattered with fatigue and excitement; I wanted a whole hour to recover even a little.

But a deluge of rain was still falling, though with that violence which generally denotes the near cessation of a storm. A few overhanging rocks afforded us some shelter from the storm. Hans prepared some food, which I could not touch; and each of us, exhausted with three sleepless nights, fell into a broken and painful sleep.

The next day the weather was splendid. The sky and the sea had sunk into sudden repose. Every trace of the awful storm had disappeared. The exhilarating voice of the Professor fell upon my ears as I awoke; he was ominously cheerful.

'Well, my boy,' he cried, 'have you slept well?'

Would not any one have thought that we were still in our cheerful little house on the Königstrasse and that I was only just coming down to breakfast, and that I was to be married to Gräuben that day?

Alas! if the tempest had but sent the raft a little more east, we should have passed under Germany, under my beloved town of Hamburg, under the very street where dwelt all that I loved most in the world. Then only forty leagues would have separated us! But they were forty leagues perpendicular of solid granite wall, and in reality we were a thousand leagues asunder!

All these painful reflections rapidly crossed my mind before I could answer my uncle's question.

'Well, now,' he repeated, 'won't you tell me how you have

slept?'

'Oh, very well,' I said. 'I am only a little knocked up, but I shall soon be better.'

'Oh,' says my uncle, 'that's nothing to signify. You are only a little bit tired.'

'But you, uncle, you seem in very good spirits this morning.'

'Delighted, my boy, delighted. We have got there.'

'To our journey's end?'

'No; but we have got to the end of that endless sea. Now we shall go by land, and really begin to go down! down! down!'

'But, my dear uncle, do let me ask you one question.'

'Of course, Axel.'

'How about returning?'

'Returning? Why, you are talking about the return before the arrival.'

'No, I only want to know how that is to be managed.'

'In the simplest way possible. When we have reached the centre of the globe, either we shall find some new way to get back, or we shall come back like decent folks the way we came. I feel pleased at the thought that it is sure not to be shut against us.'

'But then we shall have to refit the raft.'

'Of course.'

'Then, as to provisions, have we enough to last?'

'Yes; to be sure we have. Hans is a clever fellow, and I am sure he must have saved a large part of our cargo. But still let us go and make sure.'

We left this grotto which lay open to every wind. At the same time I cherished a trembling hope which was a fear as well. It seemed to me impossible that the terrible wreck of the raft should not have destroyed everything on board. On my arrival on the shore I found Hans surrounded by an assemblage of articles all arranged in good order. My uncle shook hands with him with a lively gratitude. This man, with almost superhuman devotion, had been at work all the while that we were asleep, and had saved the most precious of the articles at the risk of his life.

Not that we had suffered no losses. For instance, our firearms; but we might do without them. Our stock of powder had remained uninjured after having risked blowing up during the storm.

'Well,' cried the Professor, 'as we have no guns we cannot hunt, that's all.'

'Yes, but how about the instruments?'

'Here is the aneroid, the most useful of all, and for which I would have given all the others. By means of it I can calculate the depth and know when we have reached the centre; without it we might very likely go beyond, and come out at the antipodes!'

Such high spirits as these were rather too strong.

'But where is the compass?' I asked.

'Here it is, upon this rock, in perfect condition, as well as the thermometers and the chronometer. The hunter is a splendid fellow.'

There was no denying it. We had all our instruments. As for tools and appliances, there they all lay on the ground—ladders, ropes, picks, spades, etc.

Still there was the question of provisions to be settled, and I asked—'How are we off for provisions?'

The boxes containing these were in a line upon the shore, in a perfect state of preservation; for the most part the sea had spared them, and what with biscuits, salt meat, spirits, and salt fish, we might reckon on four months' supply.

'Four months!' cried the Professor. 'We have time to go and to return; and with what is left I will give a grand dinner to my friends at the Johannæum.'

I ought by this time to have been quite accustomed to my uncle's ways; yet there was always something fresh about him to astonish me.

'Now,' said he, 'we will replenish our supply of water with the rain which the storm has left in all these granite basins; therefore we shall have no reason to fear anything from thirst. As for the raft, I will recommend Hans to do his best to repair it, although I don't expect it will be of any further use to us.'

'How so?' I cried.

'An idea of my own, my lad. I don't think we shall come out by the way that we went in.'

I stared at the Professor with a good deal of mistrust. I asked, was he not touched in the brain? And yet there was method in his madness.

'And now let us go to breakfast,' said he.

I followed him to a headland, after he had given his instructions to the hunter. There preserved meat, biscuit, and tea made us an excellent meal, one of the best I ever remember. Hunger, the fresh air, the calm quiet weather, after the commotions we had gone through, all contributed to give me a good appetite.

Whilst breakfasting I took the opportunity to put to my uncle the question where we were now.

'That seems to me,' I said, 'rather difficult to make out.'

'Yes, it is difficult,' he said, 'to calculate exactly; perhaps even impossible, since during these three stormy days I have been unable to keep any account of the rate or direction of the raft; but still we may get an approximation.'

'The last observation,' I remarked, 'was made on the island, when the geyser was"

'You mean Axel Island. Don't decline the honour of having given your name to the first island ever discovered in the central parts of the globe.'

'Well,' said I, 'let it be Axel Island. Then we had cleared two hundred and seventy leagues of sea, and we were six hundred leagues from Iceland.'

'Very well,' answered my uncle; 'let us start from that point and count four days' storm, during which our rate cannot have been less than eighty leagues in the twenty-four hours.'

'That is right; and this would make three hundred leagues more.'

'Yes, and the Liedenbrock sea would be six hundred leagues from shore to shore. Surely, Axel, it may vie in size with the Mediterranean itself.'

'Especially,' I replied, 'if it happens that we have only crossed it in its narrowest part. And it is a curious circumstance,' I added, 'that if my computations are right, and we are nine hundred leagues from Rejkiavik, we have now the Mediterranean above our head.'

'That is a good long way, my friend. But whether we are under Turkey or the Atlantic depends very much upon the question in what direction we have been moving. Perhaps we have deviated.'

'No, I think not. Our course has been the same all along, and I believe this shore is south-east of Port Grauben.'

'Well,' replied my uncle, 'we may easily ascertain this by consulting the compass. Let us go and see what it says.'

The Professor moved towards the rock upon which Hans had laid down the instruments. He was gay and full of spirits; he rubbed his hands, he studied his attitudes. I followed him, curious to know if I was right in my estimate. As soon as we had arrived at the rock my uncle took the compass, laid it horizontally, and questioned the needle, which, after a few oscillations, presently assumed a fixed position. My uncle looked, and looked, and looked again. He rubbed his eyes, and then turned to me thunderstruck with some unexpected discovery.

'What is the matter?' I asked.

He motioned to me to look. An exclamation of astonishment burst from me. The north pole of the needle was turned to what we supposed to be the south. It pointed to the shore instead of to the open sea! I shook the box, examined it again, it was in perfect condition. In whatever position I placed the box the needle pertinaciously returned to this unexpected quarter. Therefore there seemed no reason to doubt that during the storm there had been a sudden change of wind unperceived by us, which had brought our raft back to the shore which we thought we had left so long a distance behind us.

THIRTY SEVEN

THE LIEDENBROCK MUSEUM OF GEOLOGY

How shall I describe the strange series of passions which in succession shook the breast of Professor Liedenbrock? First stupefaction, then incredulity, lastly a downright burst of rage. Never had I seen the man so put out of countenance and so disturbed. The fatigues of our passage across, the dangers met, had all to be begun over again. We had gone backwards instead of forwards!

But my uncle rapidly recovered himself.

'Aha! will fate play tricks upon me? Will the elements lay plots against me? Shall fire, air, and water make a combined attack against me? Well, they shall know what a determined man can do. I will not yield. I will not stir a single foot backwards, and it will be seen whether man or nature is to have the upper hand!'

Erect upon the rock, angry and threatening, Otto Liedenbrock was a rather grotesque fierce parody upon the fierce Achilles defying the lightning. But I thought it my duty to interpose and attempt to lay some restraint upon this unmeasured fanaticism.

'Just listen to me,' I said firmly. 'Ambition must have a limit somewhere; we cannot perform impossibilities; we are not at all fit for another sea voyage; who would dream of undertaking a voyage of five hundred leagues upon a heap of rotten planks, with a blanket in rags for a sail, a stick for a mast, and fierce winds in our teeth? We cannot steer; we shall be buffeted by the tempests, and we should be fools and madmen to attempt to cross a second time.'

I was able to develop this series of unanswerable reasons for ten minutes without interruption; not that the Professor was paying any respectful attention to his nephew's arguments, but because he was deaf to all my eloquence.

'To the raft!' he shouted.

Such was his only reply. It was no use for me to entreat, supplicate, get angry, or do anything else in the way of opposition; it would only have been opposing a will harder than the granite rock.

Hans was finishing the repairs of the raft. One would have thought that this strange being was guessing at my uncle's intentions. With a few more pieces of surturbrand he had refitted our vessel. A sail already hung from the new mast, and the wind was playing in its waving folds.

The Professor said a few words to the guide, and immediately he put everything on board and arranged every necessary for our departure. The air was clear - and the north-west wind blew steadily.

What could I do? Could I stand against the two? It was impossible? If Hans had but taken my side! But no, it was not to be. The Icelander seemed to have renounced all will of his own and made a vow to forget and deny himself. I could get nothing out of a servant so feudalised, as it were, to his master. My only course was to proceed.

I was therefore going with as much resignation as I could find to resume my accustomed place on the raft, when my uncle laid his hand upon my shoulder.

'We shall not sail until Tomorrow,' he said.

I made a movement intended to express resignation.

'I must neglect nothing,' he said; 'and since my fate has

driven me on this part of the coast, I will not leave it until I have examined it.'

To understand what followed, it must be borne in mind that, through circumstances hereafter to be explained, we were not really where the Professor supposed we were. In fact we were not upon the north shore of the sea.

'Now let us start upon fresh discoveries,' I said.

And leaving Hans to his work we started off together. The space between the water and the foot of the cliffs was considerable. It took half an hour to bring us to the wall of rock. We trampled under our feet numberless shells of all the forms and sizes which existed in the earliest ages of the world. I also saw immense carapaces more than fifteen feet in diameter. They had been the coverings of those gigantic glyptodons or armadilloes of the pleiocene period, of which the modern tortoise is but a miniature representative.[1] The soil was besides this scattered with stony fragments, boulders rounded by water action, and ridged up in successive lines. I was therefore led to the conclusion that at one time the sea must have covered the ground on which we were treading. On the loose and scattered rocks, now out of the reach of the highest tides, the waves had left manifest traces of their power to wear their way in the hardest stone.

This might up to a certain point explain the existence of an ocean forty leagues beneath the surface of the globe. But in my opinion this liquid mass would be lost by degrees farther and farther within the interior of the earth, and it certainly had its origin in the waters of the ocean overhead, which had made their way hither through some fissure. Yet it must be believed that that fissure is now closed, and that all this cavern or immense reservoir was filled in a very short time. Perhaps

1. The glyptodon and armadillo are mammalian; the tortoise is a chelonian, a reptile, distinct classes of the animal kingdom; therefore the latter cannot be a representative of the former. (Tr.)

even this water, subjected to the fierce action of central heat, had partly been resolved into vapour. This would explain the existence of those clouds suspended over our heads and the development of that electricity which raised such tempests within the bowels of the earth.

This theory of the phenomena we had witnessed seemed satisfactory to me; for however great and stupendous the phenomena of nature, fixed physical laws will or may always explain them.

We were therefore walking upon sedimentary soil, the deposits of the waters of former ages. The Professor was carefully examining every little fissure in the rocks. Wherever he saw a hole he always wanted to know the depth of it. To him this was important.

We had traversed the shores of the Liedenbrock sea for a mile when we observed a sudden change in the appearance of the soil. It seemed upset, contorted, and convulsed by a violent upheaval of the lower strata. In many places depressions or elevations gave witness to some tremendous power effecting the dislocation of strata.

We moved with difficulty across these granite fissures and chasms mingled with silex, crystals of quartz, and alluvial deposits, when a field, nay, more than a field, a vast plain, of bleached bones lay spread before us. It seemed like an immense cemetery, where the remains of twenty ages mingled their dust together. Huge mounds of bony fragments rose stage after stage in the distance. They undulated away to the limits of the horizon, and melted in the distance in a faint haze. There within three square miles were accumulated the materials for a complete history of the animal life of ages, a history scarcely outlined in the too recent strata of the inhabited world.

But an impatient curiosity impelled our steps; crackling and rattling, our feet were trampling on the remains of prehistoric animals and interesting fossils, the possession of which is a matter of rivalry and contention between the museums of great cities.

A thousand Cuviers could never have reconstructed the organic remains deposited in this magnificent and unparalleled collection.

I stood amazed. My uncle had uplifted his long arms to the vault which was our sky; his mouth gaping wide, his eyes flashing behind his shining spectacles, his head balancing with an up-and-down motion, his whole attitude denoted unlimited astonishment. Here he stood facing an immense collection of scattered leptotheria, mericotheria, lophiodia, anoplotheria, megatheria, mastodons, protopithecæ, pterodactyles, and all sorts of extinct monsters here assembled together for his special satisfaction. Fancy an enthusiastic bibliomaniac suddenly brought into the midst of the famous Alexandrian library burnt by Omar and restored by a miracle from its ashes! just such a crazed enthusiast was my uncle, Professor Liedenbrock.

But more was to come, when, with a rush through clouds of bone dust, he laid his hand upon a bare skull, and cried with a voice trembling with excitement:

'Axel! Axel! a human head!'

'A human skull?' I cried, no less astonished.

'Yes, nephew. Aha! M. Milne-Edwards! Ah! M. de Quatrefages, how I wish you were standing here at the side of Otto Liedenbrock!'

THIRTY EIGHT

THE PROFESSOR IN HIS CHAIR AGAIN

To understand this apostrophe of my uncle's, made to absent French savants, it will be necessary to allude to an event of high importance in a palæontological point of view, which had occurred a little while before our departure.

On the 28th of March, 1863, some excavators working under the direction of M. Boucher de Perthes, in the stone quarries of Moulin Quignon, near Abbeville, in the department of Somme, found a human jawbone fourteen feet beneath the surface. It was the first fossil of this nature that had ever been brought to light. Not far distant were found stone hatchets and flint arrow-heads stained and encased by lapse of time with a uniform coat of rust.

The noise of this discovery was very great, not in France alone, but in England and in Germany. Several savants of the French Institute, and amongst them MM. Milne-Edwards and de Quatrefages, saw at once the importance of this discovery, proved to demonstration the genuineness of the bone in question, and became the most ardent defendants in what the English called this 'trial of a jawbone.' To the geologists of the United Kingdom, who believed in the certainty of the fact—Messrs. Falconer, Busk, Carpenter, and others—scientific Germans were soon joined, and amongst them the forwardest, the most fiery, and the most enthusiastic, was my uncle Liedenbrock.

Therefore the genuineness of a fossil human relic of the quaternary period seemed to be incontestably proved and admitted.

It is true that this theory met with a most obstinate opponent in M. Elie de Beaumont. This high authority maintained that the soil of Moulin Quignon was not diluvial at all, but was of much more recent formation; and, agreeing in that with Cuvier, he refused to admit that the human species could be contemporary with the animals of the quaternary period. My uncle Liedenbrock, along with the great body of the geologists, had maintained his ground, disputed, and argued, until M. Elie de Beaumont stood almost alone in his opinion.

We knew all these details, but we were not aware that since our departure the question had advanced to farther stages. Other similar maxillaries, though belonging to individuals of various types and different nations, were found in the loose grey soil of certain grottoes in France, Switzerland, and Belgium, as well as weapons, tools, earthen utensils, bones of children and adults. The existence therefore of man in the quaternary period seemed to become daily more certain.

Nor was this all. Fresh discoveries of remains in the pleiocene formation had emboldened other geologists to refer back the human species to a higher antiquity still. It is true that these remains were not human bones, but objects bearing the traces of his handiwork, such as fossil leg-bones of animals, sculptured and carved evidently by the hand of man.

Thus, at one bound, the record of the existence of man receded far back into the history of the ages past; he was a predecessor of the mastodon; he was a contemporary of the southern elephant; he lived a hundred thousand years ago, when, according to geologists, the pleiocene formation was in progress.

Such then was the state of palæontological science, and what we knew of it was sufficient to explain our behaviour in the presence of this stupendous Golgotha. Any one may now understand the frenzied excitement of my uncle, when, twenty yards farther on, he found himself face to face with a primitive man!

It was a perfectly recognisable human body. Had some particular soil, like that of the cemetery St. Michel, at Bordeaux, preserved it thus for so many ages? It might be so. But this dried corpse, with its parchment-like skin drawn tightly over the bony frame, the limbs still preserving their shape, sound teeth, abundant hair, and finger and toe nails of frightful length, this desiccated mummy startled us by appearing just as it had lived countless ages ago. I stood mute before this apparition of remote antiquity. My uncle, usually so garrulous, was struck dumb likewise. We raised the body. We stood it up against a rock. It seemed to stare at us out of its empty orbits. We sounded with our knuckles his hollow frame.

After some moments' silence the Professor was himself again. Otto Liedenbrock, yielding to his nature, forgot all the circumstances of our eventful journey, forgot where we were standing, forgot the vaulted cavern which contained us. No doubt he was in mind back again in his Johannæum, holding forth to his pupils, for he assumed his learned air; and addressing himself to an imaginary audience, he proceeded thus:

'Gentlemen, I have the honour to introduce to you a man of the quaternary or post-tertiary system. Eminent geologists have denied his existence, others no less eminent have affirmed it. The St. Thomases of palæontology, if they were here, might now touch him with their fingers, and would be obliged to acknowledge their error. I am quite aware that science has to be on its guard with discoveries of this kind. I know what capital enterprising individuals like Barnum have made out of fossil men. I have heard the tale of the kneepan of Ajax, the pretended body of Orestes claimed to have been found by the Spartans, and of the body of Asterius, ten cubits long, of which Pausanias speaks. I have read the reports of the skeleton of Trapani, found in the fourteenth century, and which was at the time identified as that of Polyphemus; and the history of the giant unearthed in the sixteenth century near Palermo. You know as well as I do, gentlemen, the analysis made at Lucerne in 1577 of those huge bones which the celebrated Dr. Felix Plater affirmed to be those of a giant nineteen feet high. I have gone through the treatises of Cassanion, and all those memoirs, pamphlets, answers, and rejoinders published respecting the skeleton of Teutobochus, the invader of Gaul, dug out of a sandpit in the Dauphiné, in 1613. In the eighteenth century I would have stood up for Scheuchzer's pre-adamite man against Peter Campet. I have perused a writing, entitled Gigan—'

Here my uncle's unfortunate infirmity met him—that of being unable in public to pronounce hard words.

'The pamphlet entitled Gigan—'

He could get no further.

'Giganteo—'

It was not to be done. The unlucky word would not come out. At the Johannæum there would have been a laugh.

'Gigantosteologie,' at last the Professor burst out, between two words which I shall not record here.

Then rushing on with renewed vigour, and with great animation:

'Yes, gentlemen, I know all these things, and more. I know that Cuvier and Blumenbach have recognised in these bones nothing more remarkable than the bones of the mammoth and other mammals of the post-tertiary period. But in the presence of this specimen to doubt would be to insult science. There stands the body! You may see it, touch it. It is not a mere skeleton; it is an entire body, preserved for a purely anthropological end and purpose.'

I was good enough not to contradict this startling assertion.

'If I could only wash it in a solution of sulphuric acid,' pursued my uncle, 'I should be able to clear it from all the earthy particles and the shells which are incrusted about it. But I do not possess that valuable solvent. Yet, such as it is, the body shall tell us its own wonderful story.'

Here the Professor laid hold of the fossil skeleton, and handled it with the skill of a dexterous showman.

'You see,' he said, 'that it is not six feet long, and that we are still separated by a long interval from the pretended race of giants. As for the family to which it belongs, it is evidently Caucasian. It is the white race, our own. The skull of this fossil is a regular oval, or rather ovoid. It exhibits no prominent cheekbones, no projecting jaws. It presents no appearance of that prognathism which diminishes the facial angle.[1] Measure that angle. It is nearly ninety degrees. But I will go further in my deductions, and I will affirm that this specimen of the human

1. The facial angle is formed by two lines, one touching the brow and the front teeth, the other from the orifice of the ear to the lower line of the nostrils. The greater this angle, the higher intelligence denoted by the formation of the skull. Prognathism is that projection of the jaw-bones which sharpens or lessons this angle, and which is illustrated in the negro countenance and in the lowest savages.

family is of the Japhetic race, which has since spread from the Indies to the Atlantic. Don't smile, gentlemen.'

Nobody was smiling; but the learned Professor was frequently disturbed by the broad smiles provoked by his learned eccentricities.

'Yes,' he pursued with animation, 'this is a fossil man, the contemporary of the mastodons whose remains fill this amphitheatre. But if you ask me how he came there, how those strata on which he lay slipped down into this enormous hollow in the globe, I confess I cannot answer that question. No doubt in the post-tertiary period considerable commotions were still disturbing the crust of the earth. The long-continued cooling of the globe produced chasms, fissures, clefts, and faults, into which, very probably, portions of the upper earth may have fallen. I make no rash assertions; but there is the man surrounded by his own works, by hatchets, by flint arrow-heads, which are the characteristics of the stone age. And unless he came here, like myself, as a tourist on a visit and as a pioneer of science, I can entertain no doubt of the authenticity of his remote origin.'

The Professor ceased to speak, and the audience broke out into loud and unanimous applause. For of course my uncle was right, and wiser men than his nephew would have had some trouble to refute his statements.

Another remarkable thing. This fossil body was not the only one in this immense catacomb. We came upon other bodies at every step amongst this mortal dust, and my uncle might select the most curious of these specimens to demolish the incredulity of sceptics.

In fact it was a wonderful spectacle, that of these generations of men and animals commingled in a common cemetery. Then one very serious question arose presently which we scarcely dared to suggest. Had all those creatures slided through a great fissure in the crust of the earth, down to the shores of the Liedenbrock sea, when they were dead and turning to dust, or had they lived and grown and died here in this subterranean world under a false sky, just like inhabitants of the upper earth? Until the present time we had seen alive only marine monsters and fishes. Might not some living man, some native of the abyss, be yet a wanderer below on this desert strand?

THIRTY NINE

FOREST SCENERY ILLUMINATED BY ELETRICITY

For another half hour we trod upon a pavement of bones. We pushed on, impelled by our burning curiosity. What other marvels did this cavern contain? What new treasures lay here for science to unfold? I was prepared for any surprise, my imagination was ready for any astonishment however astounding.

We had long lost sight of the sea shore behind the hills of bones. The rash Professor, careless of losing his way, hurried me forward. We advanced in silence, bathed in luminous electric fluid. By some phenomenon which I am unable to explain, it lighted up all sides of every object equally. Such was its diffusiveness, there being no central point from which the light emanated, that shadows no longer existed. You might have thought yourself under the rays of a vertical sun in a tropical region at noonday and the height of summer. No vapour was visible. The rocks, the distant mountains, a few isolated clumps of forest trees in the distance, presented a weird and wonderful aspect under these totally new conditions of a universal diffusion of light. We were like Hoffmann's shadowless man.

After walking a mile we reached the outskirts of a vast forest, but not one of those forests of fungi which bordered Port Gräuben.

Here was the vegetation of the tertiary period in its fullest blaze of magnificence. Tall palms, belonging to species no longer living, splendid palmacites, firs, yews, cypress trees, thujas, representatives of the conifers. were linked together by a tangled network of long climbing plants. A soft carpet of moss and hepaticas luxuriously clothed the soil. A few sparkling streams ran almost in silence under what would have been the shade of the trees, but that there was no shadow. On their banks grew tree-ferns similar to those we grow in hothouses. But a remarkable feature was the total absence of colour in all those trees, shrubs, and plants, growing without the life-giving heat and light of the sun. Everything seemed mixed-up and confounded in one uniform silver grey or light brown tint like that of fading and faded leaves. Not a green leaf anywhere, and the flowers—which were abundant enough in the tertiary period, which first gave birth to flowers—looked like brown-paper flowers, without colour or scent.

My uncle Liedenbrock ventured to penetrate under this colossal grove. I followed him, not without fear. Since nature had here provided vegetable nourishment, why should not the terrible mammals be there too? I perceived in the broad clearings left by fallen trees, decayed with age, leguminose plants, acerineæ, rubiceæ and many other eatable shrubs, dear to ruminant animals at every period. Then I observed, mingled together in confusion, trees of countries far apart on the surface of the globe. The oak and the palm were growing side by side, the Australian eucalyptus leaned against the Norwegian pine, the birch-tree of the north mingled its foliage with New Zealand kauris. It was enough to distract the most ingenious classifier of terrestrial botany.

Suddenly I halted. I drew back my uncle.

The diffused light revealed the smallest object in the dense and distant thickets. I had thought I saw—no! I did see, with my own eyes, vast colossal forms moving amongst the trees. They were gigantic animals; it was a herd of mastodons—not fossil remains, but living and resembling those the bones of which were found in the marshes of Ohio in 1801. I saw those huge elephants whose long, flexible trunks were grouting and turning up the soil under the trees like a legion of serpents. I could hear the crashing noise of their long ivory tusks boring into the old decaying trunks. The boughs cracked, and the leaves torn away by cartloads went down the cavernous throats of the vast brutes.

So, then, the dream in which I had had a vision of the prehistoric world, of the tertiary and post-tertiary periods, was now realised. And there we were alone, in the bowels of the earth, at the mercy of its wild inhabitants!

My uncle was gazing with intense and eager interest.

'Come on!' said he, seizing my arm. 'Forward! forward!'

'No, I will not!' I cried. 'We have no firearms. What could we do in the midst of a herd of these four-footed giants? Come away, uncle— come! No human being may with safety dare the anger of these monstrous beasts.'

'No human creature?' replied my uncle in a lower voice. 'You are wrong, Axel. Look, look down there! I fancy I see a living creature similar to ourselves: it is a man!'

I looked, shaking my head incredulously. But though at first I was unbelieving I had to yield to the evidence of my senses.

In fact, at a distance of a quarter of a mile, leaning against the trunk of a gigantic kauri, stood a human being, the Proteus of those subterranean regions, a new son of Neptune, watching this countless herd of mastodons.

Immanis pecoris custos, immanior ipse.[1]

Yes, truly, huger still himself. It was no longer a fossil being like him whose dried remains we had easily lifted up in the field of bones; it was a giant, able to control those monsters. In stature he was at least twelve feet high. His head, huge and unshapely as a buffalo's, was half hidden in the thick and

1. 'The shepherd of gigantic herds, and huger still himself.'

tangled growth of his unkempt hair. It most resembled the mane of the primitive elephant. In his hand he wielded with ease an enormous bough, a staff worthy of this shepherd of the geologic period.

We stood petrified and speechless with amazement. But he might see us! We must fly!

'Come, do come!' I said to my uncle, who for once allowed himself to be persuaded.

In another quarter of an hour our nimble heels had carried us beyond the reach of this horrible monster.

And yet, now that I can reflect quietly, now that my spirit has grown calm again, now that months have slipped by since this strange and supernatural meeting, what am I to think? what am I to believe? I must conclude that it was impossible that our senses had been deceived, that our eyes did not see what we supposed they saw. No human being lives in this subterranean world; no generation of men dwells in those inferior caverns of the globe, unknown to and unconnected with the inhabitants of its surface. It is absurd to believe it!

I had rather admit that it may have been some animal whose structure resembled the human, some ape or baboon of the early geological ages, some protopitheca, or some mesopitheca, some early or middle ape like that discovered by Mr. Lartet in the bone cave of Sansau. But this creature surpassed in stature all the measurements known in modern palæontology. But that a man, a living man, and therefore whole generations doubtless besides, should be buried there in the bowels of the earth, is impossible.

However, we had left behind us the luminous forest, dumb with astonishment, overwhelmed and struck down with a terror which amounted to stupefaction. We kept running on for fear the horrible monster might be on our track. It was a flight, a fall, like that fearful pulling and dragging which is peculiar to nightmare. Instinctively we got back to the Liedenbrock sea, and I cannot say into what vagaries my mind would not have carried me but for a circumstance which brought me back to practical matters.

Although I was certain that we were now treading upon a soil not hitherto touched by our feet, I often perceived groups of rocks which reminded me of those about Port Gräuben. Besides, this seemed to confirm the indications of the needle, and to show that we had against our will returned to the north of the Liedenbrock sea. Occasionally we felt quite convinced. Brooks and waterfalls were tumbling everywhere from the projections in the rocks. I thought I recognised the bed of surturbrand, our faithful Hansbach, and the grotto in which I had recovered life and consciousness. Then a few paces farther on, the arrangement of the cliffs, the appearance of an unrecognised stream, or the strange outline of a rock, carne to throw me again into doubt.

I communicated my doubts to my uncle. Like myself, he hesitated; he could recognise nothing again amidst this monotonous scene.

'Evidently,' said I, 'we have not landed again at our original starting point, but the storm has carried us a little higher, and if we follow the shore we shall find Port Gräuben.'

'If that is the case it will be useless to continue our exploration, and we had better return to our raft. But, Axel, are you not mistaken?'

'It is difficult to speak decidedly, uncle, for all these rocks are so very much alike. Yet I think I recognise the promontory at the foot of which Hans constructed our launch. We must be very near the little port, if indeed this is not it,' I added, examining a creek which I thought I recognised.

'No, Axel, we should at least find our own traces and I see nothing—'

'But I do see,' I cried, darting upon an object lying on the sand.

And I showed my uncle a rusty dagger which I had just picked up.

'Come,' said he, 'had you this weapon with you?'

'I! No, certainly! But you, perhaps—'

'Not that I am aware,' said the Professor. 'I have never had this object in my possession.'

'Well, this is strange!'

'No, Axel, it is very simple. The Icelanders often wear arms of this kind. This must have belonged to Hans, and he has lost it.'

I shook my head. Hans had never had an object like this in his possession.

'Did it not belong to some preadamite warrior?' I cried, 'to some living man, contemporary with the huge cattle-driver? But no. This is not a relic of the stone age. It is not even of the iron age. This blade is steel—'

My uncle stopped me abruptly on my way to a dissertation which would have taken me a long way, and said coolly:

'Be calm, Axel, and reasonable. This dagger belongs to the sixteenth century; it is a poniard, such as gentlemen carried in their belts to give the coup de grace. Its origin is Spanish. It was never either yours, or mine, or the hunter's, nor did it belong to any of those human beings who may or may not inhabit this inner world. See, it was never jagged like this by cutting men's throats; its blade is coated with a rust neither a day, nor a year, nor a hundred years old.'

The Professor was getting excited according to his wont, and was allowing his imagination to run away with him.

'Axel, we are on the way towards the grand discovery. This blade has been left on the strand for from one to three hundred years, and has blunted its edge upon the rocks that fringe this subterranean sea!'

'But it has not come alone. It has not twisted itself out of shape; some one has been here before us!'

'Yes—a man has.'

'And who was that man?'

'A man who has engraved his name somewhere with that

dagger. That man wanted once more to mark the way to the centre of the earth. Let us look about: look about!'

And, wonderfully interested, we peered all along the high wall, peeping into every fissure which might open out into a gallery.

And so we arrived at a place where the shore was much narrowed. Here the sea came to lap the foot of the steep cliff, leaving a passage no wider than a couple of yards. Between two boldly projecting rocks appeared the mouth of a dark tunnel.

There, upon a granite slab, appeared two mysterious graven letters, half eaten away by time. They were the initials of the bold and daring traveller:

'A. S.,' shouted my uncle. 'Arne Saknussemm! Arne Saknussemm everywhere!'

FORTY

PREPARATIONS FOR BLASTING A PASSAGE TO THE CENTRE OF THE EARTH

Since the start upon this marvellous pilgrimage I had been through so many astonishments that I might well be excused for thinking myself well hardened against any further surprise. Yet at the sight of these two letters, engraved on this spot three hundred years ago, I stood aghast in dumb amazement. Not only were the initials of the learned alchemist visible upon the living rock, but there lay the iron point with which the letters had been engraved. I could no longer doubt of the existence of that wonderful traveller and of the fact of his unparalleled journey, without the most glaring incredulity.

Whilst these reflections were occupying me, Professor Liedenbrock had launched into a somewhat rhapsodical eulogium, of which Arne Saknussemm was, of course, the hero.

'Thou marvellous genius!' he cried, 'thou hast not forgotten one indication which might serve to lay open to mortals the road through the terrestrial crust; and thy fellow-creatures may even now, after the lapse of three centuries, again trace thy footsteps through these deep and darksome ways. You reserved the contemplation of these wonders for other eyes besides your own. Your name, graven from stage to stage, leads the bold follower of your footsteps to the very centre of our planet's core, and there again we shall find your own name written with your own hand. I too will inscribe my name upon this dark granite page. But for ever henceforth let this cape that advances into the sea discovered by yourself be known by your own illustrious name—Cape Saknussemm.'

Such were the glowing words of panegyric which fell upon my attentive ear, and I could not resist the sentiment of enthusiasm with which I too was infected. The fire of zeal kindled afresh in me. I forgot everything. I dismissed from my mind the past perils of the journey, the future danger of our return. That which another had done I supposed we might also do, and nothing that was not superhuman appeared impossible to me.

'Forward! forward!' I cried.

I was already darting down the gloomy tunnel when the Professor stopped me; he, the man of impulse, counselled patience and coolness.

'Let us first return to Hans,' he said, 'and bring the raft to this spot.'

I obeyed, not without dissatisfaction, and passed out rapidly among the rocks on the shore.

I said: 'Uncle, do you know it seems to me that circumstances have wonderfully befriended us hitherto?'

'You think so, Axel?'

'No doubt; even the tempest has put us on the right way. Blessings on that storm! It has brought us back to this coast from which fine weather would have carried us far away. Suppose we had touched with our prow (the prow of a rudder!) the southern shore of the Liedenbrock sea, what would have become of us? We should never have seen the name of Saknussemm, and we should at this moment be imprisoned on a rockbound, impassable coast.'

'Yes, Axel, it is providential that whilst supposing we were steering south we should have just got back north at Cape Saknussemm. I must say that this is astonishing, and that I feel I have no way to explain it.'

'What does that signify, uncle? Our business is not to explain facts, but to use them!'

'Certainly; but—'

'Well, uncle, we are going to resume the northern route, and to pass under the north countries of Europe—under Sweden, Russia, Siberia: who knows where?—instead of burrowing under the deserts of Africa, or perhaps the waves of the Atlantic; and that is all I want to know.'

'Yes, Axel, you are right. It is all for the best, since we have left that weary, horizontal sea, which led us nowhere. Now we shall go down, down, down! Do you know that it is now only 1,500 leagues. to the centre of the globe?'

'Is that all?' I cried. 'Why, that's nothing. Let us start: march!'

All this crazy talk was going on still when we met the hunter. Everything was made ready for our instant departure. Every bit of cordage was put on board. We took our places, and with our sail set, Hans steered us along the coast to Cape Saknussemm.

The wind was unfavourable to a species of launch not calculated for shallow water. In many places we were obliged to push ourselves along with iron-pointed sticks. Often the sunken rocks just beneath the surface obliged us to deviate from our straight course. At last, after three hours' sailing, about six in the evening we reached a place suitable for our landing. I jumped ashore, followed by my uncle and the Icelander. This short passage had not served to cool my ardour. On the contrary, I even proposed to burn 'our ship,' to prevent the possibility of return; but my uncle would not consent to that. I thought him singularly lukewarm.

'At least,' I said, 'don't let us lose a minute.'

'Yes, yes, lad,' he replied; 'but first let us examine this new gallery, to see if we shall require our ladders.'

My uncle put his Ruhmkorff's apparatus in action; the raft moored to the shore was left alone; the mouth of the tunnel was not twenty yards from us; and our party, with myself at the head, made for it without a moment's delay.

The aperture, which was almost round, was about five feet in diameter; the dark passage was cut out in the live rock and lined with a coat of the eruptive matter which formerly issued from it; the interior was level with the ground outside, so that we were able to enter without difficulty. We were following a horizontal plane, when, only six paces in, our progress was interrupted by an enormous block just across our way.

'Accursed rock!' I cried in a passion, finding myself suddenly confronted by an impassable obstacle.

Right and left we searched in vain for a way, up and down, side to side; there was no getting any farther. I felt fearfully disappointed, and I would not admit that the obstacle was final. I stopped, I looked underneath the block: no opening. Above: granite still. Hans passed his lamp over every portion of the barrier in vain. We must give up all hope of passing it.

I sat down in despair. My uncle strode from side to side in the narrow passage.

'But how was it with Saknussemm?' I cried.

'Yes,' said my uncle, 'was he stopped by this stone barrier?'

'No, no,' I replied with animation. 'This fragment of rock has been shaken down by some shock or convulsion, or by one of those magnetic storms which agitate these regions, and has blocked up the passage which lay open to him. Many years have elapsed since the return of Saknussemm to the surface and the fall of this huge fragment. Is it not evident that this gallery was once the way open to the course of the lava, and that at that time there must have been a free passage? See here are recent fissures grooving and channelling the granite roof. This roof itself is formed of fragments of rock carried down, of enormous stones, as if by some giant's hand; but at one time the expulsive force was greater than usual, and this block, like the falling keystone of a ruined arch, has slipped down to the ground and blocked up the way. It is only an accidental obstruction, not met by Saknussemm, and if we don't destroy it we shall be unworthy to reach the centre of the earth.'

Such was my sentence! The soul of the Professor had passed into me. The genius of discovery possessed me wholly. I forgot the past, I scorned the future. I gave not a thought to the things of the surface of this globe into which I had dived; its cities and its sunny plains, Hamburg and the Königstrasse, even poor Gräuben, who must have given us up for lost, all were for the time dismissed from the pages of my memory.

'Well,' cried my uncle, 'let us make a way with our pickaxes.'

'Too hard for the pickaxe.'

'Well, then, the spade.'

'That would take us too long.'

'What, then?'

'Why gunpowder, to be sure! Let us mine the obstacle and blow it up.'

'Oh, yes, it is only a bit of rock to blast!'

'Hans, to work!' cried my uncle.

The Icelander returned to the raft and soon came back with an iron bar which he made use of to bore a hole for the charge.

This was no easy work. A hole was to be made large enough to hold fifty pounds of guncotton, whose expansive force is four times that of gunpowder.

I was terribly excited. Whilst Hans was at work I was actively helping my uncle to prepare a slow match of wetted powder encased in linen.

'This will do it,' I said.

'It will,' replied my uncle.

By midnight our mining preparations were over; the charge was rammed into the hole, and the slow match uncoiled along the gallery showed its end outside the opening.

A spark would now develop the whole of our preparations into activity.

'Tomorrow,' said the Professor.

I had to be resigned and to wait six long hours.

FORTY ONE

THE GREAT EXPLOSION AND THE RUSH DOWN BELOW

The next day, Thursday, August 27, is a well-remembered date in our subterranean journey. It never returns to my memory without sending through me a shudder of horror and a palpitation of the heart. From that hour we had no further occasion for the exercise of reason, or judgment, or skill, or contrivance. We were henceforth to be hurled along, the playthings of the fierce elements of the deep.

At six we were afoot. The moment drew near to clear a way by blasting through the opposing mass of granite.

I begged for the honour of lighting the fuse. This duty done, I was to join my companions on the raft, which had not yet been unloaded; we should then push off as far as we could and avoid the dangers arising from the explosion, the effects of which were not likely to be confined to the rock itself.

The fuse was calculated to burn ten minutes before setting fire to the mine. I therefore had sufficient time to get away to the raft.

I prepared to fulfil my task with some anxiety.

After a hasty meal, my uncle and the hunter embarked whilst I remained on shore. I was supplied with a lighted lantern to set fire to the fuse. 'Now go,' said my uncle, 'and return immediately to us.' 'Don't be uneasy,' I replied. 'I will not play by the way.' I immediately proceeded to the mouth of the tunnel. I opened my lantern. I laid hold of the end of the match. The Professor stood, chronometer in hand. 'Ready?' he cried.

'Ay.'

'Fire!'

I instantly plunged the end of the fuse into the lantern. It spluttered and flamed, and I ran at the top of my speed to the raft.

'Come on board quickly, and let us push off.'

Hans, with a vigorous thrust, sent us from the shore. The raft shot twenty fathoms out to sea.

It was a moment of intense excitement. The Professor was watching the hand of the chronometer.

'Five minutes more!' he said. 'Four! Three!'

My pulse beat half-seconds.

'Two! One! Down, granite rocks; down with you.'

What took place at that moment? I believe I did not hear the dull roar of the explosion. But the rocks suddenly assumed a new arrangement: they rent asunder like a curtain. I saw a bottomless pit open on the shore. The sea, lashed into sudden fury, rose up in an enormous billow, on the ridge of which the unhappy raft was uplifted bodily in the air with all its crew and cargo.

We all three fell down flat. In less than a second we were in deep, unfathomable darkness. Then I felt as if not only myself but the raft also had no support beneath. I thought it was sinking; but it was not so. I wanted to speak to my uncle, but the roaring of the waves prevented him from hearing even the sound of my voice.

In spite of darkness, noise, astonishment, and terror, I then understood what had taken place.

On the other side of the blown-up rock was an abyss. The explosion had caused a kind of earthquake in this fissured and abysmal region; a great gulf had opened; and the sea, now changed into a torrent, was hurrying us along into it.

I gave myself up for lost.

An hour passed away—two hours, perhaps—I cannot tell. We clutched each other fast, to save ourselves from being thrown off the raft. We felt violent shocks whenever we were borne heavily against the craggy projections. Yet these shocks were not very frequent, from which I concluded that the gully was widening. It was no doubt the same road that Saknussemm had taken; but instead of walking peaceably down it, as he had done, we were carrying a whole sea along with us.

These ideas, it will be understood, presented themselves to my mind in a vague and undetermined form. I had difficulty in associating any ideas together during this headlong race, which seemed like a vertical descent. To judge by the air which was whistling past me and made a whizzing in my ears, we were moving faster than the fastest express trains. To light a torch under these' conditions would have been impossible; and our last electric apparatus had been shattered by the force of the explosion.

I was therefore much surprised to see a clear light shining near me. It lighted up the calm and unmoved countenance of Hans. The skilful huntsman had succeeded in lighting the lantern; and although it flickered so much as to threaten to go out, it threw a fitful light across the awful darkness.

I was right in my supposition. It was a wide gallery. The

dim light could not show us both its walls at once. The fall of the waters which were carrying us away exceeded that of the swiftest rapids in American rivers. Its surface seemed composed of a sheaf of arrows hurled with inconceivable force; I cannot convey my impressions by a better comparison. The raft, occasionally seized by an eddy, spun round as it still flew along. When it approached the walls of the gallery I threw on them the light of the lantern, and I could judge somewhat of the velocity of our speed by noticing how the jagged projections of the rocks spun into endless ribbons and bands, so that we seemed confined within a network of shifting lines. I supposed we were running at the rate of thirty leagues an hour.

My uncle and I gazed on each other with haggard eyes, clinging to the stump of the mast, which had snapped asunder at the first shock of our great catastrophe. We kept our backs to the wind, not to be stifled by the rapidity of a movement which no human power could check.

Hours passed away. No change in our situation; but a discovery came to complicate matters and make them worse.

In seeking to put our cargo into somewhat better order, I found that the greater part of the articles embarked had disappeared at the moment of the explosion, when the sea broke in upon us with such violence. I wanted to know exactly what we had saved, and with the lantern in my hand I began my examination. Of our instruments none were saved but the compass and the chronometer; our stock of ropes and ladders was reduced to the bit of cord rolled round the stump of the mast! Not a spade, not a pickaxe, not a hammer was left us; and, irreparable disaster! we had only one day's provisions left.

I searched every nook and corner, every crack and cranny in the raft. There was nothing. Our provisions were reduced to one bit of salt meat and a few biscuits.

I stared at our failing supplies stupidly. I refused to take in the gravity of our loss. And yet what was the use of troubling myself. If we had had provisions enough for months, how could we get out of the abyss into which we were being hurled by an irresistible torrent? Why should we fear the horrors of famine, when death was swooping down upon us in a multitude of other forms? Would there be time left to die of starvation?

Yet by an inexplicable play of the imagination I forgot my present dangers, to contemplate the threatening future. Was there any chance of escaping from the fury of this impetuous torrent, and of returning to the surface of the globe? I could not form the slightest conjecture how or when. But one chance in a thousand, or ten thousand, is still a chance; whilst death from starvation would leave us not the smallest hope in the world.

The thought came into my mind to declare the whole truth to my uncle, to show him the dreadful straits to which we were reduced, and to calculate how long we might yet expect to live. But I had the courage to preserve silence. I wished to leave him cool and self-possessed.

At that moment the light from our lantern began to sink by little and little, and then went out entirely. The wick had burnt itself out. Black night reigned again; and there was no hope left of being able to dissipate the palpable darkness. We had yet a torch left, but we could not have kept it alight. Then, like a child, I closed my eyes firmly, not to see the darkness.

After a considerable lapse of time our speed redoubled. I could perceive it by the sharpness of the currents that blew past my face. The descent became steeper. I believe we were no longer sliding, but falling down. I had an impression that we were dropping vertically. My uncle's hand, and the vigorous arm of Hans, held me fast.

Suddenly, after a space of time that I could not measure, I felt a shock. The raft had not struck against any hard resistance, but had suddenly been checked in its fall. A waterspout, an immense liquid column, was beating upon the surface of the waters. I was suffocating! I was drowning!

But this sudden flood was not of long duration. In a few seconds I found myself in the air again, which I inhaled with all the force of my lungs. My uncle and Hans were still holding me fast by the arms; and the raft was still carrying us.

FORTY TWO

HEADLONG SPEED UPWARD THROUGH THE HORRORS OF DARKNESS

It might have been, as I guessed, about ten at night. The first of my senses which came into play after this last bout was that of hearing. All at once I could hear; and it was a real exercise of the sense of hearing. I could hear the silence in the gallery after the din which for hours had stunned me. At last these words of my uncle's came to me like a vague murmuring:

'We are going up.'

'What do you mean?' I cried.

'Yes, we are going up—up!'

I stretched out my arm. I touched the wall, and drew back my hand bleeding. We were ascending with extreme rapidity.

'The torch! The torch!' cried the Professor.

Not without difficulty Hans succeeded in lighting the torch; and the flame, preserving its upward tendency, threw enough light to show us what kind of a place we were in.

'Just as I thought,' said the Professor 'We are in a tunnel not four-and-twenty feet in diameter The water had reached the bottom of the gulf. It is now rising to its level, and carrying us with it.'

'Where to?'

'I cannot tell; but we must be ready for anything. We are mounting at a speed which seems to me of fourteen feet in a second, or ten miles an hour. At this rate we shall get on.'

'Yes, if nothing stops us; if this well has an aperture. But suppose it to be stopped. If the air is condensed by the pressure of this column of water we shall be crushed.'

'Axel,' replied the Professor with perfect coolness, 'our situation is almost desperate; but there are some chances of deliverance, and it is these that I am considering. If at every instant we may perish, so at every instant we may be saved. Let us then be prepared to seize upon the smallest advantage.'

'But what shall we do now?'

'Recruit our strength by eating.'

At these words I fixed a haggard eye upon my uncle. That which I had been so unwilling to confess at last had to be told.

'Eat, did you say?'

'Yes, at once.'

The Professor added a few words in Danish, but Hans shook his head mournfully.

'What!' cried my uncle. 'Have we lost our provisions?'

'Yes; here is all we have left; one bit of salt meat for the three.'

My uncle stared at me as if he could not understand.

'Well,' said I, 'do you think we have any chance of being saved?'

My question was unanswered.

An hour passed away. I began to feel the pangs of a violent hunger. My companions were suffering too, and not one of us dared touch this wretched remnant of our goodly store.

But now we were mounting up with excessive speed. Sometimes the air would cut our breath short, as is experienced by æronauts ascending too rapidly. But whilst they suffer from cold in proportion to their rise, we were beginning to feel a contrary effect. The heat was increasing in a manner to cause us the most fearful anxiety, and certainly the temperature was at this moment at the height of 100° Fahr.

What could be the meaning of such a change? Up to this time facts had supported the theories of Davy and of Liedenbrock; until now particular conditions of non-conducting rocks, electricity and magnetism, had tempered the laws of nature, giving us only a moderately warm climate, for the theory of a central fire remained in my estimation the only one that was true and explicable. Were we then turning back to where the phenomena of central heat ruled in all their rigour and would reduce the most refractory rocks to the state of a molten liquid? I feared this, and said to the Professor:

'If we are neither drowned, nor shattered to pieces, nor starved to death, there is still the chance that we may be burned alive and reduced to ashes.'

At this he shrugged his shoulders and returned to his thoughts.

Another hour passed, and, except some slight increase in the temperature, nothing new had happened.

'Come,' said he, 'we must determine upon something.'

'Determine on what?' said I.

'Yes, we must recruit our strength by carefully rationing ourselves, and so prolong our existence by a few hours. But we shall be reduced to very great weakness at last.'

'And our last hour is not far off.'

'Well, if there is a chance of safety, if a moment for active exertion presents itself, where should we find the required strength if we allowed ourselves to be enfeebled by hunger?'

'Well, uncle, when this bit of meat has been devoured what shall we have left?'

'Nothing, Axel, nothing at all. But will it do you any more good to devour it with your eyes than with your teeth? Your reasoning has in it neither sense nor energy.'

'Then don't you despair?' I cried irritably.

'No, certainly not,' was the Professor's firm reply.

'What! do you think there is any chance of safety left?'

'Yes, I do; as long as the heart beats, as long as body and

soul keep together, I cannot admit that any creature endowed with a will has need to despair of life.'

Resolute words these! The man who could speak so, under such circumstances, was of no ordinary type.

'Finally, what do you mean to do?' I asked.

'Eat what is left to the last crumb, and recruit our fading strength. This meal will be our last, perhaps: so let it be! But at any rate we shall once more be men, and not exhausted, empty bags.'

'Well, let us consume it then,' I cried.

My uncle took the piece of meat and the few biscuits which had escaped from the general destruction. He divided them into three equal portions and gave one to each. This made about a pound of nourishment for each. The Professor ate his greedily, with a kind of feverish rage. I ate without pleasure, almost with disgust; Hans quietly, moderately, masticating his small mouthfuls without any noise, and relishing them with the calmness of a man above all anxiety about the future. By diligent search he had found a flask of Hollands; he offered it to us each in turn, and this generous beverage cheered us up slightly.

'Forträfflig,' said Hans, drinking in his turn.

'Excellent,' replied my uncle.

A glimpse of hope had returned, although without cause. But our last meal was over, and it was now five in the morning.

Man is so constituted that health is a purely negative state. Hunger once satisfied, it is difficult for a man to imagine the horrors of starvation; they cannot be understood without being felt.

Therefore it was that after our long fast these few mouthfuls of meat and biscuit made us triumph over our past agonies.

But as soon as the meal was done, we each of us fell deep into thought. What was Hans thinking of—that man of the far West, but who seemed ruled by the fatalist doctrines of the East?

As for me, my thoughts were made up of remembrances, and they carried me up to the surface of the globe of which I ought never to have taken leave. The house in the Königstrasse, my poor dear Gräuben, that kind soul Martha, flitted like visions before my eyes, and in the dismal moanings which from time to time reached my ears I thought I could distinguish the roar of the traffic of the great cities upon earth.

My uncle still had his eye upon his work. Torch in hand, he tried to gather some idea of our situation from the observation of the strata. This calculation could, at best, be but a vague approximation; but a learned man is always a philosopher when he succeeds in remaining cool, and assuredly Professor Liedenbrock possessed this quality to a surprising degree.

I could hear him murmuring geological terms. I could understand them, and in spite of myself I felt interested in this last geological study.

'Eruptive granite,' he was saying. 'We are still in the primitive period. But we are going up, up, higher still. Who can tell?'

Ah! who can tell? With his hand he was examining the perpendicular wall, and in a few more minutes he continued:

'This is gneiss! here is mica schist! Ah! presently we shall come to the transition period, and then—'

What did the Professor mean? Could he be trying to measure the thickness of the crust of the earth that lay between us and the world above? Had he any means of making this calculation? No, he had not the aneroid, and no guessing could supply its place.

Still the temperature kept rising, and I felt myself steeped in a broiling atmosphere. I could only compare it to the heat of a furnace at the moment when the molten metal is running into the mould. Gradually we had been obliged to throw aside our coats and waistcoats, the. lightest covering became uncomfortable and even painful.

'Are we rising into a fiery furnace?' I cried at one moment

when the heat was redoubling.

'No,' replied my uncle, 'that is impossible—quite impossible!'

'Yet,' I answered, feeling the wall, 'this well is burning hot.'

At the same moment, touching the water, I had to withdraw my hand in haste.

'The water is scalding,' I cried.

This time the Professor's only answer was an angry gesture.

Then an unconquerable terror seized upon me, from which I could no longer get free. I felt that a catastrophe was approaching before which the boldest spirit must quail. A dim, vague notion laid hold of my mind, but which was fast hardening into certainty. I tried to repel it, but it would return. I dared not express it in plain terms. Yet a few involuntary observations confirmed me in my view. By the flickering light of the torch I could distinguish contortions in the granite beds; a phenomenon was unfolding in which electricity would play the principal part; then this unbearable heat, this boiling water! I consulted the compass.

The compass had lost its properties! it had ceased to act properly!

FORTY THREE

SHOT OUT OF A VOLCANO AT LAST!

Yes: our compass was no longer a guide; the needle flew from pole to pole with a kind of frenzied impulse; it ran round the dial, and spun hither and thither as if it were giddy or intoxicated.

I knew quite well that according to the best received theories the mineral covering of the globe is never at absolute rest; the changes brought about by the chemical decomposition of its component parts, the agitation caused by great liquid torrents, and the magnetic currents, are continually tending to disturb it—even when living beings upon its surface may fancy that all is quiet below. A phenomenon of this kind would not have greatly alarmed me, or at any rate it would not have given rise to dreadful apprehensions.

But other facts, other circumstances, of a peculiar nature, came to reveal to me by degrees the true state of the case. There came incessant and continuous explosions. I could only compare them to the loud rattle of along train of chariots driven at full speed over the stones, or a roar of unintermitting thunder.

Then the disordered compass, thrown out of gear by the electric currents, confirmed me in a growing conviction. The mineral crust of the globe threatened to burst up, the granite foundations to come together with a crash, the fissure through which we were helplessly driven would be filled up, the void would be full of crushed fragments of rock, and we poor wretched mortals were to be buried and annihilated in this dreadful consummation.

'My uncle,' I cried, 'we are lost now, utterly lost!'

'What are you in a fright about now?' was the calm rejoinder. 'What is the matter with you?'

'The matter? Look at those quaking walls! look at those shivering rocks. Don't you feel the burning heat? Don't you see how the water boils and bubbles? Are you blind to the dense vapours and steam growing thicker and denser every minute? See this agitated compass needle. It is an earthquake that is threatening us.'

My undaunted uncle calmly shook his head.

'Do you think,' said he, 'an earthquake is coming?'

'I do.'

'Well, I think you are mistaken.'

'What! don't you recognise the symptoms?'

'Of an earthquake? no! I am looking out for something better.'

'What can you mean? Explain?'

'It is an eruption, Axel.'

'An eruption! Do you mean to affirm that we are running up the shaft of a volcano?'

'I believe we are,' said the indomitable Professor with an air of perfect self-possession; 'and it is the best thing that could possibly happen to us under our circumstances.'

The best thing! Was my uncle stark mad? What did the man mean? and what was the use of saying facetious things at a time like this?

'What!' I shouted. 'Are we being taken up in an eruption? Our fate has flung us here among burning lavas, molten rocks, boiling waters, and all kinds of volcanic matter; we are going to be pitched out, expelled, tossed up, vomited, spit out high into the air, along with fragments of rock, showers of ashes and scoria, in the midst of a towering rush of smoke and flames; and it is the best thing that could happen to us!'

'Yes,' replied the Professor, eyeing me over his spectacles, 'I don't see any other way of reaching the surface of the earth.'

I pass rapidly over the thousand ideas which passed through my mind. My uncle was right, undoubtedly right; and never had he seemed to me more daring and more confirmed in his notions than at this moment when he was calmly contemplating the chances of being shot out of a volcano!

In the meantime up we went; the night passed away in continual ascent; the din and uproar around us became more and more intensified; I was stifled and stunned; I thought my last hour was approaching; and yet imagination is such a strong thing that even in this supreme hour I was occupied with strange and almost childish speculations. But I was the victim, not the master, of my own thoughts.

It was very evident that we were being hurried upward upon

the crest of a wave of eruption; beneath our raft were boiling waters, and under these the more sluggish lava was working its way up in a heated mass, together with shoals of fragments of rock which, when they arrived at the crater, would be dispersed in all directions high and low. We were imprisoned in the shaft or chimney of some volcano. There was no room to doubt of that.

But this time, instead of Snæfell, an extinct volcano, we were inside one in full activity. I wondered, therefore, where could this mountain be, and in what part of the world we were to be shot out.

I made no doubt but that it would be in some northern region. Before its disorders set in, the needle had never deviated from that direction. From Cape Saknussemm we had been carried due north for hundreds of leagues. Were we under Iceland again? Were we destined to be thrown up out of Hecla, or by which of the seven other fiery craters in that island? Within a radius of five hundred leagues to the west I remembered under this parallel of latitude only the imperfectly known volcanoes of the north-east coast of America. To the east there was only one in the 80th degree of north latitude, the Esk in Jan Mayen Island, not far from Spitzbergen! Certainly there was no lack of craters, and there were some capacious enough to throw out a whole army! But I wanted to know which of them was to serve us for an exit from the inner world.

Towards morning the ascending movement became accelerated. If the heat increased, instead of diminishing, as we approached nearer to the surface of the globe, this effect was due to local causes alone, and those volcanic. The manner of our locomotion left no doubt in my mind. An enormous force, a force of hundreds of atmospheres, generated by the extreme pressure of confined vapours, was driving us irresistibly forward. But to what numberless dangers it exposed us!

Soon lurid lights began to penetrate the vertical gallery which widened as we went up. Right and left I could see deep channels, like huge tunnels, out of which escaped dense volumes of smoke; tongues of fire lapped the walls, which crackled and sputtered under the intense heat.

'See, see, my uncle!' I cried.

'Well, those are only sulphureous flames and vapours, which one must expect to see in an eruption. They are quite natural.'

'But suppose they should wrap us round.'

'But they won't wrap us round.'

'But we shall be stifled.'

'We shall, not be stifled at all. The gallery is widening, and if it becomes necessary, we shall abandon the raft, and creep into a crevice.'

'But the water—the rising water?'

'There is no more water, Axel; only a lava paste, which is bearing us up on its surface to the top of the crater.'

The liquid column had indeed disappeared, to give place to dense and still boiling eruptive matter of all kinds. The temperature was becoming unbearable. A thermometer exposed to this atmosphere would have marked 150°. The perspiration streamed from my body. But for the rapidity of our ascent we should have been suffocated.

But the Professor gave up his idea of abandoning the raft, and it was well he did. However roughly joined together, those planks afforded us a firmer support than we could have found anywhere else.

About eight in the morning a new incident occurred. The upward movement ceased. The raft lay motionless.

'What is this?' I asked, shaken by this sudden stoppage as if by a shock.

'It is a halt,' replied my uncle.

'Is the eruption checked?' I asked.

'I hope not.'

I rose, and tried to look around me. Perhaps the raft itself, stopped in its course by a projection, was staying the volcanic torrent. If this were the case we should have to release it as soon as possible.

But it was not so. The blast of ashes, scorix, and rubbish had ceased to rise.

'Has the eruption stopped?' I cried.

'Ah!' said my uncle between his clenched teeth, 'you are afraid. But don't alarm yourself—this lull cannot last long. It has lasted now five minutes, and in a short time we shall resume our journey to the mouth of the crater.'

As he spoke, the Professor continued to consult his chronometer, and he was again right in his prognostications. The raft was soon hurried and driven forward with a rapid but irregular movement, which lasted about ten minutes, and then stopped again.

'Very good,' said my uncle; 'in ten minutes more we shall be off again, for our present business lies with an intermittent volcano. It gives us time now and then to take breath.'

This was perfectly true. When the ten minutes were over we started off again with renewed and increased speed. We were obliged to lay fast hold of the planks of the raft, not to be thrown off. Then again the paroxysm was over.

I have since reflected upon this singular phenomenon without being able to explain it. At any rate it was clear that we were not in the main shaft of the volcano, but in a lateral gallery where there were felt recurrent tunes of reaction.

How often this operation was repeated I cannot say. All I know is, that at each fresh impulse we were hurled forward with a greatly increased force, and we seemed as if we were mere projectiles. During the short halts we were stifled with the heat; whilst we were being projected forward the hot air almost stopped my breath. I thought for a moment how delightful it would be to find myself carried suddenly into the arctic regions, with a cold 30° below the freezing point. My overheated brain conjured up visions of white plains of cool snow, where I might roll and allay my feverish heat. Little by little my brain, weakened by so many constantly repeated shocks, seemed to be giving way altogether. But for the strong arm of Hans I should more than once have had my head broken against the granite roof of our burning dungeon.

I have therefore no exact recollection of what took place during the following hours. I have a confused impression left of continuous explosions, loud detonations, a general shaking of the rocks all around us, and of a spinning movement with which our raft was once whirled helplessly round. It rocked upon the lava torrent, amidst a dense fall of ashes. Snorting flames darted their fiery tongues at us. There were wild, fierce puffs of stormy wind from below, resembling the blasts of vast iron furnaces blowing all at one time; and I caught a glimpse of the figure of Hans lighted up by the fire; and all the feeling I had left was just what I imagine must be the feeling of an unhappy criminal doomed to be blown away alive from the mouth of a cannon, just before the trigger is pulled, and the flying limbs and rags of flesh and skin fill the quivering air and spatter the blood-stained ground.

FORTY FOUR

SUNNY LANDS IN THE BLUE MEDITERRANEAN

When I opened my eyes again I felt myself grasped by the belt with the strong hand of our guide. With the other arm he supported my uncle. I was not seriously hurt, but I was shaken and bruised and battered all over. I found myself lying on the sloping side of a mountain only two yards from a gaping gulf, which would have swallowed me up had I leaned at all that way. Hans had saved me from death whilst I lay rolling on the edge of the crater.

'Where are we?' asked my uncle irascibly, as if he felt much injured by being landed upon the earth again.

The hunter shook his head in token of complete ignorance.

'Is it Iceland?' I asked.

'Nej,' replied Hans.

'What! Not Iceland?' cried the Professor.

'Hans must be mistaken,' I said, raising myself up.

This was our final surprise after all the astonishing events of our wonderful journey. I expected to see a white cone covered with the eternal snow of ages rising from the midst of the barren deserts of the icy north, faintly lighted with the pale rays of the arctic sun, far away in the highest latitudes known; but contrary to all our expectations, my uncle, the Icelander, and myself were sitting half-way down a mountain baked under the burning rays of a southern sun, which was blistering us with the heat, and blinding us with the fierce light of his nearly vertical rays.

I could not believe my own eyes; but the heated air and the sensation of burning left me no room for doubt. We had come out of the crater half naked, and the radiant orb to which we had been strangers for two months was lavishing upon us out of his blazing splendours more of his light and heat than we were able to receive with comfort.

When my eyes had become accustomed to the bright light to which they had been so long strangers, I began to use them to set my imagination right. At least I would have it to be Spitzbergen, and I was in no humour to give up this notion.

The Professor was the first to speak, and said:

'Well, this is not much like Iceland.'

'But is it Jan Mayen?' I asked.

'Nor that either,' he answered. 'This is no northern mountain; here are no granite peaks capped with snow. Look, Axel, look!'

Above our heads, at a height of five hundred feet or more, we saw the crater of a volcano, through. which, at intervals of fifteen minutes or so, there issued with loud explosions lofty columns of fire, mingled with pumice stones, ashes, and flowing lava. I could feel the heaving of the mountain, which seemed to breathe like a huge whale, and puff out fire and wind from its vast blowholes. Beneath, down a pretty steep declivity, ran streams of lava for eight or nine hundred feet, giving the mountain a height of about 1,300 or 1,400 feet. But the base of the mountain was hidden in a perfect bower of rich verdure, amongst which I was able to distinguish the olive, the fig, and vines, covered with their luscious purple bunches.

I was forced to confess that there was nothing arctic here.

When the eye passed beyond these green surroundings it rested on a wide, blue expanse of sea or lake, which appeared to enclose this enchanting island, within a compass of only a few leagues. Eastward lay a pretty little white seaport town or village, with a few houses scattered around it, and in the harbour of which a few vessels of peculiar rig were gently swayed by the softly swelling waves. Beyond it, groups of islets rose from the smooth, blue waters, but in such numbers that they seemed to dot the sea like a shoal. To the west distant coasts lined the dim horizon, on some rose blue mountains of smooth, undulating forms; on a more distant coast arose a prodigious cone crowned on its summit with a snowy plume of white cloud. To the northward lay spread a vast sheet of water, sparkling and dancing under the hot, bright rays, the uniformity broken here and there by the topmast of a gallant ship appearing above the horizon, or a swelling sail moving slowly before the wind.

This unforeseen spectacle was most charming to eyes long used to underground darkness.

'Where are we? Where are we?' I asked faintly.

Hans closed his eyes with lazy indifference. What did it matter to him? My uncle looked round with dumb surprise.

'Well, whatever mountain this may be,' he said at last, 'it is very hot here. The explosions are going on still, and I don't think it would look well to have come out by an eruption, and then to get our heads broken by bits of falling rock. Let us get down. Then we shall know better what we are about. Besides, I am starving, and parching with thirst.'

Decidedly the Professor was not given to contemplation. For my part, I could for another hour or two have forgotten my hunger and my fatigue to enjoy the lovely scene before me; but I had to follow my companions.

The slope of the volcano was in many places of great steepness. We slid down screes of ashes, carefully avoiding the lava streams which glided sluggishly by us like fiery serpents. As we went I chattered and asked all sorts of questions as to our whereabouts, for L was too much excited not to talk a great deal.

'We are in Asia,' I cried, 'on the coasts of India, in the Malay Islands, or in Oceania. We have passed through half the globe, and come out nearly at the antipodes.'

'But the compass?' said my uncle.

'Ay, the compass!' I said, greatly puzzled. 'According to the compass we have gone northward.'

'Has it lied?'

'Surely not. Could it lie?'

'Unless, indeed, this is the North Pole!'

'Oh, no, it is not the Pole; but—'

Well, here was something that baffled us completely. I could not tell what to say.

But now we were coming into that delightful greenery, and I was suffering greatly from hunger and thirst. Happily, after two hours' walking, a charming country lay open before us, covered with olive trees, pomegranate trees, and delicious vines, all of which seemed to belong to anybody who pleased to claim them. Besides, in our state of destitution and famine we were not likely to be particular. Oh, the inexpressible pleasure of pressing those cool, sweet fruits to our lips, and eating grapes by mouthfuls off the rich, full bunches! Not far off, in the grass, under the delicious shade of the trees, I discovered a spring of fresh, cool water, in which we luxuriously bathed our faces, hands, and feet.

Whilst we were thus enjoying the sweets of repose a child appeared out of a grove of olive trees.

'Ah!' I cried, 'here is an inhabitant of this happy land!'

It was but a poor boy, miserably ill-clad, a sufferer from poverty, and our aspect seemed to alarm him a great deal; in fact, only half clothed, with ragged hair and beards, we were a suspicious-looking party; and if the people of the country knew anything about thieves, we were very likely to frighten them.

Just as the poor little wretch was going to take to his heels, Hans caught hold of him, and brought him to us, kicking and struggling.

My uncle began to encourage him as well as he could, and said to him in good German:

'Was heiszt diesen Berg, mein Knablein? Sage mir geschwind!'

('What is this mountain called, my little friend?')

The child made no answer.

'Very well,' said my uncle. 'I infer that we are not in Germany.'

He put the same question in English.

We got no forwarder. I was a good deal puzzled.

'Is the child dumb?' cried the Professor, who, proud of his knowledge of many languages, now tried French: 'Comment appellet-on cette montagne, mon enfant?'

Silence still.

'Now let us try Italian,' said my uncle; and he said:

'Dove noi siamo?'

'Yes, where are we?' I impatiently repeated.

But there was no answer still.

'Will you speak when you are told?' exclaimed my uncle, shaking the urchin by the ears. 'Come si noma questa isola?'

'STROMBOLI,' replied the little herdboy, slipping out of Hans' hands, and scudding into the plain across the olive trees.

We were hardly thinking of that. Stromboli! What an effect this unexpected name produced upon my mind! We were in the midst of the Mediterranean Sea, on an island of the Æolian archipelago, in the ancient Strongyle, where Æolus kept the winds and the storms chained up, to be let loose at his will. And those distant blue mountains in the east were the mountains of Calabria. And that threatening volcano far away in the south was the fierce Etna.

'Stromboli, Stromboli!' I repeated.

My uncle kept time to my exclamations with hands and feet, as well as with words. We seemed to be chanting in chorus!

What a journey we had accomplished! How marvellous! Having entered by one volcano, we had issued out of another more than two thousand miles from Snæfell and from that barren, far-away Iceland! The strange chances of our expedition had carried us into the heart of the fairest region in the world. We had exchanged the bleak regions of perpetual snow and of impenetrable barriers of ice for those of brightness and 'the rich hues of all glorious things.' We had left over our heads the murky sky and cold fogs of the frigid zone to revel under the azure sky of Italy!

After our delicious repast of fruits and cold, clear water we set off again to reach the port of Stromboli. It would not have been wise to tell how we came there. The superstitious Italians would have set us down for fire-devils vomited out of hell; so we presented ourselves in the humble guise of shipwrecked mariners. It was not so glorious, but it was safer.

On my way I could hear my uncle murmuring: 'But the compass! that compass! It pointed due north. How are we to explain that fact?'

'My opinion is,' I replied disdainfully, 'that it is best not to explain it. That is the easiest way to shelve the difficulty.'

'Indeed, sir! The occupant of a professorial chair at the Johannæum unable to explain the reason of a cosmical phenomenon! Why, it would be simply disgraceful!'

And as he spoke, my uncle, half undressed, in rags, a perfect scarecrow, with his leathern belt around him, settling his spectacles upon his nose and looking learned and imposing, was himself again, the terrible German professor of mineralogy.

One hour after we had left the grove of olives, we arrived at the little port of San Vicenzo, where Hans claimed his thirteen week's wages, which was counted out to him with a hearty shaking of hands all round.

At that moment, if he did not share our natural emotion, at least his countenance expanded in a manner very unusual with him, and while with the ends of his fingers he lightly pressed our hands, I believe he smiled.

FORTY FIVE

ALL'S WELL THAT ENDS WELL

Such is the conclusion of a history which I cannot expect everybody to believe, for some people will believe nothing against the testimony of their own experience. However, I am indifferent to their incredulity, and they may believe as much or as little as they please.

The Stromboliotes received us kindly as shipwrecked mariners. They gave us food and clothing. After waiting forty-eight hours, on the 31 st of August, a small craft took us to Messina, where a few days' rest completely removed the effect of our fatigues.

On Friday, September the 4th, we embarked on the steamer Volturno, employed by the French Messageries Imperiales, and in three days more we were at Marseilles, having no care on our minds except that abominable deceitful compass, which we had mislaid somewhere and could not now examine; but its inexplicable behaviour exercised my mind fearfully. On the 9th of September, in the evening, we arrived at Hamburg.

I cannot describe to you the astonishment of Martha or the joy of Gräuben.

'Now you are a hero, Axel,' said to me my blushing fiancée, my betrothed, 'you will not leave me again!'

I looked tenderly upon her, and she smiled through her tears.

How can I describe the extraordinary sensation produced by the return of Professor Liedenbrock? Thanks to Martha's ineradicable tattling, the news that the Professor had gone to discover a way to the centre of the earth had spread over the whole civilised world. People refused to believe it, and when they saw him they would not believe him any the more. Still, the appearance of Hans, and sundry pieces of intelligence derived from Iceland, tended to shake the confidence of the unbelievers.

Then my uncle became a great man, and I was now the nephew of a great man—which is not a privilege to be despised.

Hamburg gave a grand fete in our honour. A public audience was given to the Professor at the Johannæum, at which he told all about our expedition, with only one omission, the unexplained and inexplicable behaviour of our compass. On the same day, with much state, he deposited in the archives of the city the now famous document of Saknussemm, and expressed his regret that circumstances over which he had no control had prevented him from following to the very centre of the earth the track of the learned Icelander. He was modest notwithstanding his glory, and he was all the more famous for his humility.

So much honour could not but excite envy. There were those who envied him his fame; and as his theories, resting upon known facts, were in opposition to the systems of science upon the question of the central fire, he sustained with his pen and by his voice remarkable discussions with the learned of every country.

For my part I cannot agree with his theory of gradual cooling: in spite of what I have seen and felt, I believe, and always shall believe, in the central heat. But I admit that certain circumstances not yet sufficiently understood may tend to modify in places the action of natural phenomena.

While these questions were being debated with great animation, my uncle met with a real sorrow. Our faithful Hans, in spite of our entreaties, had left Hamburg; the man to whom we owed all our success and our lives too would not suffer us to reward him as we could have wished. He was seized with the mal de pays, a complaint for which we have not even a name in English.

'Farval,' said he one day; and with that simple word he left us and sailed for Rejkiavik, which he reached in safety.

We were strongly attached to our brave eider-down hunter; though far away in the remotest north, he will never be forgotten by those whose lives he protected, and certainly I shall not fail to endeavour to see him once more before I die.

To conclude, I have to add that this 'Journey into the Interior of the Earth' created a wonderful sensation in the world. It was translated into all civilised languages. The leading newspapers extracted the most interesting passages, which were commented upon, picked to pieces, discussed, attacked, and defended with equal enthusiasm and determination, both by believers and sceptics. Rare privilege! my uncle enjoyed during his lifetime the glory he had deservedly won; and he may even boast the distinguished honour of an offer from Mr. Barnum, to exhibit him on most advantageous terms in all the principal cities in the United States!

But there was one 'dead fly' amidst all this glory and honour;

one fact, one incident, of the journey remained a mystery. Now to a man eminent for his learning, an unexplained phenomenon is an unbearable hardship. Well! it was yet reserved for my uncle to be completely happy.

One day, while arranging a collection of minerals in his cabinet, I noticed in a corner this unhappy compass, which we had long lost sight of; I opened it, and began to watch it.

It had been in that corner for six months, little mindful of the trouble it was giving.

Suddenly, to my intense astonishment, I noticed a strange fact, and I uttered a cry of surprise.

'What is the matter?' my uncle asked.

'That compass!'

'Well?'

'See, its poles are reversed!'

'Reversed?'

'Yes, they point the wrong way.'

My uncle looked, he compared, and the house shook with his triumphant leap of exultation.

A light broke in upon his spirit and mine.

'See there,' he cried, as soon as he was able to speak. 'After our arrival at Cape Saknussemm the north pole of the needle of this confounded compass began to point south instead of north.'

'Evidently!'

'Here, then, is the explanation of our mistake. But what phenomenon could have caused this reversal of the poles?'

'The reason is evident, uncle.'

'Tell me, then, Axel.'

'During the electric storm on the Liedenbrock sea, that ball of fire, which magnetised all the iron on board, reversed the poles of our magnet!'

'Aha! aha!' shouted the Professor with a loud laugh. 'So it was just an electric joke!'

From that day forth the Professor was the most glorious

of savants, and I was the happiest of men; for my pretty Virlandaise, resigning her place as ward, took her position in the old house on the Königstrasse in the double capacity of niece to my uncle and wife to a certain happy youth. What is the need of adding that the illustrious Otto Liedenbrock, corresponding member of all the scientific, geographical, and mineralogical societies of all the civilised world, was now her uncle and mine?